Iain Pears

Iain Pears is a journalist and art historian. After several years working for Reuters, he went to Yale University to complete his book, *The Discovery of Painting*, which was published by Yale University Press in 1988. He now lives in Oxford.

Iain Pears has written five other novels featuring art dealer Jonathan Argyll and Flavia di Stefano of Rome's Art Theft Squad, and is currently working on a seventh. He is also the author of the acclaimed international bestseller, *An Instance of the Fingerpost*.

An Instance of the Fingerpost

Jonathan Argyll novels
Death and Restoration
The Last Judgement
The Bernini Bust
The Titian Committee
The Raphael Affair

IAIN PEARS

GIOTTO'S HAND

HarperCollins*Publishers*

This novel is entirely a work of fiction. The names, characters and incidents portrayed in it are the work of the author's imagination. Any resemblance to actual persons, living or dead, events or localities is entirely coincidental.

HarperCollins*Publishers*
77–85 Fulham Palace Road,
Hammersmith, London W6 8JB

This paperback edition 2000

8

First published in Great Britain by
HarperCollins*Publishers* in 1994

Copyright © Iain Pears 1994

The Author asserts the moral right to
be identified as the author of this work

ISBN 0 00 649026 3

Typeset in Meridien
by Palimpsest Book Production Limited,
Polmont, Stirlingshire

Printed in Great Britain by
Clays Ltd, St Ives plc

1

General Taddeo Bottando's triumphantly successful campaign towards the unmasking of the shadowy English art dealer, Geoffrey Forster, as the most extraordinary thief of his generation began with a letter, postmarked Rome, that turned up on his desk on the third floor of the Art Theft Department on a particularly fine morning in late July.

Initially, this small hand grenade of sticky-taped and stamped information lay there until the General – a stickler for routine in the morning until he was sufficiently wide awake to improvise – completed his morning rounds of watering his pot-plants, studying the pages of the newspapers and having a cup of the coffee which came up in regular shipments from the bar across the Piazza San Ignazio.

Then, item by item, he dug his way through the mail put in the in-tray by his secretary, slowly excavating the pile of miscellaneous messages until, eventually, at about 8.45 a.m., he picked up the thin, inexpensive paper envelope and slit it open with his paper knife.

He wasn't wildly excited; the address had been hand-written, in what was very much the weak and spidery manner of old age, and so it seemed likely that it would be a waste of time. All institutions have their little collection of nutters who gather round and try to attract attention, and the Art Theft Department was no exception. Everybody in the squad had their own personal favourite among this motley, but generally harmless, crew. Bottando's own was the man in Trento who claimed to be the reincarnation of Michelangelo and wanted the Florence David back on the grounds that the Medicis had never paid him enough for it. Flavia di Stefano – who sometimes exhibited signs of a peculiar sense of humour which might have had something to do with living with an Englishman – had a weakness for the man who, concerned about the plight of the Apulian vole, kept on threatening to smear jam over the Vittorio Emanuele monument in Rome to draw the attention of the world's press. In Flavia's view, such gastronomic terrorism would probably greatly improve the horrible monstrosity, and she had to be restrained from writing back to encourage him in his project. As she said, in some parts of the world you get government art grants for that sort of thing.

Not exactly burning with anticipation, therefore, Bottando leant back in his chair, unfolded the letter, and skimmed through it. Then, frowning in the fashion of someone trying to remember a dream that is just out of reach, he went back to the beginning and read it again, this time more carefully.

Then he picked up the phone and called Flavia so she could have a look as well.

Esteemed and honourable sir, the letter began in that opulently respectful way which the Italian language still

2

preserves for formal correspondence, *I am writing to confess that I am a criminal, having been involved in the theft of a painting which was once the property of the Palazzo Straga in Florence. This crime, which I freely confess, took place in July 1963. May God forgive me, for I know I cannot forgive myself.*

With my most obedient respects,

Maria Fancelli.

Flavia, when she came into the office, read it through with only minimal attention and double checked she wasn't missing anything. Then she brushed her long fair hair back into place, rubbed her nose meditatively with the flat of her palm, and delivered her final and considered verdict.

'Pouf!' she said. 'So what?'

Bottando shook his head in a thoughtful fashion. 'So something. Maybe.'

'What makes you think that?'

'Age has its virtues,' he said pompously. 'And one of them is fragments of primeval memory which young snips like you do not possess.'

'Thirty-three last week.'

'Middle-aged snips like you, then, if that makes you feel any better. The Palazzo Straga has a familiar ring to it, somehow.'

Bottando tapped his pen against his teeth, frowned, and looked up at the ceiling. 'Um,' he said.

'Straga. Florence. 1963. Picture. Um.'

And he sat there, staring dreamily out of the window, with Flavia sitting patiently opposite, wondering if he was going to tell her what was on his mind.

'Ha!' he said with a relieved smile as his memory began behaving itself after a few more minutes. 'Got it. If you would be so kind as to look in the extinct box, my dear?'

The extinct box was a misnomer for the small broom cupboard that was the last resting place for hopeless causes – those crimes which had an almost minimal chance of ever being resolved. It was very full.

Flavia got up to obey orders. 'I must say,' she said sceptically as she opened the door, 'your memory amazes me. Are you sure about this?'

Bottando waved his hand airily. 'See what you can find,' he said confidently. 'My memory never lets me down, you know. We old elephants . . .'

So off she went, down the stairs into the basement, where she burrowed into the dust piles, ruining her clothes for half an hour, before emerging, triumphant but extremely discontented.

Her complaints to her boss were temporarily delayed by a sneezing fit when she got back to his office bearing a large and bulky file.

'Bless you, my dear,' Bottando said sympathetically as she roared away.

'It's all your fault,' she said in between interruptions. 'It's a complete shambles down there. If an entire pile of stuff hadn't collapsed and spilled over the floor, I would never have found it.'

'But you did.'

'I did. Stored, completely out of sequence, in a vast file called "Giotto". What in God's name is that?'

'Oh,' Bottando said, realization dawning. 'Giotto. That's why I remember.'

'So?'

'One of the great geniuses of his age,' the General said with a slight twitch of a smile.

Flavia scowled again.

'I don't mean that Giotto,' Bottando explained. 'I mean a gentleman of superhuman skill, breathtaking audacity, almost total invisibility. So clever, so astute, that, alas, he doesn't exist.'

Flavia gave him the sort of reproving look that such enigmatic comments deserved.

'A fit of whimsy that came out of a quiet summer a couple of years back,' he went on. 'Just after that Velásquez vanished from Milan. When was it? That's right. 1992.'

Flavia looked at him curiously. 'The portrait? From the Calleone collection?'

He nodded. 'That's the one. Convenient burglar alarm failure, someone went in, took it, left and vanished. Quick and neat. A portrait of a girl called Francesca Arunta. It was never seen again, and two years is a long time for it to be gone. Lovely picture, too, it seems, although there was no photograph.'

'What?'

'No. No photograph. Amazing, isn't it? Some people. Although in fact that's quite common. That's what gave me the idea. Lots of pictures in the house, and the only one taken was the only one which had never been photographed. In this case, there was at least a print made in the nineteenth century. On the board over there.'

He pointed to a noticeboard on the far side of his office, covered with what had been called the devil's list: photographs of paintings, sculpture and other oddments that had vanished without trace. Half obscured by a gold, fourteenth-century chalice which had presumably long since been melted down into ingots, Flavia saw a dog-eared photocopy of a print of a painting. Not the sort of thing you could easily take into court for the purposes of identification. But it was just about clear enough to give you an idea.

'Anyway,' he went on, 'it was embarrassing, not least because old Calleone was in a position to make a stink, and did. And we got nowhere; all the usual channels of enquiry went dead on us; not a regular customer, not organized crime, but obviously a real pro. So, in desperation, I started looking through all the back cases for a hint of someone who might have done it. And came up with a list of unphotographed paintings that had vanished in a similar fashion. I got quite carried away, hence the rather bulky file. Even made a few enquiries. But eventually I stepped back, had a long hard look and realized the whole thing was a total waste of time.'

'It sounds quite a good idea to me,' she said, settling herself on the sofa and placing the file by her side. 'Are you sure you were wrong?'

'Oh, in theory there was nothing wrong with it at all. Which just shows what's wrong with theory. The trouble was, once I began to think about it, I realized I now had one man, who I dubbed Giotto . . .'

'Why?'

Bottando smiled. 'Because my imaginary character was a real master at his trade, of great importance, but we knew virtually nothing about him. No personality or anything. A bit like Giotto. But, as I say, I had made this creation of mine responsible for more than two dozen thefts from at least 1963 onwards. Encompassing four different countries, in each case taking unphotographed pictures which were never seen again. Without anyone in a dozen or more specialized police units even suspecting his existence. Without a single fence or buyer ever breaking ranks and offering information. Without a single work ever being recovered.'

'Hmm.'

'And then, of course, the whole thing blew up when I came across a note from the Carabinieri saying they'd arrested someone six months previously for another job which I'd nominally pencilled in as being by Giotto's hand. Giacomo Sandano. Remember him?'

'The world's worst thief?'

'That's the one. He nicked a Fra Angelico from Padua. Got caught, of course. According to my calculations, he would have been three and a half when he committed the Straga raid, and is far too stupid ever to get away with anything for long. This is why I put the whole lot in the extinct box. It was the best proof imaginable that I was wrong. So Giotto has been gathering dust for a couple of years and, in my opinion, should return there . . .'

'Good morning, General.'

The door opened and the voice entered before the small and compact body from which it emerged. A moment later, a man who looked surprisingly like a well-fed Siamese cat entered the room, with a look of superior amusement on his face. Bottando smiled back genially, with an expression that connoisseurs like Flavia knew to be entirely false.

'Good morning, dottore,' he said. 'How nice to see you.'

Dottore Corrado Argan was one of those people that large-scale organizations periodically create for the sole purpose of making the lives of its several members virtually intolerable. He had started off as an art historian – thus giving himself somewhat dubious intellectual credentials which he played on mercilessly – then, finding the Italian and international university system far too sensible to give him a post, had gravitated into the bureaucracy, specifically the *beni artistici*, the

7

amorphous body which keeps its eye on the national heritage.

After successfully creating chaos in several areas of that fine organization's activities, he had become suffused with indignation over the way bits of the national heritage kept on going missing, and decided that what the fight against crime really needed to make it effective was the stimulus of his own powerful intellect to focus its activities.

He was not the first to imagine he might make a difference and, to give him very grudging credit, he was certainly enthusiastic. That, of course, mainly had the effect of making him more tiresome. Bottando was well-practised in dealing with periodic memoranda from outsiders demanding action, suggesting campaigns and recommending policies. Long experience had taught him the best way of agreeing profoundly with all interventions, thanking their authors and then ignoring them totally.

What he was not capable of dealing with too well was the outsider moving in, taking over office space and settling down for an extended stay to write reports based on a day-to-day monitoring of activities. Which was what the loathsome Argan had done. For six months now he had read his way through files, sat in on meetings, pipe in mouth, supercilious smile on face, making notes that no one was allowed to see and muttering things about how the department did not conceptualize its policies in a sufficiently holistic fashion.

Bottando, for once, had been rather slow off the mark in meeting the threat, and was now paying the price. Because Argan was so ludicrous, he had not taken the man seriously. Only when his secretary had undertaken a do-it-yourself espionage operation late one evening, and handed over photocopies of the innumerable reports and memoranda the man had been sending off to those in high places, did the magnitude of the problem become clear.

In brief, Argan wanted Bottando's job, and was trying very hard to get it. His line was that, in these days of international crime, old-fashioned policing (for which read old-fashioned policemen, as personified by General Taddeo Bottando) was no longer sufficient. What was needed was an efficient organization (i.e. a cheaper one) headed up by an executive skilled in man-management and resource allocation (i.e. himself). No mention in any of this of catching criminals or recovering lost works of art.

War had broken out, in a quiet and civilized fashion. Bottando found that his tardiness had blocked off the obvious response: it was too late now to chuck the man out for fear of being accused of wanting to hide something. As much as possible, he fed him false information, so that he could be made to look a fool. Unfortunately, Argan, as an art historian, didn't think facts were so important anyway and carried on regardless.

On his side, Bottando had the policing establishment, who quite rightly saw enthusiastic amateurs as a threat to them all. On the other, Argan had the bureaucracy, which believed firmly that the quality of an organization depended solely on how many jobs it provided for administrators. And they, as Bottando was aware, were the ones with the cheque books.

For the past month, Bottando's counter-offensive had run into the sand. Argan had taken full possession of all the right words, like efficiency and results and cost-effectiveness, and Bottando had not worked out a way of opposing the man without seeming old, fusty and hidebound. He was reduced, therefore, to grumbling ferociously and hoping he would make a mistake. So far, patience had not been rewarded, mainly because Argan didn't actually do anything except watch other people and say, with the benefit of hindsight, how it should have been done better.

'And how are we this morning?' said this walking insult to all the traditions of good policing. 'Still solving those crimes, I hear. I couldn't help overhearing your fascinating discourse on criminal detection.'

Bottando scowled at him. 'I hope you found it instructive?'

'Very helpful, yes. An important Etruscan site robbed overnight, I see?'

That was the other trouble with him. He always had a quick look through the overnight reports so that he had this vague patina of being on top of things. Bottando had been diverted by Giotto and hadn't got around to it yet.

'I know,' he replied steadily nonetheless. 'But there's not much we can do until we have a full report on what was stolen.' Always a safe remark, that.

'Oh, I think we should get involved a bit earlier than that. Nice case like this, looks very good. We have to keep up the department profile, after all. And the destruction of our heritage through the spoliation of sites of immense historical significance . . .'

And off he went, talking away as though he was instructing a class of five-year-olds. That was another problem with him, Bottando had once explained gloomily to a sympathetic colleague in Corruption one evening. Quite apart from the fact that he could never resist an opportunity to be didactic, Argan was more of a marketing executive than a policeman. He didn't care how effective the department was as long as it looked good.

'Not our case yet,' Bottando repeated firmly as Argan was getting into his stride. 'Unless you want to get a reputation for poaching. If you like I could telephone the Carabinieri and say you personally want to take over . . .'

'Oh, no. Of course, I bow to your experience in these matters,' Argan said. Much too smart to be caught out by an obvious ploy like that.

'So,' he went on, 'what's this conference with the lovely signorina about, then?'

The lovely signorina ground her teeth, and Bottando smiled. Argan was trying to charm his staff over on to his side. He was not really adopting the right approach with Flavia. Some of the others, however . . .

'The lovely signorina and I were planning our day,' said Bottando.

'This?' Argan said, picking up the letter disdainfully. 'I really must ask you not to read my mail without my permission.'

'Sorry,' Argan said, putting it down with an unapologetic smile and sitting beside Flavia on the sofa. She got up. 'I imagine you won't be doing anything with it. A thirty-year-old crime is hardly a high priority.'

'All crimes are a high priority,' Bottando said pompously.

'But some are more so than others, surely? And to concern yourself with an ancient affair and turn a blind eye to a robbery only last night . . .'

It was like talking to a brick wall, Bottando thought.

'How often do I have to explain that our main brief is to recover works of art?' he said testily. 'Criminals are secondary. If a painting can be recovered, it doesn't

11

matter whether it vanished last night or thirty years or a century ago. And to miss an opportunity because we don't make elementary checks would be a gross dereliction of our duty.'

'Of course,' Argan purred, giving way with suspicious grace. 'You're in charge, General. You're in charge.'

And on that ambiguous note he left. Only afterwards did Bottando calm down enough to realize that much of the Giotto file had vanished with him.

'No,' said Jonathan Argyll with suitable concern that evening, as they sat companionably on the balcony of their apartment and felt the sun go down at long last. 'It doesn't sound good. You'll have to nobble him.'

Flavia had spent much of their meal talking about the iniquities of Corrado Argan. It's difficult to avoid a degree of obsession if you've spent the better part of the morning calming your boss down and persuading him that sober reason would be a better response than foot-stamping fury.

'What was this picture, anyway?' Argyll asked, considering then postponing a decision about doing the washing up. 'Is it really worth going to investigate?'

She shook her head. 'Not a clue. It's meant to be by Uccello, a Madonna and child. Whether it is or not I couldn't tell you. There's no photograph of it and the descriptions aren't very good.'

'It's very diligent of you to take all this trouble.'

'No, it's not. It's politics. Argan doesn't want Bottando to look into this, and so Bottando, to show he's in charge, will have to do just that. Having gone on about leaving no stone unturned to recover paintings, he has to go and peek under some pebbles. Otherwise he seems slack even by his own standards.'

Argyll nodded, then stood up and gathered the dirty plates. Too many flies around this evening. 'It'll land him in trouble one day, you know,' he said sagely. 'Does he have to be so pugnacious?'

Flavia smiled knowingly. 'It's easy to tell you've never worked in a large organization. Argan's a fool, but he has such boundless self-confidence that he convinces people who don't know any better. Which means that he is constantly being put in positions of authority. So everybody else has to spend a great deal of time tripping him up. It's all part of the job.'

'I'm glad I'm self-employed, then.'

'But unlike you, we get our salaries even if we don't do anything. In fact, in Argan's case, the less he does, the more he gets.'

A sore point. Argyll remained convinced that, somewhere out there, an individual existed who desperately wanted to buy at least one of his pictures. Finding this person was proving massively difficult at the moment. So much so that he was seriously having to consider what he gloomily called alternatives. A full-blown crisis had been precipitated by the arrival of a letter from an international university in Rome which processed eager young things anxious to learn about art and culture. One of its art historians had absconded to a better job at the last moment, and they had in desperation written to Argyll. Did he want a job for a couple of years teaching from the Carracci to Canova?

Flavia had seen this as a solution to all his problems, but Argyll wasn't so sure. He'd worked hard to set up as a dealer; giving up now would seem very much like failure. And he hated the thought of being forced to give up. Besides which, teaching looked like hard work to him.

Deeply depressing. He had enough money to trickle along, but so far had failed to make a breakthrough into the next division up. He needed to buy better pictures. But to do that, he needed some capital to buy the better pictures to start off with, and he simply didn't have it. He'd grumbled away for weeks and months, and now he'd decided to go off to England to consult his old mentor and employer to see if he had any ideas.

He'd not been very good company recently. But then, nor had Flavia. She didn't mind Argyll not making much money; she did mind him not being able to make up his mind about what to do. The job offer had been lying around for nearly two weeks now, he still hadn't responded, and his constant fretting was, in her view, becoming tiresome. She was very tolerant, normally. But as he did have to make up his mind sooner or later, she didn't see why he couldn't get it over with.

'What's this Giotto idea, then?' he said as a diversion-ary tactic to make the conversation less depressing.

'Pouf! Nothing really. Just a fancy of the General's when he got snookered by a stolen Velásquez.'

'This the one he had pinned up in his office a couple of summers back? The one that got him into trouble with the ministry?'

'That's right. A well-connected owner. It was worth looking at, but he was right to junk the whole idea. He spotted a couple of dozen thefts which all seemed to be by the same hand. Houses with old collections and pic-tures that hadn't been on the market for decades, if not centuries. Badly catalogued and often unphotographed. Small pictures of high value, generally High Renais-sance. All chosen with an expert eye, and all stolen very deftly: no violence, no sign of break-ins, no damage to anything. Whoever did them all went in and out within

14

minutes, knew exactly what they were after and were never distracted. Only one picture taken on any one occasion. All indicating, so he thought, a suspiciously similar degree of patience and dexterity.'

'Sounds good to me. What's wrong with the idea?'

'Because it goes against common sense and his fundamental law of art theft, which is that thieves aren't that good. Which is perfectly true. They're greedy, impatient, clumsy and generally not very bright. They make mistakes. They talk too much. They get shopped by accomplices. They don't methodically pursue their careers for thirty years, never overreaching themselves, never making a mistake, never trusting the wrong person, always resisting the temptation to tell the world how clever they are. And most of them now work for organized crime: lone thieves are virtually extinct.

'Giotto was a figment of the imagination, and Bottando is much too sensible to be led astray by such nonsense. You know him. Your turn to make the coffee, I think.'

2

The address in the Parioli section of Rome from whence
the troublesome letter had begun its voyage to Bottando's
desk turned out to be that of a secluded, luxurious
and probably fairly expensive nursing home for the
well-heeled old and sick of the capital. It was one of
a growing number of such establishments thrown up
as pressure of work, space and modernity squeezed
out grandparents from the homes of their children and
sounded the death knell of the Italian mama.

Flavia arrived fairly early, in the hope of getting
through and back to the office before the heat became
too insufferable, and glanced around at the building
carefully before making her way inside. The highly-
polished doors, the marble flooring and the air of
efficient, kindly and expensive care were, somehow, not
quite what she'd expected from the spidery, ill-educated
handwriting of the letter.

The first hitch came at the desk, where a bright and
competent-looking receptionist said that it was not yet
visiting time. Flavia produced her badge to show she
was in the police and it still wasn't visiting time. Flavia

was explaining that, rules or not, it was important that she see Signora Fancelli, when her words were overheard by a priest who was passing by, who stopped and intervened.

'You are the person she wrote to?' he said, after introducing himself as Father Michele and assuring the receptionist that he would look after the visitor.

'She wrote to my boss,' Flavia replied. 'I was sent along to talk to her.'

'I'm so glad. So glad. She was very much in a state of anguish about what she should do. If you wish, I will show you where she is.'

Flavia nodded, and Father Michele led the way out of the door, explaining that at this time of the year most of the inmates – guests, as he called them – were wheeled out into the garden for a little sun.

'It's extraordinary how much they can take,' he said as they crossed the path and headed towards a small clump of trees. 'In temperatures that make most people faint, they're constantly calling for extra sweaters.'

'Is she well off?' Flavia asked, thinking about the proceeds of crime. 'It must cost a bomb to stay here.'

'Dear me, no. As poor as possible. Quite wretchedly so, in fact.'

'But now . . .'

'A son in America, I understand. She came here several months ago, when she began to fail, and he pays the bills. And, I must tell you, she will die here as well. She is preparing herself.'

He pointed out a frail figure in a wheelchair, staring blankly into nothingness.

'That's her there. Now, I'll leave you. Please don't think that the signora has lost control of her mind as well as of her body. She's very sick, and her attention wanders, but there's nothing wrong with her intelligence at all, although the painkillers make her drowsy. But please do not excite her too much.'

There was absolutely no doubt that the priest was speaking the truth there, Flavia thought as she approached the wheelchair, hoping the woman wasn't asleep. The grey skin, sickly pallor, matchstick-thin arms and thin, wispy hair all indicated someone with very little time left. Nor was she quite as alert as Flavia had hoped, although, when she announced herself, she could see the woman making a distinct and costly effort to concentrate.

'Signora Fancelli?' Flavia began. 'I've come about a letter you wrote. About a painting. I'd like to ask you about it.'

'Ah, yes,' she said, looking up and trying to focus on Flavia. 'I wrote to you, did I? That was a long time ago, wasn't it?'

'You appeared to be confessing to a theft. I must say that I don't find that at all likely.'

'It has been a heavy burden for me, knowing what I did,' she said. 'All these years. I'm glad to have an opportunity to talk to you. Whatever the price.'

Considering her health, and the habitual speed of the Italian judiciary, there didn't seem much chance of the price being high; not in this world, anyway. She was not that old: early sixties, maybe. But she was manifestly running out of time.

'Would you like to tell me about it?'

A long silence, before her mind focused once more on the problem. 'I didn't know what I was doing, you see. Had I known, I would never have done anything. I was poor, that was certainly true; but I was never, ever dishonest. I hope you will believe that.'

Flavia nodded patiently; until she actually said something, there wasn't much point in doing anything else.

'My parents were poor, and I was unmarried and had no one to look after me. I had to leave school and began working as a maid – a cleaner, really. Partly for a school for foreigners run by a woman called della Quercia, and partly for the Straga family. This was in Florence. Did I say that already?'

Even though it was not yet eleven o'clock, and they were in the shade of the trees, it was already getting hot, and the time of year when the warmth is invigorating had long since passed. It was a blisteringly hot summer, and the worst was yet to come. Flavia reacted to the warmth quickly; and bit by bit, her chin was sinking lower, and her attention was wandering. She was beginning to sweat in the heat, and this vague discomfort was about the only thing stopping her from falling asleep entirely.

'I admit, I was looking for someone to marry,' the woman was saying, somewhere to the far left of Flavia's diminishing consciousness. 'People do not worry about that any more, but then, if you weren't married by the time you were eighteen, it was assumed there was something wrong with you. People laughed at me all the time. The old maid. But I was romantic. I didn't just want a husband; I wanted to be swept off my feet by someone exciting, and dashing.

'There was one man who used to hang around with the girls. Geoffrey, his name was. Geoffrey Forster. An Englishman. Very good-looking, very charming. Rich, or so he said. Constantly referring to famous people as though he was their best friend, spending money, driving fast cars.

'Naturally, when he turned his attention to me I was

flattered, and got delusions. I thought he was in love with me; no one had ever treated me like that before. It was only a dream, of course; I soon found out the truth. But, before I did, he took me on holiday.'

Out of sheer politeness – the story was evidently costing the old lady a great deal to tell – Flavia nodded sagely, and told her to continue.

'He asked me one day if I wanted to go to Switzerland with him, for a romantic weekend. Naturally, I agreed, and it never crossed my mind that there might be anything wrong. I'd never even been out of Tuscany before; the prospect of going to Switzerland, staying in fancy hotels, was a dream beyond anything I had ever imagined. I assumed it was merely a preliminary, and then soon we'd be making those trips together. I already thought that I might be pregnant, you see.'

Flavia was more interested now, and jerked awake by the harshness and bitterness in the woman's voice. With renewed attention, she watched Signora Fancelli carefully, still not saying a word to interrupt her narrative.

'He took a parcel with him,' she said, gesturing with her hands to indicate something less than half a metre square, then giving up as the effort was too much. 'And he didn't tell me what it was. He said it was a favour for a friend. I knew that was untrue, of course, and, foolish as I was, thought that lovers should have no secrets from each other. So, as the train went north, I opened it up. Just enough to peek inside.

'It was a painting of Our Lady. I recognized it because I'd seen it regularly in the Palazzo Straga and thought it so pretty. Not that I knew anything about it. Anyway, I sealed it back up again, and eventually Geoffrey went out with it under his arm, and came back without it.'

'What did he do with it?'

'I don't know. We went to this lovely hotel – I felt as though I was really living the high life. I was too much in love to ask questions, or wonder.'

'And then?'

'Then we came back to Florence, and a week or so later I told Geoffrey I was pregnant.'

'I gather he wasn't overjoyed?'

She shook her head. 'It was terrible,' she said. 'He ranted and raved. Then he denied that it had anything to do with him. Called me all sorts of names and told me to go away. My employers heard about it and I was fired. If it hadn't been for the kindness of one of the girls there, I don't know what I would have done.'

Flavia considered the story. It all fitted quite nicely; the Uccello stolen from the Palazzo had been a Madonna. It had been assumed that it had been spirited out of the country, and it had all taken place around this time. One or two details, however . . .

'Tell me, what made you think it was stolen?'

She looked puzzled for a moment, then her forehead cleared. 'When I got back. Everybody knew,' she said. 'All the girls at the school at various times visited the Palazzo. When it was broken into, everyone knew very quickly. I found out when I got back from Switzerland. There had been a ball at the Palazzo, you see. The signora always got her pupils invited every year. He must have taken it then.'

'And you said nothing? You didn't feel like getting your revenge on this man?'

She managed an ironic and derisive look. 'And that is what they would have assumed I was doing, wouldn't they? Who would have believed me? I couldn't say who had the picture, because I didn't know. And I was terrified that I would be locked up as well. It would have been just like him, to do that to me. To say I was a conspirator.'

'And did you ever see this Forster again?'

'I left, and came to Rome to get another job. I had my baby and sent him to relations in America. It wasn't easy, you know. Not like nowadays.'

A touch inconsequential, this, but she seemed to be heading in the general direction of saying something, so Flavia again sat there and waited.

'So now you write to us. Why, might I ask?'

Signora Fancelli gestured at her wasted frame, as though that was answer enough. 'The priest,' she said. 'Father Michele said it might make me feel better. It does.'

'Very well, then. We will, of course, have to check your story thoroughly. And you will have to make a statement.'

'And will there be any trouble?'

Flavia shook her head. 'Good heavens, no. Unless you've made this up and have been wasting my time . . .'

'For him, I mean. For Forster,' she said with a sudden hatred that Flavia found almost shocking.

'We will investigate your statement fully. That's all I can say. Now, perhaps we can get this down on paper . . .'

'Geoffrey Arnold Forster,' Flavia told Bottando when she got back to the office, dumped her bag and was swept off to a small restaurant to discuss the matter over lunch, 'was born in England on 23rd May 1938, so he's fifty-six. Brown eyes, height about one metre eighty-five.'

Bottando lifted a sceptical eyebrow. 'You mean to tell

me that she could remember all that after more than thirty years? Remarkable lady.'

'That's what I thought. However, it makes some sort of sense. She knew she'd have to fill out a birth certificate when the child was born, and she didn't want the space under "father" to remain blank. So she copied down the details from his passport before the row broke out between them.'

'She must have suspected he was going to put up a fight, then,' Bottando said as he stirred sugar into his coffee and then sipped at the thick syrupy mixture that made life worthwhile.

Flavia shrugged. 'It seems a reasonable precaution to me. She was poor, uneducated, pregnant and nearly ten years older than him. Anyway, that is how we have such detail. The question is, what do we do with it? Going to Parioli for a thirty-year-old crime is one thing. Going all the way to England and involving all sorts of international requests is quite another. Quite apart from the possibility that the man could even be dead.'

Bottando thought it over, then nodded. 'No. You're right. It's a waste of time. Too much trouble. If it was easy to find out who Forster was, then we might go through the motions, I suppose. But as the chances of actually recovering the picture are zero, there doesn't really seem much point.'

'I'll check through the beastie book to see if Forster's a regular customer. Just to be on the safe side.'

The General nodded. 'Yes. And I suppose a modest report just to tidy things away. Mark it not to be followed up. Did you get a proper statement?'

'Yes. She was too frail to come in herself, so I took it all down and got her to sign it. She's going out fast, poor old thing. Although she's still incredibly bitter about

Forster. She reckons he destroyed her life, and she's never forgiven him.'

'If she's telling the truth, then she's probably right.'

'Tell you what,' she went on, a thought passing through her mind. 'Jonathan's going off to England tomorrow. I could get him to ask around. Just to see if anyone's ever heard of this man. And while he's doing that, I could go and see if this woman's story checks out in Florence. If there's anybody at all left alive to tell me.'

Bottando thought about it, then shook his head. 'No,' he said. 'Not worth it. A waste of time.'

'Oh,' she said, slightly disappointed. 'All right. If you say so. But talking of time wasting,' she said as the bill came, 'how's friend Argan?'

Bottando frowned. 'Don't try and manipulate me by bringing him into it. This has got nothing to do with him.'

'Of course not.'

'Besides, he's being awfully nice – at the moment.'

'Oh yes?'

'Yes. He's in his office and hasn't stuck his nose in anything all day. Sweet as pie.'

'So you've decided he's OK?'

'Certainly not. I've decided he's up to something. So I don't want to make a false move until I discover what it is.'

'I see.'

'So if you have an opportunity to find out what's putting him in a good mood . . .'

'I'll see what I can do.'

3

Argyll's reintroduction to his native country the following day took the form of a valiant battle with the antique
state of the London underground system. He was in a
bad mood, and had been ever since he'd arrived at the
passport section at Heathrow airport to discover that
most of the globe had touched down a few minutes
ahead of him. Then it took an age to recover his luggage
and, on top of that, the tube trains into London were
all delayed by what a scratchy announcer said, with
not the slightest apology in his voice, were technical
problems.

'Welcome to England. You are now entering the third
world,' he muttered to himself half an hour later as
he hung desperately from an overhead support in the
train which rattled and squeaked out of the station, so
crammed full of jet-lagged travellers it was difficult to see
how anyone else could possibly squeeze in. But they did
at the next station, only to have the thing stop dead for
fifteen minutes a few hundred yards down the tunnel.
About an hour later he emerged at Piccadilly Circus,
feeling like Livingstone after cutting his way through a

particularly dense piece of jungle, and went into a café to restore himself.

Mistake, he realized the moment the coffee was delivered; a grey, weak solution with a smell which, whatever it was, had nothing to do with coffee. Dear God, he thought when he discovered that it tasted as bad as it looked, what's happening to this country of mine?

He gave up after a while and wandered back out into the street, walked down Piccadilly then turned up into Bond Street. A few hundred yards up was his destination. He shivered. Moving from Rome to England in July can be something of a shock to the system: the skies were dark grey and leaden, he was under-dressed and had forgotten to bring an umbrella. He had a feeling already that he was merely wasting time and money for no other reason than to sidestep decision-making for a few days.

'Jonathan, dear boy. Good trip?' Edward Byrnes said as Argyll walked into the empty gallery and found his former employer carrying what looked like a painting by Pannini from one side of the room to another.

'No,' he said.

'Oh.' Byrnes put the painting down, looked at it for a few seconds, then called an assistant from the back and told him to hang it just there while he was out. 'No matter,' he went on when this was done. 'Let's go straight out for lunch. That might restore your flagging spirits a bit.'

There was that to be said about the trip. Byrnes had always been something of a *bon viveur*, and liked a good lunch. At the very least, Argyll was going to spend the rest of the day feeling well fed. Byrnes led the way out of the gallery door, leaving his minion in charge of the Pannini and with strict instructions about what to do in the unlikely event of a client coming in, then walked at a brisk pace into increasingly narrow streets then, finally, down a set of shabby steps into a basement.

'Nice, don't you think?' Byrnes said complacently as they emerged into what was presumably a restaurant at the bottom.

'Where are we?'

'Ah, it's a dining club. Set up by a group of art dealers who were getting fed up with the vastly inflated prices that all restaurants charge round here. The sort of place you can bring the more potentially lucrative client without having to double the price of their purchase to pay for their entertainment. Marvellous idea. We get good food and wine, partly own a new business and have somewhere civilized to sit. Splendid, eh?'

For his part, Argyll preferred not to have to associate too closely with colleagues all the time; the idea of having to eat with them, as well as attend auctions with them, didn't strike him as such a good idea. On the other hand, he could see the attractions for an incorrigible gossip like Byrnes. The idea of having a large chunk of the art market under his eye at the same time as a plate of food lay on his table was, probably, as close to paradise as he could envisage.

'Come, dear boy,' he said with mounting enthusiasm as his eyes grew accustomed to the gloom, 'I'm starving.'

They sat down, ordered drinks and Byrnes beamed at him for a few seconds before curiosity got the better of him and his gaze wandered off to survey the surrounding tables.

'Hmm,' he said meditatively as he spotted a smooth, moon-faced young man attentively pouring a glass of wine for an elderly lady with an elongated nose.

'Ah,' he continued, moving on to a group of three men, their heads conspiratorially close together.

'Well, well,' he mused thoughtfully at the sight of another pair, one wearing a fine piece of Italian tailoring for the well-to-do male, the other in slacks and sports jacket.

'Are you going to fill me in on any of this? Or just keep it to yourself?' Argyll asked in a tone that just avoided a slight touch of pique.

'I am sorry, I thought you didn't approve of gossip.'

'I don't,' Argyll replied. 'That doesn't mean I don't like to hear it, though. Come on. A few names and faces. That foppish character over there? The one talking to the old witch in the corner?'

'Ah, that's young Wilson. Keen as mustard and the IQ of a sunflower seed. Thinks that charm will get him anywhere. If that is his latest client, I imagine he will shortly be learning the lesson of his life.'

'What about the three musketeers in the corner?'

'I know two of them,' Byrnes said, treasuring the sight with all the appreciation of a true connoisseur. 'One is Sebastian Bradley, a man of high ambition and limited morals who has worked hard in the last few years to relieve Eastern Europe of its most precious treasures.'

'Legally?'

'Shouldn't think so for a minute. The person next to him is called Dimitri. I don't know his other name; but he supplies Sebastian with works of art – paintings, furniture, statuary, just about anything as long as it's fallen off the back of a lorry. His ethereal friend I don't know.'

'Nor do I.'

Byrnes sighed. 'You really don't pull your weight, you know.'

'Sorry. What about the other pair? The smoothy talking to the shaven-headed gent by the pillar?'

'Jonathan, *really*. I sometimes despair of you. The smoothy – I admire your perception, by the way – is the appalling Winterton, who, as he would be the first to tell you, is the most famous and distinguished dealer in the world. If not the known universe.'

'Oh,' said Argyll humbly. He had heard of Winterton: Byrnes's only serious rival for the title of the best-connected dealer in London. Naturally, they disliked each other intensely.

'And the other one is Andrew Wallace, chief buyer for . . .'

'Oh, yes. I know. I wonder if he wants a Guido Reni sketch I bought six months back . . .'

'Oh, I don't think you'd want to sell anything to him, you know. It's really not worth it. Just kill yourself; it's pleasanter and cheaper in the long run.'

Conversation ceased awhile as they studied the menu and Byrnes got over the shock of having to dine in the same room as Winterton. Then he recovered himself and beamed at Argyll once more. 'Now then, how's business?' he asked.

Argyll shrugged. 'All right, I suppose,' he said grudgingly. 'The Moresby Museum still sends my monthly retainer for services I rarely provide, and that pays the bills. And I've sold some drawings recently for a reasonable amount. But that's it. The rest of the time I hang around listening to the clock tick. I'm getting really sick of it.'

They sighed in sympathetic unison. 'I know. I know,' Byrnes said nostalgically. 'Ah, the glory days of the 1980s. When greed, selfishness and vulgar ostentation swept all before them. The Holy Trinity of the

31

Fine Arts. When will these underrated virtues ever return, eh?'

They mournfully considered the sudden outbreak of frugality in the world and tutted over the retrograde and inconsiderate desire of people to live within their incomes. A lengthy complaint by Byrnes about his virtual bankruptcy ended with his recommending the foie gras with truffles to start. Quite acceptable, he said. For the time of year.

'So,' Byrnes went on, when he noticed that Argyll's glumness was more than his habitual tendency to professional pessimism. 'What can I do for you?'

'You can give me advice, if you want. I'm not selling anything, and I've got this job offer. If you were me, what would you do? I can't sit around for the rest of my life hoping something will turn up.'

'Ah, no. Indeed not,' the older man said. 'It can be very depressing if you hit a slow patch. I speak from experience. Especially if you don't have much in the way of reserves. What you need is a backer, of course. Either that or a magnificent discovery of unparalleled importance. A hundred thousand or so would set you up nicely.'

Argyll snorted. 'Both discoveries and backers are even rarer than customers at the moment. Besides, I don't have much of a track record. Why would anyone think that investing in me would be a good bet?'

'Now, now,' Byrnes said reassuringly. 'Gloom is one thing, despair another. You've sold one or two very nice things.'

'One or two, yes,' said the unrepentantly pessimistic Argyll. For some reason, talking to the vastly successful Byrnes was not yet making him feel much better. 'One or two is not a career, though.'

'What do you want, exactly?'

'I want to sell paintings. There's not much point being a dealer otherwise. That's about it. I mean, I don't particularly want to make untold millions or anything like that. But I don't know what I'm doing wrong.'

'You're not doing anything wrong,' Byrnes said kindly. 'No one is selling anything at the moment. Not for a profit, anyway. Of course, that may be the trouble.'

'What?'

'Not doing anything wrong. Honesty is a great virtue normally, but a bit of a handicap in the art trade. And I do think that sometimes you take the upright posture too far. Remember that Chardin?'

Byrnes was referring to a small painting that Argyll had bought in a sale a year or so previously. He thought, but wasn't sure, that it was a Chardin, and persuaded a buyer to take it for a considerable amount of money. The following week he had discovered it was not by Chardin at all, and had been painted by someone very much less reputable.

'It was a clean, honest deal,' Byrnes said disapprovingly. 'And you went straight round, presented the man with the evidence that he would never have found for himself, proved it wasn't by Chardin and took it back, giving a full refund. Now, frankly, I admire your integrity. But not your acumen.'

'But I thought it was a good idea,' Argyll protested. 'He was an important collector and I was building up his trust. He would have bought more from me . . .'

'Had he not himself been arrested for corruption and links with organized crime three weeks later,' Byrnes pointed out gravely. 'You were being scrupulous with his money. Splendid. Except for the tiny little fact that it wasn't his money to start off with.'

33

'I know, I know,' Argyll said glumly. 'But I just don't like that part of the business,' he confessed. 'I know I should shave as many corners as possible. But when an opportunity to be cunning or a bit sharp presents itself, my conscience mans the barricades. And there's no point your telling me all this. You're exactly the same yourself.'

'There is a difference, though. I hate to have to point it out, but I have a lot more money than you do. I can afford to indulge my conscience. And it's an expensive luxury.'

Argyll looked even glummer, so Byrnes hammered on. It was, he thought, necessary. He'd been meaning to say it for some time. He liked Argyll and had a high opinion of him, but he did need educating in the realities of life a little.

'You have to face the facts, Jonathan,' he said kindly. 'You like your clients and you like pictures. Both are rare attributes in dealers and, frankly, neither is very helpful. Your job is to get as much money as possible and give as little as possible in return. It is to spot things and keep quiet about them. Telling the world that a Chardin is not a Chardin is fine for a connoisseur or an historian; not so smart for a dealer. You have to choose between your scruples and your income. You can't have both.'

And so the conversation went on, Byrnes being kind, sympathetic and saying everything that Argyll knew perfectly well already and didn't want to hear. Ultimately, Byrnes concluded that Argyll's only real option, if he didn't want to take up the offer of a job teaching, was simply to wait until the market recovered again. 'It'll never be like the good old days,' he said. 'But it's bound to pick up eventually. If you can survive another year or so, you'll be fine.'

Argyll wrinkled his nose with dissatisfaction. Obviously, he'd been foolish to think that Byrnes – who was well disposed towards him – was going to come up with a magical solution. As the man said, a major discovery, preferably cheap, would do the trick. Dream on, he thought.

'Oh, well,' he said. 'I'll have to think about it some more.'

'I'm not being much help, I'm afraid,' Byrnes said sympathetically.

'Nothing you can do, really. Except maybe order another bottle of wine . . .'

No sooner said than done. For some reason, knowing that even Byrnes couldn't think of anything slowly began to cheer him up. Partly because it confirmed that at least he wasn't missing anything. And secondly because even Byrnes, it seemed, was going through a lean period. If you're going to suffer, then it's somehow better not to be on your own.

'Let's talk about something else,' he said when the bottle had come, a glass had been poured out and he'd drunk half of it. 'I can't take any more reality today. Does the name Forster mean anything to you? Geoffrey Forster?'

Byrnes looked at him cautiously. 'Why?'

'Flavia. Somebody said he stole a painting. Decades ago. She wanted me to see if I could find out who he was. It doesn't really matter, but I'm sure she'd appreciate anything I can dredge up. It's nothing hugely important, I think, but you know what she's like. Who is he?'

'A dealer,' Byrnes said. 'At least, he was once. I haven't seen him for years. When the end of the eighties hit, he diverted into freelance expertise.'

'Oh yes? What does he do?'

'Vulturing mainly,' Byrnes said half admiringly. 'Picking over the semi-dead bodies of old families. You know, advising impoverished aristocrats and selling off their collections for them. He's got a sort of half-permanent post with some old lady in Norfolk. Lives up there now. As an example of how to sit out troubled times, it's a line of business you might investigate.'

'Lucky him.'

'Yes. Useful sideline. His great problem is that he's a bit difficult.'

'What does that mean?'

'Well, I didn't like him. Quite charming, in a way, if you like that sort of thing, but not many clients could stand him over the long term either. That was why he was never very successful. There was something a bit insidious about him. Hard to describe, really.'

'Crooked?'

'Not that I've heard, no. And if he was, then no one would have been reticent about saying so. What is this picture?'

Argyll explained the circumstances.

'Youthful indiscretion?' Byrnes suggested. 'Perfectly possible. Does Flavia want to nail him?'

Argyll shrugged. 'Not desperately. But if it was something that could be wrapped up quickly I'm sure she'd love to give him a hard time. Although as far as I can see there's not much chance of doing anything else.'

'No. Not after so many years. Even if you could prove it. Are you meant to be skulking round and finding out?'

'Not really. But, on the other hand, I've not got anything else to do, and I have a day or so here, so I might as well contact him, at least. Do you know what his address is?'

Byrnes shook his head. 'No. But he rents space from Winterton. Just to give him a respectable address and telephone number, really, and I don't think he's ever there. It's only five minutes from here. You could walk up and see. They'd know.'

The older man's benign sympathy and good taste in wine, if it was of no practical help, had ultimately managed to lift his spirits off the floor, and the prospect of doing something which had no connection to his own career furthered this process. By the time he got to Winterton Galleries, he was almost in a decent mood, even though it was very much on probation.

He explained his business, or part of it, to the secretary inside. Was Geoffrey Forster around?

No, he wasn't.

Did she know where to get hold of him?

Why?

Business. He was on a flying visit from Italy and wanted to talk to him before he flew back.

Very grudgingly, she said he was undoubtedly at his house in Norfolk. He virtually never came here. If Argyll thought it was really important, she could ring him.

Argyll did think it was really important.

Forster had one of those voices which are very much the stock in trade of a certain sort of English art dealer: the type of accent and intonation that can make a nineteenth earl feel socially inferior at a distance of several miles. It was one reason Argyll quite liked Italy. Even over the phone, he felt his hackles rising when Forster asked him, in a tone of drawling impatience, what exactly he wanted.

He explained that he was after information about a

painting, and understood that Forster may have had it once.

'What is this? A guessing game? Tell me which picture. I have handled one or two in my time.'

Argyll suggested that it might be better if they met. It was a delicate matter.

'Don't be such a damned fool! Tell me what it is or stop wasting my time.'

'Very well. I wish to ask you about an Uccello, which was in your possession shortly after it was stolen from the Palazzo Straga in Florence in 1963.'

There was a long silence from the other end, followed, rather irritatingly, by what sounded very much like a laugh. The secretary in the gallery was impressed as well.

'Was it indeed?' Forster said. 'Well, well. Maybe I should talk to you about that. Whoever you are.'

He managed to say it with something approaching a contemptuous sneer. Argyll disliked him intensely already, but nonetheless agreed to meet him, in Norfolk, at eleven the next morning. It was, he thought as he put the phone down, a pity he couldn't persuade Flavia to take a more active interest in locking the man up.

'Know what you mean,' said the secretary in the flat accent of south London, interpreting the sour look on his face with accuracy. 'Real bleeder.'

Argyll glanced at her, and decided to be forthcoming. 'Is he as bad as he sounds?'

'God, yes. Worse. Luckily, he almost never comes here.'

'Why does he come here at all? I thought he had a job with some old lady?'

'Oh, she died at the end of last year. Her successor took one look and kicked him out. So he's a bit short of money. God knows why he's allowed in here though. The boss loathes him, but somehow he's part of the fittings. Every time he turns up my life's a misery. No creep like an old creep. Hey, what's all this about then? Been a naughty boy, has he?'

Argyll shrugged noncommittally. 'If anything, he's been a very clever boy, I think,' he said, unashamedly doing his best to blacken the name of a man who, for all he knew, might be as innocent as a new-born babe.

'Oh, yes? Did you mention something about a stolen picture? Lifted it, did he? When was this?'

Even Argyll, however, retained some shred of discretion. So he looked vague, said he really didn't know all the details, and asked about how to get to the village of Weller, Norfolk. The girl was disappointed in him, and in a disapproving voice told him that Liverpool Street was the place to start.

Outside, he stood on the street and thought about it. Could he be bothered? He did have some time to kill before the plane back, but on the other hand was reluctant to go interfering in Flavia's job too much. Over the years, he'd decided that the more policework was left to her, the safer their relationship was. It was only the purely malicious desire to cause this arrogant voice on the other end of the phone some discomfort which prevented him from dismissing the idea entirely.

He decided he'd sleep on it. He had friends to visit, and he'd go and see them that evening. Then he'd rest, relax and consider. In the morning, he would decide what to do.

4

While Argyll was distracting himself in this fashion, Flavia was similarly stuck with activities which, in her opinion, made no sensible contribution to the maintenance of Italy's slightly shaky grasp on law and order. She was, for much of the day he left, doing her paperwork.

It had been building up for days. Vast quantities had made their way to her desk, liked it, and settled down to nest and produce offspring. This was the disadvantage with having made yourself semi-indispensable over the years. Sometimes she didn't quite understand why it was that certain administrative matters required her attention, but there it was. A mountain of reports on thefts, a hillock of reports on arrests and a virtual Alpine range of standard nonsense about all sorts of things. Archives wanted a new photocopier. What about Susannah's day off next Thursday to go to her ex-husband's wedding? An odd request, that one, but why not? No harm in being broad-minded. Accounts wondered whether another researcher had really needed to stay in the most expensive hotel in Mantua on a routine trip recently.

And on, and on. What would happen, she wondered absently, if she shredded the whole lot? No; that wouldn't work. Lose an entire art gallery and no one turns a hair; lose a copy of an invoice and the whole world gets turned upside down until it is found. She decided instead to experiment with a holding action. On top of every form, note and memorandum she wrote her initials in large letters, and then sent them all back to where they'd come from. See how long it takes to figure that out, she thought.

That taken care of, she turned to the real reports and, to cheer herself up, began with the arrests and recoveries. Only two of those, one concerning a stash of seventeenth-century ceramics in a left luggage locker at Naples railway station, which came with the observation that they had probably been stolen and did anyone know where they'd been stolen from? And an exultant note from Paolo, announcing that the case of the Leonardo man had finally been wound up. Flavia took it up to Bottando. It wasn't often they managed to bring a case to a decided end, complete with an arrest, confession and evidence, and he liked to know on the rare occasion that it did happen.

'Oh good,' Bottando said as she told him and handed over the report. 'Thank heavens for that. Who is he?'

She grinned. 'Just an art student, trying to earn a bit on the side. Bit of a problem what to do with him, really.'

True enough. The Leonardo man had attracted more than his fair share of attention in the press, which had pounced on a nice story of Italian criminality. It was simple enough; someone had been producing, and peddling, what were claimed to be Leonardo juvenilia on to an imbecile, and generally foreign, public. At least half a dozen people had trotted off home bearing bits of paper supposedly produced by a youthful, but already inquisitive, Renaissance genius.

As far as forgeries went, they were not in the top class: the handwriting was OK, but the paper was new and the ink was so obviously ballpoint that it shouldn't have deceived a child. And the subject matter had made Flavia gurgle with merriment when confronted with the first in a series of outraged collectors. Had they honestly, she asked, taken seriously something claiming to be a design for a late fifteenth-century vacuum cleaner? Quite ingenious, and might have worked had you persuaded some servant to set to work on a pair of bellows large enough, but *really*. And what about the hand-cranked, Renaissance food-processor? Personally, she thought that if people were daft enough to be taken in by such an obvious joke, she didn't see why they should be helped out, at the taxpayers' expense, by the Italian legal system.

But, of course, it had got into the papers, and Corrado Argan decided that something had to be done. And so last night they'd hauled him in. A nice lad, apparently, who'd used his skill to pay for a lifestyle marginally above the penurious level at which Italian art students habitually live. What's more, he'd implicated a dealer, who he claimed had been behind the entire thing.

'I suppose we interview him, make clucking noises and see if we can get him off with a caution or a suspended sentence.'

'I guess.'

Then Bottando rethought. 'On the other hand, it's about time we were seen to be cracking down on something. Tell you what, get the magistrate in Florence to lock him up for a week or so. Who is it?'

'The magistrate? Branconi, I think.'

'Oh, that's all right then. Yes. Get the dealer and bung him in the bin too. Then when all the interest has died out, let him go. Besides, there's no harm in giving him a good scare. Maybe a severe interrogation or two. Frighten the wits out of him.'

'I'll send Paolo. He could do with a day out.'

'Ah, no. I was going to send him to Palermo for a couple of days. Could you do this yourself?'

She nodded. 'Sure. I can go tomorrow if you like. Does this mean I can check out Maria Fancelli's statement? As I'm going to be there anyway?'

Bottando smiled at her persistence. 'Oh, very well. But remember . . .'

'Don't waste any time on it. I know. Oh, by the way,' she fumbled in her handbag and took out an envelope.

'What's this?'

'Copies of Argan's computer disks. I took the liberty of popping in when he was out for lunch yesterday. I thought you might want them. In the interests of departmental coordination.'

'Flavia, you're wonderful.'

'I know.'

She went off to Florence the next day with a full shopping list of little tasks to accomplish to make the trip worthwhile and fit in with Bottando's strictures about efficiency. While she could have done most by phone, there was undoubtedly a lot to be said for taking care of many of them in person and in one day. She had to collect reports on thefts, inspect a few sites of robberies, have a brief chat with the local police, interview the Leonardo man, talk to the magistrate about what should be done with him, interview someone Bottando thought might be suitable for a job, and so on.

But the first stop was the establishment of Signora della Quercia, whose continued existence had been ascertained by that most sophisticated tool of police enquiry, the telephone directory. Had she not been in Florence anyway, she would probably not have bothered. But she had half an hour to kill before her first appointment, and it was a cheaper way of spending the time than sitting in a café. At first sight she appeared to live in one of the very grand places occupied by the well-heeled Florentine establishment, a few hundred metres away from the Piazza della Repubblica down a dark but nonetheless imposing side street. At second sight, however, it was clearly an old town palazzo that had been sold, rehabilitated and turned into a set of offices for some vast and anonymous company selling who knew what. Flavia hesitated, then went in and asked the secretary guarding the gate. She assumed the signora had moved; did she know where she had gone?

The secretary was surprisingly talkative and, having nothing better to do, gave her the whole story; more, in fact, than she really wanted to hear. The signora had sold up about twelve years previously, but all the money had gone to her son, who'd effectively stolen it. He now lived in considerable splendour in Milan while the signora was left virtually penniless. The new owners, partly out of charity and partly because of the legal costs and bad publicity that would have gone with evicting her, allowed her to live in the attic, in what were the old servants' quarters. They had assumed it would be a temporary measure, but the old lady had lived on, and on, and still showed no signs of dying. It must be the exercise she got from climbing up and down six flights of stairs every day. She was at least ninety, the woman said, and as mad as a hatter. She was the last of the old inhabitants: even the Palazzo Straga was now the headquarters of a firm importing computers. If Flavia wanted to see her, she should go up. But it would probably be a waste of time.

Flavia walked to the back of the courtyard where the dark stairs to the servants' floor began and paused. Six flights of stairs? Was anything worth climbing up six flights of stairs?

It was pitch black, chilly despite the weather, and very unwelcoming in the stairwell, and Flavia had to pause periodically to make sure she didn't arrive at the top too breathless to introduce herself. The trip took some time, but eventually she stood outside a thin wooden door and knocked loudly on it.

She stood quietly, listening for signs of life, and eventually heard the sound of creaking floorboards and someone coming towards her. A tiny woman, bent over with age, opened the door, and peered at her quizzically. Flavia announced herself.

'Eh?' she said, cupping her hand to her ear.

Flavia bellowed that she was a policewoman and wanted to talk to her.

The old woman didn't believe it, and stood there, shaking her walking stick, as if to indicate that if Flavia put one foot wrong, she'd beat her to within an inch of her life. Flavia admired her spirit, but not her realism; she could have picked her up with one hand.

'Can I come in?' she yelled.

'Come in, then,' said Signora della Quercia in a thin, high-pitched voice, as if it had been her idea.

The room in which the old lady lived was about four

metres by three, and one of the most crowded places Flavia had ever seen. There was a bed, a wash basin, a sofa, an armchair, two dining chairs, three tables, a wooden bookcase, half a dozen carpets, pot-plants, a small cooker, three lights, one of which glowed dimly, and such wall space as wasn't covered with furniture was crammed with photographs, crucifixes, framed letters and other mementoes of an exceptionally long life. It wasn't possible to take more than one step without tripping, and Flavia, without bothering to be asked, weaved her way carefully through the obstacles and sat down to avoid breaking something.

Signora della Quercia hobbled behind, and fluttered down to perch on a chair opposite.

'I need to ask you about one of your old employees,' Flavia screamed in her direction.

'I am a Medici, you know,' she said.

'I believe you used to run a school. For foreigners. Is that right?'

'I ran a school. For foreigners. One of the finest. Only the very best young ladies came here. The cream of Europe, they were. Such charming girls.'

'I want to know about a woman called Maria Fancelli,' Flavia shouted hopefully.

'They were always so grateful to me. They used to regard me as their second mother. Of course, I didn't encourage such intimacy. Girls like that needed to maintain a proper sense of position, don't you think?'

'I understand you fired her. Is that correct?' Flavia bellowed, despite the strong feeling that the room was witnessing two conversations simultaneously.

'The English,' della Quercia twittered, blithely ignoring the question. 'The English, now. They always had a strong sense of themselves. Very formal and dignified, most of them. Admirable. Of course, I do believe they have degenerated in recent years.'

'Fancelli?' Flavia called hopefully.

'And very respectful of Italian civilization, of course. Quite unlike the French. Just the sort of girls my school was designed for. The best. The cream of Europe. And married the cream as well.'

'Maid-servants?'

'None of that vulgarity that so disfigures modern womanhood, even though they could be so kind. A gentler age, it was, in those days. But then my young ladies began to get ideas. No chaperones any more, and some were even drinking at parties and dancing with people to whom they'd not been formally introduced. Can you imagine that?'

Flavia shook her head sadly.

'I'm so glad you agree. Shortly after that I began to think of retirement. Just as well, the things you read in the papers these days. Can you imagine it? Well brought up ladies, of good families, having ideas below their station?' She snorted derisively. 'I used to tell them, if God had wanted you to work he would have made you working class. If he had wanted you to bring up your own children, he would have made you a bourgeois. They always listened to me. They respected me, you know. As a Medici, you understand.'

'Forster?' Flavia screamed, hoping that the word might trigger some old and dusty memory. The interview, after all, seemed to be proceeding by association. There wasn't much point in asking proper questions.

'Fortunately, I never had any major scandals,' she fluted. 'Although I believe I was lucky. Some of the boys hung around my girls like flies round a honey pot. Flies. Round a honey pot. Beasts. I always insisted on receiving only pure young girls, and always sent them back that way as well. Can you imagine the disaster if one had been returned damaged?'

Flavia sighed, resigned herself to the passive role of just sitting there, and looked surreptitiously at her watch. Time was running on.

'Such things only happened to servants,' she rambled on. 'And what would one expect from them? Although some of the boys who were presented here as escorts scarcely deserved the name of gentlemen. Yes, I remember. Now, why did I think of that? Something must have put it into my mind. It was the year that Miss Beaumont attended my school, a servant disgraced herself and had to be dismissed. Maria, her name was. I knew she would come to no good, of course.'

By this time, Flavia's mind was proceeding by association as well, and was beginning to leap ahead. She had mentioned Forster, and the word had triggered the old woman into talking about a servant called Maria. But that wasn't good enough for her line of business.

'Forster,' she yelled again, on the off-chance.

'The boy involved was quite shameless. He'd been hanging around Miss Beaumont like a dog after its owner, trying to ingratiate himself. She treated him with the contempt he deserved, knowing what he was, and he consoled himself elsewhere. Which, if I may say so, was perfectly typical. Like always ends up with like. She married very well later, of course, as did so many of my girls. Now what was his name? Foster? Forster. That's it. Now, why did I think of that?'

'Can't imagine,' Flavia said. 'What was her name?' she demanded, even more loudly than before.

'Of course, that was one of the high years, where I entertained the daughters of two dukes simultaneously.

And one American millionaire. I was naturally a bit dubious about her, even though she came highly recommended. And I was quite right, as I discovered. She spent too much time talking to the servants. Such a lowly characteristic. No really well-bred person would do that. Not even an American. Breeding will out, you know.'

'Her name?'

'Emily, I believe. Emily Morgan. She came from Virginia. I believe that is in America. I can't say I have ever wanted to go there myself, of course.'

'Not her. The servant.' She stood over her, glowering, willing her to act sane just for a few seconds. 'What was the name of your servant, Maria?'

She shrank back in the chair, shocked out of her reverie.

'Fancelli,' she said. 'Maria Fancelli.'

'Ah,' said Flavia with relief, and tripped over the sofa as she stepped back in exhaustion after her effort.

'Of course, I got rid of her as quickly as possible, you know. It wouldn't have done at all. And fortunately, the event did not become common knowledge among the select circle with whom I associated at that time. Not like now, of course.'

'Ah, yes,' said Flavia, no longer paying much attention.

'Signorina Beaumont was very upset, but I consoled her by telling her that people like that would sink to their own level, no matter how refined an example they were set. I believe that she tried to help the girl, thinking that she was merely young and foolish. I knew better, though.'

Flavia grimaced in a way she hoped could pass muster as a sympathetic smile. Horrible old woman, she thought.

'Ah, those days are long gone,' the old snob rabbited on. 'Once the cream of Europe came here, and felt it a privilege. Now what do they do? Back-packs, camping, noisy music and all sorts of inappropriate social mixing. I always say, if the aristocracy of Europe wishes to continue, it will have to avoid mixing with the lower orders. Do you know, signorina, I fear for the future. I really do.'

'Do you really,' she said, and gave up the unequal struggle.

It was partly because she had been so roundly defeated by the chaotic senility of Signora della Quercia that Flavia spent the entire evening getting her revenge by interrogating Giacomo Sandano with quite unnecessary vigour.

The poor man, after all, had done little to merit such treatment and as he had paid his debt to society over the little matter of the Fra Angelico, he scarcely deserved to be bothered; but as she'd gone to a considerable amount of trouble to find out where he was, it seemed a pity to waste the effort. She was mindful of Bottando's strictures, and wanted to demonstrate her thoroughness, if nothing else.

She tracked him down in a bar in one of the seedier outskirts of the city after having discovered that he was not, as she'd anticipated, back in jail again. Sandano was, in fact, one of those ever-hopeful types who are permanently convinced that this time his plan is foolproof. That was partly why the department loved him so dearly; every time he was tempted off the straight and narrow, they could count on another successful arrest and prosecution shortly afterwards.

He was, in brief, a rotten criminal, and a judge

had once told him so. He was more of a danger to himself than anyone else and his compulsive thieving and swindling brought him so little personal gain that nobody could really understand why on earth the man bothered.

Take his most recent exploit of trying to steal some candlesticks from a church, which had apparently landed him with only a short sentence. As the prosecutor remarked when preparing the case, it was quite a good idea to think of hiding inside the altar until the place was locked up for the night. It wasn't quite so brilliant to choose Christmas Eve, the one day when it wasn't locked up and remained full of people until near dawn.

Sandano had wedged himself in the box at six in the evening, and had finally given himself away at two in the morning when his body became so racked with cramps that he'd cried out in agony. It took some time before the priest and congregation got over the shock at what appeared to be a divine voice emerging from the altar, but when they'd recovered, they dragged him out, revived him with brandy, called the police and Sandano was, once again, returned to jail.

He was sitting over his drink, a hunched-up, weedy sort of man in his thirties, with an unhealthy demeanour and surrounded by a faint but permanent aroma of stale cigarettes. Slob, she thought as she walked up behind him. Could at least make an effort.

'Gotcha!' she said cheerfully, clapping her hand on his shoulder. Sandano nearly leapt out of his skin.

'Confess, Giacomo, confess,' she went on, to soften him up a little.

'What?' the verminous little man said in terror. 'What?'

'Just trying,' she said. 'A joke. Thought I'd buy you a

drink. I was passing through, and I thought, "I haven't seen my old friend Giacomo recently. Must look him up." How are you?'

He shook his head and recovered himself as much as possible. 'Fine,' he said cautiously. 'What do you want?'

Flavia looked sad. 'Conviction rates are really down,' she said. 'So we – Bottando and I – thought. What better than arresting old Giacomo? we thought. He's bound to have been up to something.'

Sandano twitched. 'I'm going straight,' he said. 'Those days are over for me. You know that.'

'Nonsense,' Flavia said. 'And I'm sure you'll realize it's nonsense after a night in the cells.'

'Look, what do you want?' Sandano said plaintively. 'Why don't you leave me alone?'

'Because I don't want to. I want to lock someone up. And you're as good a candidate as any. Better than most, in fact. Those candlesticks. How long had you been out of jail before you tried that one? Go on. Be honest?'

'A week,' he said sullenly. 'But I was short of money.'

'What had you been in for? Now, what was it? A picture, wasn't it? Fra Angelico, if I remember. We were quite surprised. A bit out of your league, that sort of thing. Got off very lightly, as well. How long was it? Six months?'

'Nine,' he said.

'Tell me about it. You were caught on the border, weren't you? So near and yet so far. How did you steal the thing in the first place without getting caught?'

Sandano fiddled with his drink and lit a cigarette. Then, very reluctantly, he said: 'I didn't.'

'Didn't what?'

'Didn't steal it.'

She raised an eyebrow. 'Come now. You admitted it. And you were caught with it in the back of your car.'

'I still didn't steal it.'

'So why plead guilty?'

''Cos I was offered a deal. I'd help the local Carabinieri to clean that one up without the need to call you lot in from Rome, and they agreed to forget one or two other little matters as well.'

'Was this the Meissen?' she asked, referring to a highly valuable eighteenth-century porcelain dinner service he'd stolen from a house by dropping it from a third-floor window into the arms of a waiting accomplice. As usual, his planning had slipped up.

'Yes,' he said sorrowfully. 'My own silly fault, that one. No doubt about it. Still haven't figured out why my brother was waiting round the other side of the building. But otherwise it was a good idea. It was only the noise of the stuff smashing that alerted the police, you know.'

'Yes. Tough luck, that. So you just confessed to stealing a picture when you hadn't? That's a bit stupid, isn't it?'

'No need to get personal. They told me that they knew I'd done it, and wouldn't budge no matter how much I said I was only the courier. They said that if I'd confess, they'd get a light sentence for me and forget the Meissen.'

'They kept their word, didn't they?'

'Oh, yes. I'm not complaining about that. But the fact remains that I didn't do it.'

'Ah, poor you,' she said sympathetically. 'Don't tell me. You really found the picture in a dustbin, and thought it would make a nice present for your mum.

So you put it in the car and before you could gift-wrap it and hand it over, these horrible suspicious police jumped you.'

'Close.'

Flavia gave him the sort of look appropriate for a person who is becoming extremely tiresome.

'Look, I'm telling you the truth,' he said indignantly. 'I was rung up and asked if I wanted a job. As a runner, to take a package over the border. Five million lire for a day's work. Two and a half million in advance. So I asked what it was, and this man said a package . . .'

'Which man?'

Sandano looked scornful. 'A friend of a friend of a friend. Someone who occasionally puts a bit of work my way. None of my business who's behind it all. I was to pick it up from the left luggage at the railway station, and deposit it in the left luggage at Zurich. Then I was to send the key to a post office box number in Berne. When it arrived safely, then I'd be sent the rest of my money.

'Before you ask, I had no idea then who it was. At the time. That was why my story didn't convince the Carabinieri.'

'At the time,' Flavia repeated. 'What does that mean?'

'Why should I tell you?'

'Because I can make your life hell if I want to. And because I will look favourably on your case the next time you get pinched for something. Which is only a matter of time. Think of it as an insurance policy. Who did steal it?'

Sandano twiddled his fingers and looked furtive, cunning and then sly as well. An ugly combination.

'You won't mention my name?'

'Heaven forfend.'

'And you remember people who do you favours?'

'Giacomo. Do I look like someone who forgets her friends? Or her enemies? Tell me what you know.'

Sandano paused and took a deep breath. 'OK. But I'm trusting you, mind.'

'Get on with it.'

'I didn't know who it was at the time. Like I say, it was done on the phone. I never saw anyone. Just a simple commission, and the less I knew the better, as far as I was concerned. It went wrong, as you know, and I got pinched, and did my time. Fair enough.

'But three months ago, I had a visit. This man turned up and asked me about the Fra Angelico. What had gone wrong. He was very smooth, and knew all about it. He wanted to be sure I hadn't told anyone anything. I told him I'd hardly have gone to jail if I had, and he seemed satisfied. He gave me some money, and said that he was impressed by my discretion.'

'And?'

'And nothing. That was it.'

'How much did he give you?'

'Three million lire.'

'And now the big question. Do you know who he was?'

'Yes.'

'Who?'

'An Englishman.'

'Name?'

'Forster.'

5

Constable Frank Hanson was a methodical, cautious man well suited to the routine of being a policeman in the English countryside. He had rounds that he made pretty much every day in his car, driving regularly through village after village, stopping periodically to talk to people to show that he was interested in community policing, occasionally turning a blind eye to the little infringements of law that went on all around him, and generally being a good, conscientious sort of person who was appreciated by those who actually noticed his existence.

Personally, he thought he was rather overworked; his beat had been devised in the far-off halcyon days when country life was safe, with virtually nothing but the occasional pub brawl or bit of domestic to occupy his time. Now he reckoned there was not much difference between the small patch of Norfolk that was in his care and the worst parts of London, or even Norwich, in which towns he was convinced sudden death was a way of life and sin the dominant occupation of the inhabitants.

Urban evil had now come to afflict him here. In the past few years, burglaries, rapes, arson, car theft and all manner of city blights had swept across the local villages, rendering his life miserable as he drove perpetually from one hamlet to another, jotting down details and reassuring people, quite untruthfully, that there was some chance that those responsible would be punished.

He was on his way to such a monstrosity now. Jack Thompson, a large and successful farmer, had just rung up, spluttering with indignation, to report that his dairy herd was three cows smaller than it had been the previous evening. It seemed that the Norfolk constabulary was now going to have to add cattle rustling to the various unnatural crimes it had to cope with.

Cattle rustling, he thought gloomily as he drove at several miles an hour above the speed limit through the village of Weller. What next? Piracy? He snorted with disgust. Gangs of yobs from Norwich boarding canal boats in the smoke and sinking them with cannon fire? Wouldn't surprise him at all, he muttered to himself as he sped along.

No discipline any more, he continued, reverting to one of his favourite themes. Not just thieves, either. The whole country was crumbling. Just selfishness; that's all that was left. He blamed the government for setting a bad example. And not paying public servants like himself enough.

I mean, he thought, look at that idiot there. Country road with lots of traffic and with a perfectly decent side path for pedestrians to walk on. And what does he do? Does he think of the danger he's putting himself and others into? No. Instead, he goes prancing around in the middle of the road as though he owned it.

Eleven o'clock in the morning and probably drunk already.

It was too much. The man was leaping up and down like someone who'd been returned to the community – another one of PC Hanson's grumbles – completely regardless of all danger. Hanson slammed his foot on the brakes, and slowed down to give the man a good talking to.

'You saw me,' the man said as the car stopped. He spoke clearly, although with an agitated tone, and was tolerably well dressed with fair hair and slender hands that he was wringing together nervously.

'Could hardly avoid that, could I, sir?' said Hanson drily, in the best traditions of constabulary repartee. 'Don't you think you might be safer on the pavement?'

'But I wanted to attract your attention. It's urgent.'

'Oh, yes, sir? And why's that?'

The man gestured vaguely in the direction of a pathway a hundred yards or so further on. 'There's a man in there,' he babbled.

Constable Hanson, offered such an opportunity for wit, could hardly decline it. 'Well, that's not so surprising, is it, sir? It's a house. People live in houses, sir. Now, had it been a chicken coop . . .'

'Yes, I know that,' the man said impatiently. 'I mean that he's dead. That's why I was trying to wave you down.'

'Is he now? Well, we'd better have a look at that, then.'

And so, reporting his position on the radio, and deciding that Farmer Thompson's cattle had probably already been turned into hamburgers and could wait, he drove into the driveway of the Old Mill House, with the, man who'd stopped him jogging along behind.

'Now, sir,' he said as he got out of the car, 'would you mind telling me your name?'

'Argyll. Jonathan Argyll. I came up to see someone called Forster, and when I got here there was no reply. The door was ajar, so I walked in and there he was. Still is, I imagine.'

'Aha! Shall we go and see then?'

PC Hanson walked over to the door, pushed it open lightly, and stepped into the hallway.

There was no trouble with Mr Argyll's powers of observation, at least. The body at the bottom of the stairs was most definitely dead, and the unnatural, skewed angle at which the head joined the neck instantly suggested a reason, as did the way in which the thinning, fair hair was matted with blood. PC Hanson had known Geoffrey Forster at a distance; he knew the man was something arty, who worked for the people at Weller House. Had done so, anyway, until Miss Beaumont died.

As there had been a spate of burglaries in the area in the past few weeks, his immediate thought was that this was another, or it was quite simply an accident. These old buildings that city dwellers so liked were, to his mind, hopelessly inconvenient, uneconomical and dangerous. Pretty enough, he supposed, with their thatch and whitewash, but nothing would ever persuade him to live in one. The staircase, now, was twisted, highly polished and slippery. He walked up it, and noticed that the top stair was loose and wobbly. It struck him, as he walked out of the house to radio for assistance, that it was well within the bounds of possibility that the man had simply slipped downstairs, bashing his head and breaking his neck as he went. He would have to wait before he could tell if anything had been stolen.

'Oy!' he called after he'd sent the radio message and emerged from the police car once more. 'Where do you think you're going?'

Argyll, who'd been walking in the direction of the front gate, looked back nervously. 'Just looking around, you know,' he called back. 'To see if I could find anything useful.'

Oh God, Hanson thought. One of those. He reckoned this stranger had a bit of explaining to do in any case.

'Well, don't. Come back here where I can see you. Who are you, anyway?'

Argyll crunched his way back up the gravel path until he was next to Hanson, then explained himself. 'I'm an art dealer. I came here to talk to Mr Forster about a picture.'

'And what picture was that?'

'It's a picture he may have owned. Had. Stolen, in fact,' he said apologetically. Hanson's eyebrow lifted in response.

'Oh, yes?' he said flatly.

'Yes,' Argyll went on nervously. 'So I was going to ask him about it. That's why I'm here.'

'And what concern might this be of yours? Do you own this picture?'

'Oh, no.'

'Did he steal it from you?'

'Heavens, no.'

'I see. Well, sir, I suggest you just stand there. Don't touch anything, and wait until we're ready to take a statement.'

'Would it be useful for me to look around the house, to see if I can spot anything?'

'No, sir,' Hanson said with exaggerated patience. 'Just don't move. All right?'

And so Argyll, hands in pockets, spent the next half hour shivering in the wind, wishing he'd remembered what a cold thing an English summer was, and standing mournfully next to the police car, waiting for reinforcements to come and take his statement.

He did, however, provide one or two useful services for the police, the main one being fending off the spectators who walked past on the way out of the village, noticed the police car, stopped and came in to ask what was going on.

'Accident. Best leave it to the experts,' he told an old scruffy man with a mangy dog and a plastic bag full of frozen food who appeared at the gate first of all. This one raised an eyebrow with a knowing look, then ambled off.

'Accident,' he said again to a thuggish, thick-set young man who came along a few moments later and stared at the scene with an air of almost malicious fascination. 'Maybe a burglary.'

He noticed that this made the man scowl and hurry away in a furtive sort of way.

'Accident. Move along, please,' he said again to a greying woman in her mid-fifties with bright, curious eyes who also walked in to see the events. He'd always wanted to tell someone to move along, please.

'Don't be ridiculous,' this one replied briskly, brushing aside his spurious authority with the contempt it deserved. 'I'll do no such thing. Hanson!' she called out in an unexpectedly loud voice to the policeman who'd disappeared back into the house. 'Come out of there.'

And Hanson did, with surprising speed. Argyll was impressed. The man didn't quite touch his forelock, but he was plainly very much more friendly than he had been when dealing with him.

'What in God's name is going on here?' she asked briskly.

'It's Mr Forster, Mrs Verney. He's dead. Broken neck, by the look of it.'

Mrs Verney seemed taken aback by this, but lost none of her poise and certainly wasted no time with conventional expressions of regret, shock or horror.

'When?'

Hanson shook his head. 'Some time, I think. The body's cold. He appears to have fallen down the stairs. This gentleman here' – he indicated Argyll with a nod of his head – 'found him.'

'About ten minutes ago,' Argyll offered. 'Eleven o'clock, or thereabouts. I had an appointment.'

'I'd be grateful if you'd keep me informed,' the woman said, ignoring Argyll completely after giving him a rapid look over. 'It used to be our house, after all. I knew we should have had that staircase fixed. Is it the top stair? It's always been a bit wobbly. I did tell him once . . .'

Constable Hanson said that sort of thing would have to wait until the experts arrived. So she stood there, hands in pocket, thinking for a moment.

'Well,' she said after a while. 'If I'm going to be sued for selling someone an unsafe staircase, I'd like to know about it as soon as possible. Come along, Frederick,' she went on, whistling at the labrador that had been snuffling around the rose bushes. It occurred to Argyll that, had there been any useful hints like footprints in the soil, they probably weren't there any more.

And then she marched off down the pathway and disappeared up the road.

'Who was that?' Argyll asked the policeman, thinking that the common assault might make a useful bridge to establish more cordial relations.

'Mrs Mary Verney,' the policeman said. 'The local landowner, not that she's really local, or owns much land any more, I gather. Quite a nice woman, but not really from these parts. She only took over when her cousin died recently.'

'Ah.'

But any further opportunity for conversational bonding was lost, because at that moment the full range of policemen arrived to do their several duties.

And so the slow, ponderous wheels of justice began to inch forward. Photos were taken, distances were measured, brows were furrowed, windows were peered at, chins were scratched. Bodies were removed and statements were taken. It lasted for hours, and as far as Argyll could see, didn't accomplish a great deal.

The local police, however, were very pleased with themselves. Fingerprint men danced around, puffing away like a bunch of manic hairdressers. Other miscellaneous experts also gave it as their preliminary view that, at a rough guess, Geoffrey Forster had met his end by falling down the stairs. They were not so bold as to say how this unfortunate event had come about.

Deprived of anything really meaty by way of discoveries, rather like Flavia with Sandano, they turned their full attention on to Argyll in revenge, and he spent the next several hours stating his business, explaining his presence and accounting for his movements. He recommended that, if they wanted testimonials to his good character and general usefulness to the police, they should contact the Art Theft Department in Italy. A Signorina di Stefano, he added, spoke good enough English to praise him to the skies in language they would understand.

With some reluctance, the collective mind of the police

edged slowly towards the conclusion that, if Forster had been given assistance in his final descent, then it was unlikely that Argyll had provided it, especially as the doctors later offered a preliminary opinion that he had been dead for twelve hours at least and Argyll could prove relatively easily that he had been in London at the time. While not ruling out some devious piece of skulduggery entirely, it didn't really fit. Moreover, Bottando, in Flavia's absence, did his duty by saying that in his opinion Argyll was a generally law-abiding type.

'And this picture,' Inspector Wilson said, 'did you believe that Mr Forster had it in his possession?'

'No. I'd be very surprised if he did. Anyone who kept a stolen painting for more than two decades would be a bit silly. Why bother to steal it in that case?'

'But it was your impression that he knew what you were referring to. When you mentioned it on the phone?'

'Oh yes. It seemed so. He said he'd talk to me about that. The "that" was emphasized, you see.'

'You know what this picture is?'

'I have an approximate description. I was told about it a few days ago. Before that I'd never heard of it. It was a Madonna and child.'

'You don't have a photograph, I suppose?'

Argyll shook his head and said that nobody had one.

'Very useful, sir. Thank you. Now, you got here . . .'

And on they went, stating, typing, witnessing, confirming, signing. Eventually it was all over.

'Oh, and one other thing, sir. Your passport.'

'What about it?'

'Could I have it, sir?'

'What? Why?'

Wilson smiled apologetically. 'You'll get it back in a few days, I'm sure.'

'You mean I'm going to be stuck here?'

Wilson smiled again.

'But what about my job? I live in Italy, you know.'

'I know. That's why we want your passport.'

'But I'm not under arrest? You don't suspect me of anything?'

'Oh, no. But we might want to talk to you again, and it would be much easier for us if you were close to hand.'

He was very polite about it, but quite firm. Argyll, scowling and a little alarmed, handed the document over. He'd never realized it could be confiscated like that. Now it was gone, he rather missed it.

After he'd been told that a further statement would be required in due course, he was left at his leisure, although how he was to fill it in a village like Weller he was not entirely sure. As he walked past the bus stop in the only real street the place possessed, he realized that he was in a bit of a pickle: the last bus to Norwich had gone and there was not much chance of getting a train back to London. He would have to throw himself on the mercy of the constabulary and beg for a lift somewhere. Unless, that is, he could find a place to stay.

He was also out of cigarettes, so went to stock up and make enquiries.

'Five packets of Rothmans,' he said to the surly, pasty-faced woman on the other side of the counter in the tiny village shop-cum-post office, and grabbed one of the packets that were put down in front of him. He glanced around for emergency rations so that he could maintain a small supply of provisions. Alas, everything was in tins, had been deep-frozen for aeons, or was covered in a thin layer of dust. He decided to leave them be, and settled for some biscuits. One thing about Italy, it doesn't know much about good biscuits. Not with chocolate on top.

'Tell me,' he went on to the woman, who struck him as a fine example of the dangers of in-breeding and bad diet, 'is there a hotel around here somewhere? Where I can get a room for the night?'

'You in the police?'

'No.'

'Twelve pound fifty.'

'What?'

'For the cigarettes. Twelve pound fifty.'

'Good God,' he said, reluctantly handing over much of his cash. 'What about a hotel?'

'No hotel.'

'There is a pub though,' said a cheerful and familiar-sounding voice from behind. He turned round and saw Frederick the labrador standing in the open doorway of the shop. 'But the rooms are a bit dicey.'

'Rats,' he said in disappointment.

'That's right,' agreed Mary Verney evenly, following the dog in. 'But you might survive a night or two. You have to stay around because of Geoffrey, do you?'

Not the discreet type. Argyll could see, out of the corner of his eye, the large pale cigarette server moving slightly downwind so she could hear better. He in turn edged towards the door, and Mrs Verney accompanied him.

'What's your name?' she asked as they emerged into the fresh air again.

She talked in a pleasing, well-modulated voice that was, nonetheless, strangely lacking in accent. Argyll decided this was merely because she talked normally: none of the thick rusticity of the locals, nor the tonsil-strangling accents normally associated with the English aristocracy.

Argyll introduced himself, then turned his attention more directly to his fellow customer. A pleasant, very English-looking lady, lots of tweed and labrador hair. Good bones, as they say, and the sort of skin that retains its freshness through decades of being lashed by fresh, cold rain while out in pursuit of furry animals.

'D'you want some tea, by the way? I'm just about to make some. It's just so I can pump you dry about Geoffrey and what's been going on there. Be warned. The police are being damnably uncommunicative, and I'm dying to know.'

Argyll considered, then accepted. It would make a pleasant change. Besides, while he was providing her with information, she might do the same for him.

So he walked by her side back through the main street of the village, then down a broad avenue that branched off to the left, with his new companion chattering away about the family of jays nesting in the oak tree, the depredations of Dutch Elm disease which had quite transformed the area. Her remarks were punctuated by whistles and shouts at Frederick the dog who lolloped alongside, snuffling his nose joyously into every patch of summer mud that presented itself for inspection.

On the whole, it was not a bad village, he decided, located as it was in one of those small sections of East Anglia which are not flat as a pancake and windswept by icy gales coming straight from the North Pole. Clearly, though, it had come down in the world in the past few centuries. It probably had less than a thousand inhabitants, most of whom lived in minuscule cottages along the diminutive main street and in outlying farmhouses and labourers' cottages. The church, on the other hand, would have done a fair-sized city proud. It was vast, with enough space to sit every villager and still have room to spare. The square, grim tower dominated the entire landscape and the lack of any other building of comparable grandeur nearby only emphasized that the village had not yet fully recovered from the Black Death.

Apart from that there was a small, self-enclosed settlement of modern houses on the outskirts built for people who wanted to live in the country but had no desire to give up either the form or appearance of suburban life, and Weller House itself.

This lay at the end of a grand, if a little neglected, avenue and had been built, so Argyll guessed, in the late seventeenth century. Subsequent modernizers had Greekified one side in the nineteenth century, and a few decades later had Gothicized the other so that the house looked strikingly like an example from a text-book of architectural styles. The result was charming, though. Just the right size, too. Not a gigantic palace, but something you could live in and still impress every neighbour for twenty miles around.

Quiet and tranquil as well, he added to himself. About three-quarters of a mile out, cut off from the rabble by still-extensive – if overgrown – grounds which turned into scruffy woodland, a tall stone wall and a large, rusty iron gate that gave on to the main road. Once upon a time the stone wall was to keep the peasants at bay; now it served to keep out all the noise of the modern age. Adaptability, that was the thing.

Alas, more than stone walls were needed. Just as Argyll was thinking how quiet it was, there came another low rumble from somewhere over the horizon.

As he stood there, trying to work out what sort of storm was in the offing, the sound grew in volume and changed from something that resembled a slow-motion roll of thunder into an ever more high-pitched whine. Then, with an explosive blast that made the ground beneath his feet vibrate, two black and very threatening shapes shot through the air a few hundred feet above him, flashing through the skies at an almost unbelievable speed. Then they disappeared over the line of trees at the far end of the grounds, and the noise slowly dissipated once again.

'What in God's name was that?' he asked his new hostess, who appeared to pay no attention to the phenomenon. She merely glanced at her watch.

'Five-thirty,' she said mysteriously. 'Must have been bombing Scotland again.'

'Eh?'

'They're F1-11s,' she explained with all the indifference that long familiarity breeds. 'American bombers,' she added, lest Argyll's aircraft recognition skills be rusty. 'Their base is about five miles away, and we're underneath their flight path. When they're feeling a bit perky, they see the avenue cut through the trees, and can't resist belting up it for all they're worth. Bloody noisy, aren't they?'

'Can't anyone stop them? The house'll fall down if it vibrates like that.'

She pointed up at the house, and one long crack coming down the side. 'I'm trying to persuade the Americans it's all the fault of their pilots and that they should pay for it. In fact, I suspect that crack appeared before the Wright brothers were even born, but never mind. With a bit of luck they'll cough up before they go.'

'Go where?'

She shrugged. 'Wherever they come from. The base is closing, as they think there's nothing to defend us from any more. Disaster.'

'Why? It'll be much quieter.'

'Yes. And that's the problem. No commuters want to live here because it's so noisy; so when they pack up, Weller will become another bedroom community. Also, the Americans were incredibly generous. They so wanted to be liked they paid for every house for miles around to have double-glazing; repaved all the roads their lorries used, and threw annual parties and excursions for the local children. Wonderful people. Much better than the local council. And the party's over. The general feeling round these parts is that it's all the fault of the Russians for being so weak and feeble. Come along.'

Digesting this strange analysis of geo-politics, Argyll followed Mrs Verney through the big wooden doors covered with peeling and blistered paint, and into the hallway. He waited patiently, examining distinct signs of woodworm in the dark brown panelling, while she worked herself up into an artificial fit of indignation and then telephoned the base commander to protest about his pilots using her arboretum for target practice. Yet again, Colonel, yet again, as she put it so primly.

'Now, then,' she said afterwards. 'Tea. And gossip. But tea first.' Then she led the way down a grim staircase to a kitchen so ancient that it might well have been transported complete for an exhibition on Edwardian domesticity, and began to brew up.

'No modern equipment, and no servants to work the old equipment either,' she observed. 'The worst of both worlds. I spend my life trying to fix the fuses when they blow. It's amazing how much you learn about electrical circuitry when you join the landed gentry.'

'I thought you were born into it. Isn't that the whole point?'

'Depends on how resilient the breed is. In the case of my family, not very. They die like flies. I'm about the last. My Uncle Godfrey, who reduced the place to the dire state which you can see, dropped off his perch about fifteen years ago. His daughter died last winter. Leaving me this bloody mausoleum, for which generosity I was not overly grateful. And her dog, of course. Worst day of my life, when I inherited this place. The dog's OK, though.'

'You don't have to live here, do you? Couldn't you just close it up and move into a comfortable bungalow?'

She sighed as she poured the boiling water into a kettle the size of a bathtub. 'Then who'd fix the fuses when they blow? Or the plumbing when it gets stuck? Or the roof when it leaks? Without constant attention this baroque slum would fall down in a week. You can't just walk out and leave it. And before you suggest it, don't think I haven't thought about it. Fat insurance policy, nice fire, and me crying my eyes out as I cash the cheque.'

Argyll sat down at the kitchen table and grinned at her.

'But, of course, I'd get caught, wouldn't I? And I'm damned if I'm going to spend the rest of my life in jail for this place.'

'You can't give it to someone?'

She snorted. 'Who? I'm the only Beaumont who's ever earned a penny. If I can't manage, that lot certainly couldn't. The only thing to be said for them is that they're too sensible to try. They know a loser when they see one.'

'What about the National Trust?'

'They'd take it. But not encumbered with debts, which is the problem at the moment. So I'm stuck with it, unless I can lay my hands on some cash. Funny world, isn't it? I don't suppose you have a couple of million you have no use for? We could turn the place into a conference centre, or fill it with geriatrics and squeeze every last penny out of them.'

'Not on me.'

'Pity.'

'No children, then?'

'Three. Twins and a single. They're all scattered to the winds, thank God. I mean, I love them dearly, but now they're off learning for themselves how beastly life is, I find my existence is very much calmer. Quite like being young again.'

'Goodness.'

'Now, tell me about yourself. Who are you? Where do you come from? Do you live alone? Are you married? What, most importantly, is going on in the village? And are you responsible for it?'

So Argyll sang for his tea, giving the details of his life as the vivaciously waspish woman opposite nodded and asked supplementary questions. Her eager cross-questioning over the death of Geoffrey Forster would have done a skilled lawyer proud. For the first time since he got off the plane, he felt relaxed, and as a result he stayed chattering much longer than he should.

'But are you a *good* art dealer, dear?' she asked after she'd exhausted the topic of Geoffrey Forster and moved on to excavate Argyll's personal life.

He shrugged. 'I'm not bad at the art bit. It's the dealing side that lets me down. I'm told I lack the killer instinct.'

'Not ruthless enough, eh?'

'That's the general opinion. In fact, the main trouble is not having enough money to buy pictures in the first place. The really major dealers start off either with oodles of their own, or a backer who will put up capital. But I haven't noticed the queues forming.'

'I wish you luck.'

'Thank you.'

And so the conversation harmlessly meandered along and it was nearly eight before he glanced at the clock on the wall, gave a start and stood up.

'Are you in a hurry?' she asked.

'Not exactly. But I should go; I have to find somewhere to stay the night.'

'Stay here.'

'I couldn't possibly do that.'

'Please yourself. How long are the police going to be interested in you?'

'I've no idea. I can't imagine what else they might need. But they seem to expect me to hang around. And they've got my passport as well.'

She nodded. 'A bit of a captive, then. Tell you what, if you're still here tomorrow, come for dinner. I can guarantee that the food will be better than the pub, if nothing else.'

Argyll said he'd be delighted.

6

Flavia got back from Florence in a fairly jolly mood, and before knocking off for the evening, went into the office to tell Bottando of her findings. 'Is he about?' she asked Paolo, who was standing by the coffee machine.

'Think so,' replied the colleague. 'Go carefully, though. He's a real misery this afternoon. I was going to ask him for a day off, as a reward for catching the Leonardo man. I thought better of it when I saw his face. It was his compulsory overtime on a Sunday face.'

'Why?'

'Don't know. Just getting old, I guess. However good you were once, too long doing the same thing . . .'

Aha. Forewarned is forearmed. Paolo had gone over to the enemy. She mounted the stairs with a proper mixture of sympathy and caution, to present her findings.

When she told him about her trip, however, he didn't seem impressed. Just nodded in an absent-minded fashion.

'What's the matter?' she asked. 'Paolo said you were an old sourpuss today.'

'Did he, indeed? Very indiscreet of him. Nor is it

accurate. I am, in fact, more furious than I have ever been in my entire life.'

'Argan?'

Bottando nodded.

'Those disks I gave you?'

He nodded again. 'Argan absconded with much of the Giotto file, read it, and has now written and circulated an enormous memorandum. Talking about how we waste our time, use up resources concocting fictions, have not the slightest idea about what modern crime is all about. He pours fun on the whole exercise, manages to get across the idea that the Giotto material is taken seriously, which it isn't. That we are working on it at the moment, which we are not. And that I personally am so obsessed with my own theories that the smooth running of the department is being sacrificed to my daft ideas. Using your going to this Fancelli woman as evidence. And your trip to Florence, although how he found out you were doing anything on it there I don't know.'

'Whoops.' Not a brilliant comment, but justifiable. Flavia wondered whether Paolo might have been making his bid for promotion with the new broom.

'The general thrust is that I personally am ineffective, if not actually senile, that action is required immediately so that the department can be placed in a pair of safe hands who understands how to run things properly.'

'Hands which are attached to the body of Corrado Argan?'

'Even he doesn't say so directly, but that's the idea.'

'Wipe the disk.'

'What would that accomplish?'

'It would win you some time.'

'Not much. Besides, it's too late. He's already printed fifteen copies and sent them out.'

'Fifteen?'

'Top copy to the minister. And everybody else down.'

'Oh, dear.'

'Is that all you can say? I'll kill the little bastard.'

'Now, now. Calm down.'

'Why? What is there to be calm about? I don't want to be calm.'

'Evidently. But I don't think it'll do much good at the moment. You're turning Argan into a demon. And that's not the best way of reacting.'

'So what do you suggest? I wouldn't be so mad, except for the fact that today of all days, fragments of evidence suggest that the lead this woman gave us might go somewhere after all. I don't know where, of course. Except that I can't risk doing anything about it.'

'What do you mean?'

'Your Jonathan. The English police rang to ask about him. He found out that Forster was an art dealer who has just been found dead. Possibly murdered.'

'Ah,' said Flavia with interest. 'Tell me all.'

Bottando gave her what little information he had.

'That is a little awkward,' she said when he finished. 'But it does make him interesting enough to investigate, doesn't it?'

'Not if it turns out that it was an accident.'

'Anything else?'

'Just that they want us to let them know if we have anything on Forster, if he had any contacts or business here. Awkward.'

'Why? That won't take us long. And it's fairly routine.'

'I know. But it will be a formal, on-the-record request which will no doubt note the fact that we are already interested in the damn man. Which will make my insistence to Argan that we are not seem even more duplicitous. I mean, I could have passed off your efforts as the inexperienced enthusiasm of a junior . . .'

'Thank you.'

'But official bits of paper, noting my conversation with them re Forster. That's more difficult. Your Jonathan was trying to be helpful, I suppose, and accomplishing the exact opposite. As usual. You *did* tell him not to bother with Forster?'

'Ah . . .'

'Oh.'

'But it's just as well he did,' she said robustly. 'Because I talked to Signora della Quercia. She's completely loopy, but her ramblings seemed consistent with what Fancelli told us. Even remembered Forster and Fancelli.'

'Hmm.'

'More importantly, I also had a chat with Sandano. Who now maintains that he didn't steal that Fra Angelico. He was railroaded into confessing by the Carabinieri, so he says, which is quite possible. He reckons he was just delivering it for someone.'

'Oh yes?'

'An Englishman called Forster.'

Bottando looked at her stolidly. 'Oh, God.'

'He's not the most truthful of people but I was thinking about it. That Padua job was very neat. Well executed, no hitches at all. It only went wrong because of a keen customs man. Now, does that really sound like Sandano to you?'

Bottando considered. 'Not really. So, we have a couple of very interesting leads . . .'

He rubbed his chin and drummed his fingers on the desk and sighed. 'It's a gamble, isn't it? We investigate Forster and come up with something, then we can cobble together something to prove we weren't wasting our time and make Argan seem vindictive. Investigate him and come up with nothing . . .'

'You'll have to rely on your instincts.'

'My instincts say something very odd is going on, and that makes me cautious.' He thought some more, then slammed his open palm on the desk. 'No,' he said. 'I've had enough. Let's see what we can find out. If Argan says it's a waste of time, then there's bound to be something worthwhile there.'

7

Argyll was leaning against the bar of the pub and, very much less chirpy than before, considering the miserable choices before him. He had arrived just before nine, and went to the bar for some food before seeing about somewhere to stay for the night.

Scotch egg, pickled onion, pork scratchings, came the reply. Or we could do you a nice ham sandwich, if you like. There might be one left over from lunch-time.

He shook his head in mixed sadness and horror. A pint of bitter and a packet of crisps, please.

'Don't blame you,' came a voice, clearly not local and more likely hailing from somewhere in the vicinity of Wisconsin. He looked to the end of the bar, and spied two men, one old, gnarled, bright-eyed and local and the other young, fresh-faced, glum and foreign. He was in uniform and the one who had roused himself to comment on the quality of the traditional pub fayre.

'You're new around here, aren't you?' asked the wizened old duffer perched on the stool, taking over the conversation.

'You're the person I saw in Forster's house this morning,' he continued accusingly. 'The one who told me to move along. You in the police then?'

There was going to be no escape, that was clear. Probably everybody in East Anglia knew who he was by now and wanted a private conversation about Geoffrey Forster. But, as with Mary Verney, that was all right as long as it was mutually advantageous. Argyll knew of no reason why he should be discreet.

'No,' he said. 'I just found the body.'

'You kill him?'

The question rather took Argyll aback. It seemed a bit rude, really. He hastened to explain that he had only ever seen Forster dead.

'Who did kill him, then?'

'I really don't know. What makes you think anyone killed him?'

'Hope they did,' the old man said, and the Wisconsin flyer looked glumly into his beer.

'Right,' he said. Not a brilliant conversationalist.

'This is Hank,' the old duffer continued. 'He's got another name, but there's no point telling you what it is. It's unpronounceable. That's because he's foreign. I'm George.'

Argyll nodded politely.

'So, who do the police think did it?' he continued methodically, lest he leave a loophole for Argyll to hide relevant information in. 'Anyone seen leaving the scene of the crime?'

'Not as far as I know. And I don't even know it was a crime,' Argyll repeated.

'Met Mrs Verney already, I gather,' George continued, switching direction rapidly.

'Oh. Yes. I met her. Nice woman, I thought.'

'A dark one, her.'

'Oh yes? Why's that?'

'She's a foreigner. Only came here when she got Weller House. When Miss Veronica died.'

'So I gather.'

'Not got the ways, you know.'

'What ways?'

'Tries hard, I'll give her that. But she doesn't really know. Take the village fête.'

'What about the village fête?' Argyll asked politely. He wished he could find a way of steering the conversation back to Forster. Oddly, they didn't seem to want to talk about him. He would have thought that a real murder would have got them chattering away like crazy.

'Refused to turn up. Too busy, she said. That's the trouble, y'see. She's not here so often. Always going down to London and places. Miss Veronica, now. She never missed a fête in her life, even though she was sick all the time.'

'Now, George, don't go prattling,' said the barman easily as he came over to return a pint glass to its rightful place. 'This gentleman doesn't want to hear about Mrs Verney.'

'Quite right,' Argyll said, deciding that the direct approach might be better. 'I want to hear about Geoffrey Forster.'

'Pfuff! A piece of scum, he was,' was George's considered opinion on this. 'And I'll say this for Mrs Verney, she'd have no truck with him. She may be odd, but she's no fool.'

'So why did she sell him a house?'

'That was Miss Veronica's doing,' he said. 'Thought he was wonderful, she did. Thought the sun shone out of his backside. Course, she was a bit . . .'

'George,' said the barman sharply. 'Now you shut up. I'll not have that sort of idle gossip here.'

What sort of gossip? Argyll thought. Come along, you old fool. Don't listen to him . . .

'It's not gossip,' George protested, 'I'm not saying anything . . .'

'Can I buy you a drink?' asked the gossip-hating Argyll.

'Don't mind if I do. Pint, please. And a half for the dog.' A small mongrel looked up expectantly from the floor, with bright eyes and a slightly alcoholic expression. The American airman said he had to get back to base, and wandered off with a couple of comrades who'd been playing a surprisingly good game of darts.

When master and dog both had their snouts stuck in a bowl of bitter, Argyll resumed the hunt. He decided he'd start discreetly.

'And what about Miss Beaumont? What was she like?'

George scowled as he swivelled round to see if the barman was in earshot, decided he had a brief opening as the man drew a Guinness at the far end of the bar, and then discreetly tapped the side of his head.

'Barking, if you know what I mean,' he said in a loud stage whisper that could be heard outside in the car park. 'Of course, it was all kept private. But I was told she ate lots of pills. That's what killed her, you know, the pills. Poor Mrs Verney found her. She was staying as Miss Veronica was ill. Only relation who'd have anything to do with her. Anyway, Mrs Verney went out to London for a day, came back, and there she was, dead in her bed.'

'What about Forster, then? You don't seem to have liked him.'

George made a facial expression consistent with not liking someone. 'Nasty man. Glad he's dead. And it's a pity you didn't kill him, young man.'

'Oh? Why?'

''Cause if you had, I'd buy you a drink.'

'You're going to buy me one anyway,' Argyll said. 'It's your round. What was wrong with Forster?'

'Dishonest, crawling, mean, vicious.'

'A good start,' Argyll conceded. 'Anything more specific?'

'Nothing that I'd tell you. But I will say I was always surprised that a respectable woman like Miss Veronica would have anything to do with him, if you see what I mean, and him married to that poor downtrodden woman who should have left him years ago.'

'Oh,' Argyll said, a confused enlightenment dawning.

'Not someone who was ever seen in here, I can tell you that for nothing,' the barman added from his side of the counter.

Sipping his beer, Argyll decided that this wasn't really all that interesting. Nothing such as you might call a full curriculum vitae, so to speak. If he did indeed keep himself to himself, then no one in the village was going to know much about his art dealing. Only Mary Verney might be able to help there. Which meant that he was going to have to get her into a much longer conversation.

'Tell me,' he said abandoning the search for knowledge in the bar, 'do you have a room for the night?'

A few minutes later he was led up into a bleak, cold chamber, the very sight and feel of which made shivers run up and down his spine. If one wanted to kill oneself, or maybe even write a neglected masterpiece in a romantic sort of way, it would have been ideal.

If you wanted a good and comfortable night's sleep, it wasn't right at all. When the barman – who did have the grace to look embarrassed – mentioned the price, his spirit rebelled.

And a useful idea came to him. A bit of a nerve, of course. On the other hand, she had offered.

He marched back up the road, turned in at the gates once more, encouraged by the fact that lights were burning cheerfully in a couple of rooms on the ground floor, and knocked with more certainty than he felt on the door.

'Hello again,' he said with an apologetic smile as it swung open and an enquiring face appeared.

'Jonathan! What a pleasant surprise. I was afraid you were the local burglar come to visit me at last. Do come in. I'm having my late-night cocoa by the fire. Trying to keep warm.'

'Is that why you're wearing a mac?'

'Eh? Oh, no. I was bringing in some wood. Chopped with my own fair hands. It's another skill you learn when you're privileged. Come in. Would you like some cocoa? Slice of cake?'

Try as he might to avoid salivating, something about him must have given off strong hints about what he thought of a mere slice of cake.

'Are you hungry?' she asked with a motherly concern.

'Umm,' he said hesitating between politeness and self-interest.

'You are, aren't you?'

He smiled regretfully, abandoning the politeness option.

'I am absolutely starving,' he said. 'I've never felt so hungry in my life. I haven't eaten all day.'

'Oh, you poor thing. The state of the cuisine in the pub

doesn't reach great heights, does it? It was the sausage rolls that put you off, I suppose?'

'A sausage roll I could have managed. The Scotch eggs, though . . .'

'Ah, yes. I ate one of those once. I can do you a plate of bacon and eggs, with some fresh bread and butter. Not wonderful, but I'm afraid that's about all there is, until I go shopping tomorrow. But they're fresh eggs, at least. I have a hen, you know. I keep it in the state bedroom.'

'You really mustn't,' he said, hoping she would brush the objection aside as mere politeness.

Being a well brought up lady, she did exactly that. 'Why not? The bedroom's not used for anything else. And hens are quite clean, if you treat them properly. Now,' she went on, 'come down to the kitchen and do as you're told. This won't take long.'

'Is there really a local burglar?' he asked as he settled himself down and surrendered to the comforting feeling that being cooked for by a woman old enough to be your mother brings with it.

'Oh, yes,' she said, as she broke the eggs and fiddled with the bacon. 'At least, it strikes me it's a local.'

'Why?'

'Because all the houses burgled belong to the foreign interlopers.'

'The Americans?'

'Lord, no. No one would dare. They're convinced all Americans sleep with machine guns under their pillows. Just the English foreigners, if you see what I mean. The police reckon it's because they have the bigger houses, but I think it's the countryman's revenge. No one's bothered me, mind you. I'm not exactly thought of as a local, but a sort of resident alien. An honorary citizen, so to speak.'

'So who's your suspect?'

'There's a lad called Gordon. A bit wild. Lots of dubious friends who drive around in cars they can't possibly afford on their incomes – not that many of them have jobs. He's the one I'd put my money on.'

She put the eggs in the oven, and turned her attention to the bread, slicing thick lumps and putting it on the table. Argyll got down to business.

'I didn't think they had crime in the countryside,' he said.

'Considering you may have discovered a murder this morning, that's not very observant of you. It's a bit like the wild west round here at times. You should see them getting drunk and beating each other up on a Friday night.'

'The locals do that?'

'When they're not beating their wives.' She looked at him with a grin. 'I can see you've never lived in the country. You think it's all thatched cottages and cider and merrymaking in the hay.'

Argyll smiled at the absurdity of the thought.

'Not a bit of it, my sweet,' she went on. 'All human life, red in tooth and claw, can be found in an English village. Incest, adultery, you name it. We even have one suspected axe murderer. He's a church warden. Jane Austen didn't know the half of it.'

'You're joking.'

'Maybe. But he didn't get on at all well with his brother, who mysteriously managed to cut off his own leg with a chain saw and bleed to death in a field. Many years back, this was. Conclusions, as they say, could be drawn. Not that the police bothered.'

'Didn't his family protest?'

'There was only his wife. And it was her affair with

the brother that caused all the trouble in the first place. So they say.'

'Oh,' he said with his mouth full.

'You are hungry, aren't you?'

He nodded. 'But I hope you don't think I came to visit in the hope I'd be fed.'

'I wouldn't have minded if you did. Living on your own, children flown the coop, is all very liberating, but it occasionally gets a bit solitary in the evenings. Especially in this bloody great barn.'

'Ah.'

'Here's your bacon and eggs and cocoa,' she said, changing the subject. Conversation lapsed while Argyll ate. After some consideration he decided that it was not merely because he was so hungry; they really were delicious. She had taken the bacon, cut it into strips and grilled it, then laid them in a thin blanket on the bottom of a dish. Then put a knob of butter and three fresh eggs on top, added a healthy slug of cream on top and liberally covered with fresh pepper. All into the oven to cook. Wonderful.

'Forgive me for asking,' Argyll said when his head, slightly yellowed round the mouth, finally lifted itself out of the bowl, 'but have you ever lived abroad?'

'What makes you think that, Sherlock?'

'The bacon and eggs are unorthodox to the point of being heretical,' he said.

'Ah, yes. You're right. It's details like cooking that give me away, I'm afraid. You know: not boiling the beans for three quarters of an hour before eating them. Please don't let on though; it's bad enough the locals think I come from London. But I'm surprised you concluded that from my food.'

'Why?'

'Because you've evidently been to the pub. I would have thought they would have filled you in on my life history in the time it took for you to cast an eye over the food tray.'

'There was a comment or two,' he said. 'Nothing scandalous, alas, although not turning up for the village fête seems to have knocked your reputation rather badly.'

'Oh, God, that,' she said despairingly. 'I shall never live it down. It's about the only village function I've missed since Veronica died, you know. I spend my life turning up to things. I never realized that being privileged was such a lot of work. I've admired so many prize peonies and babies and pigs I wake screaming in the middle of the night. And if I ever eat another scone again I shall throw up. I had to go away on the day of the fête. Simple as that. The vicar opened it instead and did a better job than me, I've no doubt. These people don't realize that any form of life exists outside Norfolk.'

'I believe you.'

'Sorry. Sometimes this place drives me crazy. What else did they tell you?'

'Not a lot, really. I was trying to find out about Geoffrey Forster.'

'And?'

'And not much. I gathered that your cousin liked him and sold him the house, that you didn't like him, and that was about it.'

'George Barton, was it?'

'I think so. Old chap with a dog.'

'That's him. He's the village radar set.'

'He seems a bit gloomy.'

'I would have thought he'd be celebrating. Forster owned his cottage and was about to evict him. He was going to develop it into a weekend cottage for rich

Londoners. Presumably, George has a stay of execution now. If that's not an unfortunate way of phrasing it.'

Argyll said he thought that was very interesting. Local colour. He liked that.

'Tell me,' she went on, 'if you didn't come for my cooking, why did you come?'

'An even bigger favour, I'm afraid.'

'Go on.'

'You sort of offered me somewhere to stay . . .'

'No room at the inn?'

'Well . . .'

'Not exactly the Hilton, is it? Of course; a pleasure. I can hardly claim not to have room. You can have any one of, I believe, twelve bedrooms. Most of which have not been slept in for a decade or more.'

'That sounds like the pub.'

'Better decorated, though, where the rain hasn't brought the wallpaper off. Although probably just as chilly. Are you married?'

'Eh?'

'You. Married?'

'Oh. No. Not exactly.'

'Getting married?'

'I think so. Maybe.'

'You think? Maybe? Not exactly?'

'Flavia's very slow in some departments. Quick as lightning generally, but a bit retarded when it comes to making up her mind over things like getting married.'

'Maybe you should make up your mind instead?'

'Pardon?'

'Sorry. None of my business.'

'It's all right. You're probably right. Anyway . . .'

'Is she in the art business as well?'

'Who?'

'Your fiancée.'

'Sort of,' Argyll conceded. 'Do you mind putting me up like this? It's an awful lot to ask, I know. I feel very guilty about imposing . . .'

'Either stay or go. But don't stay and feel guilty. It's a waste of time.'

'Oh. Well. In that case, I'll stay.'

'There you are. That wasn't so hard, was it?' she said with a pleasant, but slightly mocking smile. 'And I don't mind at all. I'd love the company. Especially if you can tell me what happened to Geoffrey Forster. It's about the most exciting thing to happen in Weller since the Saxons invaded.'

8

'Ha!' said Flavia with pleasure when, at 11 o'clock the next morning, 10 o'clock Norwich time, she put the phone down after a conversation with Argyll. He had rung to ask what, exactly, she thought he should do. Very nice part of the world, East Anglia, apart from the danger of catching a cold in the chill, but he did feel he was imposing a little.

On whom? she had asked, and he had explained at some length about the famous hospitality of the English aristocracy, their surfeit of bedrooms and his discovery that their central heating was not up to the rigours of an English summer.

'Far be it from me to get unpaid labour out of you, but if you could just hang around and listen, then that might be useful for us. And if you could find that Forster was a thief, preferably on a big scale, then we'd be eternally grateful. Bottando is fighting back.'

'Ah. I don't know that I understand what you're on about, but no matter.'

'Could you go through Forster's business papers?'

'I shouldn't think so for a moment. If I were a police-man, I wouldn't let me look at them. I'll try, if you like.'

'Thank you. Apart from all that, how did you get on in London?'

'Oh,' he said, dragging his mind back to the distressing subject of his career. 'You mean Byrnes? All right, I suppose. That is, his general view is that I should be a little more ruthless in my approach. And make up my mind about this teaching job.'

'Good. I'm glad to hear it. Are you going to listen?'

'I'm not sure I agree with either of you. Or Mrs Verney, in fact, even though you all seem to tell me the same thing. But I have decided to decide by the end of the week. About this job.'

'That's progress. So what's this woman like? Your hostess?'

'Oh, she's splendid. Quite delightful.'

'She doesn't want to buy any pictures?'

'Afraid not. She's about as strapped for cash as I am. On a grander scale, of course, but I suppose these things are all relative. She's more likely to sell some.'

'Are there any?'

'Quite a few. I had a look around this morning when she was out. They're OK, but nothing special. The Beaumont family wasn't adventurous in its tastes, and I gather Forster sold anything worth much. But I thought I might double check, in case he missed something.'

'Who did you say?'

'Forster. He sold things from the collection.'

'Not him. The other one. Did you say Beaumont?'

He agreed that he had. 'It seems to be the family name,' he explained. 'Why?'

'Because there was a woman called Beaumont at

Signora della Quercia's. Whom Forster was keen on, so it seems.'

He grunted. 'It sounds like cousin Veronica. Mrs Verney doesn't seem the finishing school type. Shall I ask?'

'If you could.'

And then she went to report to Bottando, who was, yet again, in an ill humour. Argan, he said, was lobbying for the Leonardo forger to be clapped in irons and was going around accusing everybody of being slapdash over a raid on an antiquities gallery in the via Giulia. Someone had driven a small truck through the window, loaded up and driven off. Happened every day of the week, almost. Why Argan was in such a fuss over this one had escaped him, until someone pointed out that the gallery was owned by his brother-in-law. And, of course, it served to make the department look bad.

'I did say the fake Leonardos were entirely trivial, but that, of course, is not the point. It got into the papers, and so there's an opportunity for the department to have a high profile.'

'The paperwork will take me at least a month.'

'Will it?'

'If you want it to, yes. I could spin it out indefinitely, if that's what you want.'

Bottando nodded. 'Splendid,' he said with satisfaction. 'We'll make an apparatchik of you yet. Now, Forster. What is the state of things there?'

'Interesting, since you ask. Signora Fancelli points the finger, and much of her story is supported by della Quercia. Sandano reckons Forster was behind the Fra Angelico. He was working in some way for a woman called Beaumont who was also at della Quercia's. And he's dead, of course. As far as I know, the police in

England have not yet decided whether he fell or was pushed.'

'Hmm. Anything there to indicate he was a bit light-fingered?'

'Not as far as Jonathan knows. On the other hand, he rightly points out that the police aren't exactly going to take him into their confidence. Relying on him for information isn't the best thing to do.'

Bottando nodded thoughtfully. 'Which, roughly translated into clear and unadorned prose, means you think you ought to go and see for yourself. Is that what you're getting at?'

Flavia confessed it had crossed her mind.

'And what about friend Argan? He thought you going to the other side of Rome a gross waste of resources.'

She looked at the ceiling and studied the cobwebs growing across one corner. 'He hasn't got your job yet, has he?'

Bottando scowled. 'You know what I mean. Will this be worth it? Or will it merely provide Argan with more evidence to be used against us?'

She shook her head. 'That's politics, not policing. From my lowly point of view, there is enough to look at Forster. You have to decide about Argan. Do you want me to give up a perfectly legitimate enquiry because he wants your job?'

Bottando sighed and rubbed his face. 'Curse the man. And you. Of course I don't. But make it quick, eh? Either find something or get back here. Don't mess about. I'm not going to be hanged by the neck until dead by your expense account.'

Flavia did her best not to look happy; it was some time since she'd been let out of the office on a jaunt, and it would make a nice change. Besides, there was a small possibility that it might even produce something of interest. She drained the dregs of her coffee cup, and went off to get down to business.

As far as the Norfolk police were concerned, the lad called Gordon Brown was the most likely place not only to start but also to end the investigation into the murder of Geoffrey Forster, if that was what his death was going to be.

At first sight, there was a lot going for him. Even his friends agreed that he was a bit of an oaf, and inclined to violence when roused or with a pint or two too many inside him. Next, of course, came his reputation as the local burglar, the man who had done over several of the houses in search of unearned income. He was a well-connected village figure in his way; the son of Mary Verney's part-time housekeeper and married to Louise, the elder daughter of George Barton. Relations between the Brown and Barton families had never recovered from the union, George Barton being the sort of person who did not approve of the likes of Gordon Brown, especially the way he treated his daughter.

While nobody seriously doubted that Margaret Brown the housekeeper had, as she'd claimed, spent the evening with her feet up in front of the television, and that Louise the wife couldn't possibly help in any way due to the fact that she had spent the entire evening with her sister and knew nothing whatsoever about her husband's activities and didn't want to either, such credulity did not extend to the mother's insistence that Gordon, the loyal and devoted son, had been by her side all the time. If he was, Constable Hanson said, it would be the first time in living memory, except for those occasions when he was so blind drunk he couldn't move.

In his favour, however, was the expressed opinion that young Gordon was far too cowardly to go around killing people, and that robbing art dealers was not really his style. If a colour television or video recorder vanished, then Gordon was your man. Everybody knew *that*, although unaccountably no one had yet managed to catch him at it. But no more.

Undeniably, however, he was someone who needed to be eliminated from police enquiries, so they hauled him out of bed at ten in the morning and carted him off for a good going-over.

Much to police merriment, the fact that he and his mum hadn't managed to synchronize their stories helped enormously. Although he started off being obstinate, then angry, it required little skill on the part of the policeman interrogating him to note that there was something of a discrepancy between his mother's account of a blissful evening together, and Gordon's memory that he had, instead, spent the entire period in his bedroom listening to music.

Even when Gordon obligingly changed his story to try and help out, the policeman was, with barely controlled delight, able to point out that while he maintained they had watched the football on BBC-1, his mother was strangely convinced they'd been watching the film on ITV.

'Film about football, was it, Gordon? Or maybe you've got two televisions, one in each corner of the room?'

Gordon, however, was not someone who knew how to give way gracefully. 'We watched the film, then the football,' he explained.

The policeman pulled a copy of yesterday's paper out of his pocket, and opened it at the television guide.

'Odd,' he said, 'I can't see any football on offer yesterday. What match was this, Gordon?'

Gordon snarled, and lapsed into a sullen silence.

'Have it your own way, then. But I must tell you, Gordon boy, it's not looking too good for you. Why don't you just tell us what you were up to?'

'Don't know what you're talking about.'

'And killing that man. Tut, tut. I'm surprised at you. Not your sort of thing, really, is it? Murder, that is, Gordon. Nasty.'

Gordon blanched. 'Didn't kill no one,' he said. 'What are you talking about? Who said anything about murder?'

The policeman ignored the question. It had been worth a try after all, even if the pathologists had still not made up their minds. All they knew so far was that he'd broken his neck by falling down the stairs, had a reasonable amount of alcohol in his blood supply and appeared to have eaten lamb chops and carrots for dinner. All very interesting; unfortunately, they were dithering and taking refuge in technicalities when it came to the important question.

'Of course,' the policeman went on, trying one last time to hurry things along. 'We might accept manslaughter. Or even self-defence, if you ask us nicely, and make our lives simple.'

But Gordon's limited mental faculties had shut down. He sat there morosely, words like 'brutality', 'persecution' and 'harassment' half forming on his lips.

The policeman sighed and got up. 'Ah, well. I've no doubt we'll be seeing you later, Gordon.'

'These police are a bit secretive, dear,' Mary Verney said when Argyll ambled back to Weller House after a morning stroll and hung around the place wondering what to do. He ended up helping her chop vegetables for lunch. 'It's the modern age. Ask them the time and they look as though you're a spy or something. You have to be firm with them. And talking of being firm, your fiancée rang. Flavia, is that right?'

'Yes,' he said, a bit surprised at the connection.

'She sounds quite charming,' she went on. 'Very good English. She asked me to tell you she'd be coming to England this evening and would call when she got in. After she's seen the police in London.'

'Aha!' Argyll said brightly.

'Which means you have a little explaining to do, if you please.'

'About what?'

'The seeing the police in London bit.'

Argyll considered this, and decided it was a reasonable request. 'Simple enough,' he replied after a moment. 'She's in the Italian police. The Art Squad. And recently there have been one or two little questions about Forster.'

'Oh, yes?'

'It's all a lot of nonsense, really, but I gather they're quite keen to find out whether he stole lots of paintings, starting with an Uccello in Florence years back. The man in charge had this theory about some shadowy professional criminal working for umpteen years, and then some little old lady in Rome pointed the finger at Forster.'

'Really? And is there anything in it?'

'How should I know? But, of course, there are billions of unsolved thefts they would dearly love to pin on to somebody.'

'No doubt. But I'd drop Geoffrey if I were them,' Mary said after giving the idea careful thought. 'I've always had this idea that master criminals should be dashing, flamboyant, romantic figures. If a little runt like Geoffrey Forster turned out to be one I would be profoundly disillusioned. I mean, he was a cheat and a bit of a bastard. But I don't think he would have had the endurance to plan anything and carry it through.'

'No. On the other hand, people have been talking, and so it has to be investigated.'

'I suppose so,' she said meditatively. 'But that's something else you have to explain.'

'What?'

'What has this got to do with you?'

'Nothing. I was merely asked to find out what I could as I was in England. I rang, Forster said he wanted to talk to me, and . . .'

'Pop. Dead on arrival, so to speak,' she said. 'Now, don't you think that's a bit odd?'

'I do. More annoyingly, so do the local police. Which is why I'm still here.'

'I'm not cooking up a nice meal for a murderer, am I?'

Argyll shook his head.

'Oh, good. That *is* a relief. Now, what are you going to do while you wait for your Flavia to turn up?'

Argyll opened his mouth to mention having a good look at her family art collection. But before he could even begin, she went on: 'How are you at plumbing?'

'Plumbing?'

'There's a leak in the roof. It's coming through into one of the bedrooms, and I'm a bit hopeless at that sort of thing. Electrics I can manage. Plumbing's a closed book.'

Argyll began a lengthy anecdote about what happened last time he tried to change a washer on a tap in his apartment, using lots of biblical allusions to Noah and arks to get across the idea that trusting him with water tanks was not the best idea. Paintings, he said. That was more his line of business.

But she brushed the idea aside; far more urgent matters to hand than a bunch of old pictures, she said; the chances of there being anything valuable in the house after Geoffrey had swept through it were minuscule. Believe her, she'd looked. Come and look at the water tank instead, at least.

So he dutifully followed her up the grand staircase, then diverted into the bedroom where the large drip was coming through the ceiling, which was stained and growing a greenish mould from excessive damp.

'You see?' she said plaintively. 'Look at it. The ceiling will come down soon if I don't do something. And the prices that plumbers charge these days. Outrageous.'

Argyll listened to the first part of the complaint, but completely missed the second. Instead, his attention had drifted off to contemplate a drawing on the wall.

It was love at first sight, which happens, every once in a while. It was badly framed, tucked away in a dark corner, forlorn and neglected and scruffy, a little ragamuffin of a thing, and all the more endearing for it. Byrnes, no doubt, had he been aware of the way in which Argyll studied it so obviously, would have instantly pointed out that this was his great weakness as an art dealer. Argyll did not see it, and scent a profit. Nor did he recognize the likely author, and wonder who it could be sold to. He merely saw and liked: the more so because the poor little thing was so anonymous and untended. It was its lack of value that attracted him. A failing of his.

It was just a sketch of a man's palm, with one finger and a thumb. The sort of thing art schools have drilled their students in for hundreds of years. there is probably no part of the human anatomy more difficult to get right. Small, no signature, covered in damp spots and foxing.

'What's this?' he asked Mary Verney, with no attempt to hide his appreciation. Another weakness of his.

'That?' she said. 'I've not a clue. I think it's always been there. Done by a member of the family in the days when young women were taught that sort of thing, I expect.'

'Isn't it sweet?'

She shrugged. 'I can't say I've ever looked at it.' She moved over and peered more closely. 'Now you mention it, it is handsome, if you like thumbs.'

Argyll did not reply, but merely examined it more closely. It looked a *bit* better than the average family amateur class of thing to him.

'Valuable?' she went on. 'I don't remember the men from the auctioneers noting it; it was Forster's last service before I kicked him out. They came in to tot up the house after Veronica died and paid no attention to it. More to the point, I can't remember Veronica ever enthusing about it. She was the one who claimed to have taste and discernment.'

'And did she?'

'I don't know. But she did make a fuss about running around gurgling over galleries.'

'Oh, yes? She didn't go to a finishing school in Florence, did she?' he asked, obeying orders to the letter.

'I'm sure she did. Just the sort of silly snobby nonsense she'd go in for. Why do you ask?'

'This woman who mentioned Forster also referred to a woman called Beaumont.'

'Ah. Well, there you are, then.'

'Listen, there wouldn't be any documentation on your pictures, would there? I might be able to find . . .'

She shook her head. 'Doesn't exist. Forster looked and reported that there was nothing at all. No inventories, no account books, nothing. God knows what happened to them. But surely, if this is a good drawing . . .'

'Irrelevant,' Argyll said airily. 'People aren't prepared to spend money on pictures. It took me a long time to learn that. They buy pedigree. Like dogs. Or horses. Or aristocrats,' he went on, wondering whether he was pushing his metaphors a bit too far. 'A signature and a provenance are worth ten times as much as a painting, and works without pedigree are often treated with suspicion.'

'Aren't people silly?'

'They are. Maybe Forster missed the papers?'

She shrugged. 'Maybe. Although he wasn't that much of a fool. And he had a good reason to find them if they were there. I suppose it would have helped him get a better price for all the stuff he sold.'

'Could I check? Just to make sure?'

She sighed at his persistence. 'Oh, very well. But you won't find anything. What there is will be in the attic. If there's anything.'

'Wonderful.'

'Along with the water tank,' she went on.

'Oh. All right,' he conceded. 'I'll see what I can do.'

So he followed her up the next, more rickety staircase, then up what was little more than a stepladder into the attic, where the air was filled with the sound of nesting pigeons.

'Bit dusty, I'm afraid,' she observed, with a true and sure grasp of the art of understatement. 'And smelly. But

I think the tank is over there. And the boxes of archives and things ought to be in the other direction. Might not be, of course,' she added doubtfully.

Argyll reassured her that he would do his best on both counts. In the case of the water tank, it wasn't a great deal. It took about five minutes to locate the leaky joint that was causing all the trouble, realize that it was far beyond his level of competence and conclude that a plumber was necessary. This task completed to his satisfaction, he then turned his attention to more interesting matters, and began poking around in the pile of boxes at the other end of the attic. Huge quantities of paper. Fired by a brief flicker of optimism, he quickly glanced through them, in the hope that all the stuff that Forster hadn't been able to find was in there.

It didn't take that long to realize it wasn't. Some concerned marriage settlements, the eternal haggling over property that was the solid foundation of love in the seventeenth century; and, it seemed, well into the twentieth, as the last batch concerned cousin Veronica's betrothal. Others were very routine documents concerning the management of the estate in the nineteenth century and more recent correspondence to and from members of the family. Not a reference to pictures in any of them, he thought, picking up one box at random and peering in. The contents were bound up in string with a little label attached. 'Mabel', it read.

No, he told himself as he opened it up, none of your business. No time to waste on this, he added as he took out a bundle of letters which he rapidly realized had been written by his hostess's mother. Besides, he thought as he settled down for a good read, Mary Verney would not forgive such a gross violation of her privacy. And quite right too.

His conscience registered its protest and, for once, was ignored, leaving Argyll to read with growing astonishment about Mabel Beaumont who, although she had made a promising start as the dutiful eldest of five daughters, slowly transformed in the course of dozens of letters into someone who, to put it mildly, manifested a certain eccentric streak in her character. She was, it seemed, a woman at war with herself and everybody else, and the battle took her away from home and the prospect of a life spent marrying, raising children and opening fêtes, and instead made her roam across Europe until she died, according to the death certificate which was the last document in the box, in a hotel room in what Argyll knew was a particularly seedy part of Milan. Her daughter, just turned fourteen, was the only person with her and had tended the sick woman herself as there was no money to pay for doctors. There was a letter in a girlish hand, asking for help; the box contained no reply.

Argyll sneezed meditatively as he digested this cautionary tale of inter-war wildness, and absent-mindedly flipped through the rest of the box, most of which concerned family negotiations to have Mary placed under their guardianship and sent to school. 'She is wild, intelligent but apparently immune to discipline,' said the one and only school report. Good for her, he thought briefly before remembering that this was not what he was there for. So he tied the whole lot back up, replaced the box, and reluctantly applied himself once more to the plumbing, and after another half hour, with little bits of plastic and string and much struggling and stubbing of fingers, he eventually managed to slow the flow of water. But, as he said later when fending off her thanks, it wasn't a very good job. Sooner or later, she'd have to call a plumber.

9

For all Bottando's strictures about her expenses, Flavia took a taxi from the airport; she had a busy time ahead of her, and no time to waste saving money. First stop was the British police, to explain herself. Nothing ever upsets people more than foreigners wandering around the place. And she thought that she might well need their assistance; all the more reason to be as open as possible with them.

'Good evening, miss. Welcome to England.' The man in charge was unusually youthful; no more than his late thirties and most unlike any other English policemen she'd ever come across. Generally, the need to plod the beat before going on to more intellectually challenging activities makes British policemen a bit dull; the more lively ones balk at the prospect of spending a few years breaking up pub brawls and do something else instead. Such, at least, is their European reputation.

Manstead was a bit different. He managed to project a level of intelligence and alertness that was rare. On the other hand, it quickly became clear that he knew almost nothing about his job at all. After the preliminaries were taken care of – the journey, the weather, the traffic – he expressed his pleasure at having the opportunity to meet a member of the continent's longest-surviving Art Squad.

'We're just getting going,' he explained with a sigh. 'A policy change again. The old Art Squad was set up a long time ago; then it was shut down and merged with local forces, then the party line shifted and we were reborn – but only after all the contacts and expertise and files had been dispersed.'

'Do you all have a background in the art market?'

He snorted derisively. 'Oh, no. Of course not. Put in people who know something about the job? What an idea. No. We were just assigned detectives who were interested, and told to get on with it.'

'So you rely heavily on outside advisers?'

'Would do, if we had the money. But we don't have a big enough budget to pay people with any regularity. So we have to survive on people being willing to do us favours.'

'Sounds pretty dire.'

'It is. It's all politics. If we had some resounding success that got splashed over the newspapers, we'd attract attention and be given more. To he who hath, shall be given. It should be our motto. Still,' he said, reluctantly abandoning a favourite topic, 'you haven't come here to listen to me complaining about the collapse of the British police.'

Flavia smiled apologetically. 'I reckon we could match you, atrocity for atrocity. What I need to hear about is this man Forster.'

Manstead nodded. 'Nothing to do with us. That is, we've looked through our files and there is no mention

110

of him at all. Not even a whisper. We're asking around for you, though.'

Flavia looked disappointed, even though she was not surprised. Bottando's Giotto was not the sort of person whose proclivities would have been common knowledge. If he existed, he would be an absolutely, squeaky-clean, one-hundred-per-cent good citizen. In some ways, the lack of a file on him in British hands made her more prepared to entertain the notion of him as bent. 'Not even any gossip?' she asked.

Manstead thought carefully; he was a carefully-thinking sort of man. 'Nobody seems to have liked him much; there is that to be said. But when I asked whether, now he was dead, they felt like saying what they thought of his business practices, everyone denied ever having heard a thing.'

'I see. So if someone, for example, suggested he'd ripped off every major collection in Europe over the past twenty-five years, you reckon they'd be surprised?'

'I think everyone would be astonished,' Manstead said. 'Is that what your boss is on about? Is that what you think as well?'

She shook her head. 'Not really,' she said regretfully.

'But your boss does?'

'Not exactly. Somebody in the administration doesn't.'

Manstead eyed her with a faintly amused whisper of a smile. 'I see,' he said slowly. 'At least I think I do. One of those, eh?'

Flavia sniffed with a disapproval that came directly from a sense of embarrassment.

'So what's your interest in his death?' Manstead asked, deciding that if she didn't want to burden him with details that was fine by him.

'None whatsoever, which I imagine will make life

111

a good deal easier for everyone. Except, of course, it would be much more interesting if he was murdered.'

'Of course. But unfortunately, the evidence is very ambiguous there. It's really only the fact that this colleague of yours . . . What's his name?'

'Colleague?' Flavia was a little puzzled for a moment. 'Oh. Jonathan. Yes. What about him?'

'Well, it's only really because he was on the scene, talking about theft and pointing out coincidences, that the police are taking it so seriously. Otherwise, I think they might well have concluded he drank a wee bit too much, and slipped on a loose stair. And they may well still do so.'

'And who knows, they may well be right,' Flavia added.

'Who knows indeed?' Manstead said easily. 'But I'm sure we will get to the bottom of it eventually. Now, would you care for a drink yourself?'

At about the same time that Flavia's plane was squeaking to a halt at Heathrow, Argyll's time and labour was being redirected from late nineteenth-century English plumbing into areas where he could more reasonably claim some sort of expertise. This was the doing of Manstead who, being conscientious, rang the Norfolk police to tell them that such was the international interest in Forster that a very high-ranking expert from Italy was flying in especially to offer assistance.

So he exaggerated a little, and alarmed the local police quite considerably. Their response was to go round and collect Argyll. Not that they thought for a moment he was perfect, but he did answer a practical need: which was to put a stop to any form of interference from London. Forster's death may have had something to do with paintings. They didn't know much about the workings of the art market so, if they weren't careful, they would have to hand over large chunks of the case to Manstead who, desperate as he was for a bit of publicity, might well claim whatever credit was going should the case be solved satisfactorily. Consequently, they had to bone up on things artistic as quickly as possible, and try and tie that end of the case up to avoid being burdened with Manstead's help.

But people knowledgeable about old masters are a little difficult to get hold of in the countryside at short notice. So they decided they would have to make use of the only one readily to hand, and get him to give Forster's papers a quick look over: if there was reference to something dodgy in there, Argyll might spot it for them.

So he was taken back to the house and allowed to wander around under the discreet and watchful eye of Constable Hanson. The house was bigger than it appeared from the outside, with a roof space that had been converted at some stage into a long, low room that had evidently functioned as Forster's office. At one end were all the trappings of the modern art dealer – the books, the telephones, the fax machines and the filing cabinets. At the other end were those bits of his stock in trade that were not hanging on the walls of the dining room, hallway or sitting room downstairs. In a corner was the stairwell which began with the board whose wobbly state may well have precipitated Forster's fall. Argyll trod carefully as he went up and down.

Then he went through Forster's stock of paintings methodically, rapidly and with a combination of mounting disapproval and superior disdain. Nasty, crude stuff; all of it shoddy and most of it ugly. The prices listed were outrageous. He himself was no success as a dealer, he knew, but at least he liked the stuff he couldn't unload on to others. This was the sort of tat only a real cynic would deal in, not someone with much of an eye. And not someone like Giotto – a person who'd stolen an example of work by almost every master of the Renaissance would hardly deal in stuff like that. On the other hand, he thought, thinking along the same lines as Flavia with Manstead, what better disguise than to have everybody associate you with the second rate, the tawdry and the ugly? Who, seeing this stuff, would ever dream . . . ?

Then he turned his attention to the contents of the filing cabinet, although these were not at all interesting. Inventories and the rudimentary accounts that art dealers make out for themselves and the taxman are generally little more than one small column of fanciful numbers which end in an equally fanciful total at the bottom. Even Argyll, who had little talent in mathematics, could manage, although he generally sought the help of Flavia.

'What do you mean?' she'd said the first time she'd helped him out, 'where are your expenses?'

'Didn't really have any,' he replied.

'We went on holiday, didn't we? You went to a museum during the holiday?'

'Yes. So?'

' "Item, one research trip." How much do you reckon? Three million lire? Now, the car. You delivered a picture in it once. So, maintenance, petrol and depreciation. Let's say another million.'

'But . . .'

'Oh, use your imagination, Jonathan,' she had said crossly, and proceeded to go through the entire form, adding a nought here, subtracting one there until, by the end, his little business as an art dealer had unaccountably swung from a small profit into a sudden and alarming loss. For the next six months, he'd been convinced that any day a taxman would come knocking on the door. Just needing a little clarification, Dottore Argyll.

The point was that Geoffrey Forster's accounts made his own modest efforts look like something produced in a primary school. Figures all over the place, and Argyll was damned if he could make any sense of it at all. After about three hours of work, the only conclusion he'd come to was that the police had picked on the wrong man if they wanted help from him. He was as bad an accountant as he was a plumber.

He'd developed a thudding headache by the time he came to the end. Nor was it particularly enlightening: Forster's income was variable but often quite high, so much so that he had bought not only his own house but two cottages in the village a few years back, although efforts to raise the money to tart them up and sell them to Londoners for weekend houses had not progressed too far. One of the cottages, he remembered, was inhabited by George Barton. His turnover of paintings – officially, at least – had dwindled to virtually nothing in the past couple of years, no doubt being hit by the recession like everyone else.

Several years back, his income had received a boost from being given a salary – not a huge one, he noted – by Miss Beaumont for what were ambiguously called services, but this stopped abruptly in January – presumably when Veronica died and Mary Verney gave him his marching orders. What, exactly, he had done for his money was far from clear. Nor did he seem to have bought all that much recently; like many dealers, he kept the catalogues of auction sales where he'd bought things, but there were no more than a couple of dozen of these, going back over five years. Not nearly enough to generate much of an income.

All in all, he appeared to be a man with some financial problems. Unless, of course, there were sources of money which he had kindly decided he needn't waste the taxman's time with. Certainly, it wasn't obviously the financial profile of supposedly the finest art thief of his generation. But you would expect the finest art thief to be a bit of a whiz in financial skulduggery as well: it was hardly likely that his tax forms would be full of entries like 'item: one stolen Uccello' . . .

That, however, was an unproductive line of enquiry. As was the fact that when Forster severed his ties with Weller House, he had apparently not bothered to return some of the papers concerned with it: at least, Argyll assumed that was why there was a probate inventory of the Weller House paintings in one of the files. Dated some fifteen years back, so Argyll assumed that it had been drawn up on the death of Uncle Godfrey. Not hugely illuminating, as the seventy-two paintings and twenty-seven drawings mentioned were treated in a somewhat cursory fashion. But as it might be the only listing there was, and as it clearly wasn't Forster's property anyway, he slipped it into his pocket for return to the rightful owner. He noted that the drawing of the hand was described as anonymous French eighteenth-century, which didn't satisfy him, although it was better than Mrs Verney's assessment. It had also been given a value of thirty pounds, which did seem about right.

Argyll yawned from sheer boredom and decided to rest on his laurels. He marked his place, shoved the whole lot in a drawer of the desk, locked it to comply with police wishes on security, and told the ever-patient Hanson that he was finished. There was still three-quarters of the filing cabinet to go through, but that could wait until tomorrow. The police could have a quick job, or a thorough one. On their behalf, Argyll decided they would have the latter: he needed a drink, and the now off-duty Hanson readily accepted the invitation to come along as well.

He arrived back at Weller House at half past seven on the dot, as the last F1-11 of the day rocketed through the chimney pots, bearing a bottle of not very good wine which he'd bought at the pub after turning down old George's offer of a pint.

'There you are,' she said. 'What have you been up to?'

'I've been helping the police with their enquiries, in a manner of speaking.'

'Rumbled you at last, eh?'

'Certainly not. I've been reading Forster's accounts and papers.'

'Profitably?'

'Nope. The finer points of accountancy have never been my great strength. He could be as pure as a Trappist or as bent as Al Capone, and I wouldn't notice.'

'Neither sounds right to me.'

'Hmm. I did find this, though.' He handed over the inventory. She looked at it without much interest.

'He took it, did he? Doesn't surprise me. If there's anything else there which belongs to me, could you bring that back as well?'

'As long as the police don't mind. But it's curious that he told your cousin there was nothing like this at all.'

'Maybe he didn't want her to know what he was up

to. Still, too late to worry about that now. What's gone is gone. I hope you like rabbit.'

'I love rabbit.'

'Good. I strangled it myself. Mass murder is another skill of mine. Some people in these parts can't see a furry animal without wanting to disembowel it. Killing things is a country occupation.'

'So it seems.'

'Eh?'

'Forster. I gather they've arrested someone.'

'Oh, that,' she said dismissively. 'Gordon. I know. More wishful thinking on their part, I fear.'

'You're very trusting of your neighbours,' Argyll observed.

'Am I? In what way?'

'Well, I tell you Forster may have been a crook, and you pooh-pooh the idea, even though you loathed him. The police arrest Gordon and you dismiss the notion that he might be a murderer, even though you reckon he's a burglar.'

She shrugged. 'I prefer to think that I reach a balanced account of people. I mean, please don't stop trying to prove Geoffrey was a thief: nothing I'd like better. Who knows, you may even be right. I'm willing to be persuaded. Give me that cooking wine, will you? On the side over there.'

'Oh. Tell me more about him,' he said directly, sitting himself down at the kitchen table in a companionable fashion and, rather shamefacedly, pouring the contents of his own contribution into two glasses.

'More? What do you want to know now?'

'Everything. Did you know him well? What was he like?'

'Ah,' she said, stirring thoughtfully. 'Complicated

118

story.' She paused for a while as she added a bit of pepper to her potatoes, then stirred furiously again. 'Why not, though? Everyone's dead. You know he was my cousin's lover?'

'It was hinted at in the pub,' he replied. 'But it was a little ambiguous.'

'That's unlike them. They're normally quite graphic. Anyway, Forster met her a long time back, I gather. He knew the family off and on, and got his foot in the door when Uncle Godfrey died, helping with fending off the inheritance taxes. But he really locked on to her a couple of years before she died. Pure exploitation, of course.'

'In what way?'

'Veronica was not the world's most attractive person, alas. I don't mean physically, but she was – well, not exactly a warm and vibrant personality, if you see what I mean. And you may have heard that she was a little unstable. Forster spotted her weakness, and when his business got into trouble, he laid siege to her, simply to get his hands on the family silver, as far as I can see. I'm not entirely certain what he sold; nor was Veronica, she always said she trusted him and what was the point of expert advisers if you had to check up on them all the time? I'll give him this, he was a great actor.'

'Meaning what exactly?'

'I mean, one knew he was loathsome: that was obvious to everyone except Veronica. But one never knew quite why he was loathsome, or what he was up to. You just knew that he wasn't to be trusted. God knows how his wife ever put up with him.'

'Ah, yes. The wife. Where is she?'

'I gather on the grapevine that she was spending a few days in London when he died. She should be back any moment. At least she isn't going to be suspected of giving him a good shove.'

'Why do you say that? Is that you just being optimistic about human nature again?'

She looked puzzled for a moment at the need to explain. 'Because it's absolutely inconceivable, that's why. Though the Lord knows, she has motive.'

'What's she like?'

'Simple and innocent, swept off her feet by an older man with forked tongue before she's old enough to know any better. Not that age had much to do with it, in her case, I fear. Very, very stupid. One of life's victims. Not much character, I'm afraid: a bit colourless. The sort who looks as though she washes her face in bleach every evening. Doesn't know how to look after herself. She's quite sweet, but no resilience; she put up with him for years and years. Why should she suddenly snap now?'

'People do.'

'They do. But if she'd killed him, she would have had to go to her sister, sneak back to push him down the stairs, then slip away again. Which would need a bit of forward planning. That sort of cold calculation is not her style.'

Argyll gave her a disapproving glance, and she smiled reassuringly.

'You look sceptical. You shouldn't be. You haven't met her. Besides, as far as I can tell, it's far from certain he was killed deliberately. Why do you assume he was?'

'Simply because it's an awful coincidence that he died just before I got to talk to him.'

'Look on the bright side: it spared you an unpleasant encounter.'

'I'm being serious.'

'I know. But it's only a coincidence if Geoffrey was indeed a thief.'

'He said he'd talk to me about a stolen painting.'

'Probably just to threaten to sue you for slander.'

'But you didn't like Forster. Or trust him?'

'That's about it. He used people, and dumped them when he'd finished, and he was a liar and a cheat. Maybe that's helpful if you're an art dealer. Perhaps you should try it.'

'So what did your cousin see in him?'

'He had a certain charm. If you like that sort of thing, which I don't very much,' she conceded. 'Handsome enough in a sort of slick fashion. And poor old Veronica was a bit unhappy. She married and her husband died young. Silly ass got drunk at their fifth anniversary junket, fell into a pond and drowned in five inches of water. Too sozzled to roll over. Even Veronica thought he was a bit hopeless; that was why she went back to using her own name: she reckoned the Beaumont was more worthwhile preserving than Finsey-Groat. And she never found anyone else worth sacrificing the family name for.

'So, no husband, no children, no friends. Easy meat for someone to come along and fleece her.'

'Is that what he did?'

'Well, he was selling stuff off, never producing any accounts, and I'm certain he was keeping a large chunk of money for himself. I tried to make her see sense, but she was too goggle-eyed. Dimwit.'

'When did she die?'

'January. I was here; she'd had an attack and I was summoned by Dr Johnson yet again to see what was to be done with her this time. No one else would come. She was a depressive, you know.'

'It was mentioned.'

'She had these turns. For ages she'd be fine, then she'd go crazy.'

'What sort of crazy?'

'Oh, all sorts of crazy. She'd go on a fugue; just disappear for a week or so; nobody ever knew where she'd been. Or she'd lock herself in the house and refuse to see anyone. Or she'd sit and drink. Or something. When she died, she was in a big one and just overdid the drink and the pills.'

'Why did you look after her?'

She shrugged. 'There was no one else. She refused proper treatment and when she was really bad I was the only person who could do anything with her at all. She was virtually intolerable, I must say. I went out one day and she killed herself. I like to think it was an accident, although I'm not sure.'

'What do you mean?'

'Well, it's silly, but we'd just had a fight. About Forster, in fact. It was beginning to dawn on her that he wasn't that wonderful after all. She asked me what I thought, and I told her to get rid of him. At which point she blew up and called me all the names under the sun. I marched out in a huff, and she consoled herself with half a bottle of whisky and half a bottle of pills. Had I been a bit more resilient . . .'

'You feel you're to blame?'

She shook her head. 'Only when I'm in a bad mood. When I'm in a good mood I realize it was a disaster waiting to happen. Sooner or later she would have pushed it too far. It's just a pity she couldn't have left me out of it. Typical of her, really.'

'Were you close?'

'Not so you'd notice. In fact, I don't suppose we liked

each other, if truth be told. But she left this place to me simply because she wanted it kept in the family, and I was the closest relation who wasn't a total deadbeat. Although I can't say I have enough to keep it up, or the inclination either. More rabbit?'

'I couldn't.'

'Some summer pudding, then? It's very good.'

'I'd love some.'

She spooned it out, covered it with thick cream, and allowed Argyll a few moments to eat, admire and eat some more.

'Where do you fit into this family of yours?' he asked, desperate for a bit of context into which he could place his nosing through the family papers.

'On to me now, are we? OK. I'm the daughter of the family black sheep, Mabel,' she said, 'who went to the bad. Although she had a much more interesting life than anyone here. Until she got sick, at least.'

'That sounds interesting.'

'It was, in a way. Mother was artistic, which in gentry-speak is always a euphemism for being unbalanced, if not actually certifiable. This is why I always had more sympathy for Veronica than most people. More practice. Mother spent a typical youth and was supposed to inherit Weller House – there were no sons, despite my grandmother's conscientious efforts – find a rich husband who would rebuild the finances and generally do her duty. Instead, she got all sorts of ideas, and suddenly upped and left to become a war nurse in Spain, which shocked the family enormously. Being bountiful to the unemployed was one thing; wiping Bolshevik bums was quite another, and so naturally they disinherited her. From their point of view it was a natural thing to do, and I don't know

123

that Mother minded much. I was born under what you might call ambiguous circumstances just before the war started. She died when I was fourteen. The family, very reluctantly, took me over and tried to make a lady out of unpromising material, and I suppose failed quite badly. End of story. Am I boring you?'

'Lordy, no. Tell me more.'

'Not much else to tell, really. I married, had children and my husband and I parted company, giving me an adequate settlement.'

'That's the Verney bit?'

'That's it. He was a decent soul, really. I just hated him. At which point my life story becomes very dull and uninteresting. I moved around from place to place, settled in London, did this, that and the next thing.'

'You never married again?'

She shook her head. 'No suitable candidates presented themselves. Not for the long term, anyway. By the way,' she went on, making one of those leaps of the imagination which Argyll was beginning to find alarming. 'Flavia rang again.'

'Oh?'

'Could you meet her in London tomorrow at lunchtime?'

'Oh. That's a pity. I was quite beginning to enjoy myself here.'

'Are you indeed? Splendid. In that case you can come back. Will she be coming here as well?'

'I've no idea. Wouldn't surprise me.'

'In that case, I hope she will make less of a fuss about staying here than you did. Coffee?'

10

Flavia began her researches into the life and times of Geoffrey Forster after an amiable lunch the next day with Argyll and Edward Byrnes at the dining club. Inspector Manstead, who never passed up an opportunity of either a free lunch or meeting a possibly important contact, came as well, and then decided to accompany her on her travels just to add a gloss of officialdom, as he put it, to her efforts.

Fortunately, London still retains its old local character for some of its trades. Many other occupations, which used to cluster together for protection, have long since been scattered to the winds: not many tailors still sew around Savile Row, journalists are too dispersed to fill the pubs of Fleet Street and complain about how they are unappreciated, and publishers have been cast to the winds, no longer making Covent Garden an interesting place to visit. Doctors do still dominate Harley Street, but are much too fine a bunch of people actually to talk to each other.

But enough art dealers do hang out in the area around Bond Street and St James's to give the place a particular character and, even though they might not like each other much, mutual interest and propinquity ensures that at least some show of professional solidarity remains. Thus, when Edward Byrnes made a face and telephoned Arthur Winterton for her, Winterton reluctantly made time to see Flavia.

One might think that the fact that both men were of advancing years, both had enjoyed as much success as they could reasonably desire, and both were quite unfairly wealthy, would have had a mellowing effect on them, blunting the competitive edge and allowing them to survey the art scene with the detachment that comes of total security. Not a bit of it. Both men had been profoundly jealous of each other for decades, and neither was going to give up now. Without the desire of Winterton to beat Byrnes, and without the fervent wish of Byrnes to trounce Winterton, both men might well have remained modest dealers of only limited prominence, rather than the two contesting giants of Bond Street.

For Argyll, who wanted little out of life except to be left in moderately affluent peace, watching how easily the veneer of urbanity was stripped off Byrnes by the mention of the word Winterton was a never-ending source of instruction. He had always assumed a couple of million in the bank would bring peace and contentment. It was a shock to realize that it did nothing of the sort. Winterton's superior contacts on the American museum circuit could still make Byrnes incandescent with a jealousy of a very primitive variety. Byrnes's knighthood, on the other hand, was quite capable of keeping Winterton awake until dawn if he should chance to think about it late at night.

He had, on occasion, mentioned his former

employer's Achilles heel to Flavia in the past and so she, as she walked into Winterton's rival gallery three hundred yards up the street, was keenly looking for reasons to explain how such rivalry could be generated.

Certainly, style was important, she decided as they waited for the great man to appear. Whereas Byrnes's gallery self-consciously cultivated the slightly old-fashioned, scholarly air, the high-quality faded look, Winterton had gone very much for the modern style in which everything was restored and interior designed to within an inch of its life. The difference was reflected in the men themselves, she realized as Winterton emerged; Byrnes had gone grey at least ten years previously and much of his hair had vanished, while Winterton had a full head of suspiciously black stuff despite his nearly sixty years. Byrnes, in a word, was expensively shabby in appearance, Winterton was expensively elegant. She had learnt – or rather Argyll had explained to her – that such things can indeed trigger conflict in a country like England which, despite its reputation, is more concerned with appearance than any other. The English may not dress well by continental standards, but the way they dress badly is of enormous importance.

Flavia and Inspector Manstead (himself a member of the cheap and dowdy tendency in couture) were whisked off into Winterton's office and plied with tea and coffee. Winterton sat himself behind his desk and placed the tips of his fingers together to indicate that he was taking the proceedings seriously and would, of course, do his best to help the police with their enquiries.

'Inspector Manstead and I are attempting to get some details about paintings which passed through the hands of the late Geoffrey Forster,' Flavia began. Winterton nodded to indicate that he was paying attention.

'To be frank, there is a question mark over the provenance of some of them.'

'You mean some were stolen?'

'Just so.'

Winterton nodded impatiently. 'Yes, yes. I see. Might I ask what these paintings were? I do very much hope you are not going to ask me whether *I* knew about this?'

Flavia shook her head at the very idea. 'No. But obviously we do need to know about Forster. Friends, associates, that sort of thing. We need some sort of idea how this might have happened. Did you know him well?'

Winterton shook his head. 'Oh, no,' he said with clear relief. 'Fortunately, our association was only very loose.'

'And your impressions?'

Winterton thought carefully. 'He was a man utterly devoid of anything that might be termed the finer feelings. To him, the value of everything was in how much cash you could get for it. To use the old cliché, he knew the price of everything, the value of nothing. I know it is old-fashioned, I can think of no better way of describing him than to say he was a scoundrel and a fake. Geoffrey Forster was just the sort of person who would expect to buy stolen works of art.'

'But Mr Winterton, you have a high reputation, I believe. Why would you go into business with someone of whom you had such a low opinion? Surely that could only have harmed your standing in the art world?'

Winterton frowned with annoyance at the question, probably because it was quite a good one. He waved his

128

hand vaguely to indicate the passage of time and the vagueness of the art dealing business.

'A sign of the times,' he said with a sigh. 'We must all try to make the best use of our assets, until the economy picks up. In my case, I had this large building which was rather under-used, so I rented out a couple of rooms at the top to people who want an impressive business address but can't afford their own gallery. Forster is one of three; he very rarely used the place: that was one of the conditions of letting him have it in the first instance, to be frank.

'And once he did me a favour, which saved me some potential embarrassment. I must say, I didn't like the man, but I owed him in return. You know how it is.'

'Aha. I see. Could you tell me what this favour was?'

'I don't think that is at all relevant.'

Flavia smiled sweetly, and Manstead scowled threateningly. Between them, they managed to convey how pleased the police would be with an answer, and how much trouble they might cause if he kept quiet.

'Very well, then. It was about three years ago. I had undertaken to dispose of a painting for the executors of the estate of a Belgian collector who had recently died. A very distinguished man. Whose name I will not provide. Forster heard about it as I was arranging for it to go to Christie's. He alerted me to the possibility that it was not all it seemed.'

'What did it seem?'

'It seemed to be a fine, but undocumented Florentine school painting of the mid-fifteenth century. Quite valuable, in its way, although, without any proof of identity, not in the first league. Which is why I was not proposing to try and find a private purchaser.'

'And what was it?'

129

'I could never prove it, of course.'

'But . . .'

'But it did appear to bear a superficial resemblance to a painting of St Mary the Egyptian by Antonio Pollaiuolo which was stolen in 1976 from the Earl of Dunkeld's Scottish house.'

'And so you instantly reported this to the police?'

Winterton smiled grimly. 'Certainly not.'

'Why not?'

'Because there was absolutely no proof one way or the other. I could not in good conscience undertake to sell the painting myself, of course. But to drag the name of a famous collector through the mire – for that is what would have happened – by calling in the police over a painting which might very well have been bought quite legitimately, seemed irresponsible. I did check, and there was no indication of how the painting had arrived in the collection.'

'So you walked away?' Manstead interrupted indignantly.

Winterton grimaced with slight pain at the vulgar way this was put.

'Where is the picture now?' the English policeman went on.

'I do not know.'

'I see. So, let's get this straight. You were selling a hot picture, Forster takes one look at it and tells you it was stolen. You pull out in case someone notices it. And you didn't for a moment consider you might have been doing anything wrong?'

Winterton raised an eyebrow in surprise. 'Of course not. I knew the Pollaiuolo painting had been reported stolen, of course. On the other hand, I didn't know it actually *had* been stolen.'

Manstead positively fulminated at this comment. 'That seems like splitting hairs to me.'

'I don't care one way or the other what it seems to you. But I suspect Miss di Stefano here knows exactly what I mean. A painting is stolen; the owner registers the loss and collects on the insurance. Has it really been stolen? Or has the owner sold it through a dealer and faked the theft so he can be paid twice? Does the new owner think he is buying a stolen work, or does he think he is buying a legitimate painting which is being sold discreetly for fear of having to hand over too much to the taxman? What some previous owner has done fifteen years ago and in another country is not my concern: making a living at art dealing is hard enough without going out of your way to find trouble. In my case, I decided the best thing to do would be not to get involved.'

'And give Forster office space upstairs as a little thank you for heading you away from trouble?'

Winterton nodded. 'I would prefer to say that my opinion of him lifted a little after that. But not that much.'

Manstead felt decidedly ruffled at this, but noticed that Flavia remained perfectly calm, dealing with Winterton's explanation as though it was the most natural thing in the world. Indeed, he got the distinct impression she even approved of his decision. Certainly, she didn't bother to follow it up.

'Now,' she said, taking control of the questioning once more, 'how did Forster know it was stolen? That's the important thing, isn't it? If he had no finer feelings, spotting something as obscure as a Pollaiuolo would hardly come easily to him. So how did he know? Not a famous theft, or a famous collection.'

Winterton shrugged.

'He didn't say, "I know it's stolen because I stole it myself"?' she suggested.

Winterton looked ruffled, a state which Flavia found a great improvement. 'Of course not,' he said eventually. 'Firstly, I doubt he had it in him. And if he did, he would hardly tell me, would he? A bit stupid, even for him?'

'Not necessarily,' Flavia said thoughtfully. 'After all, I assume you would have sold it on the London market, wouldn't you? And it might have been awkward had it reappeared. After all, I assume you are good at your job – you must be to have achieved your current position – so you would have done a proper check on the painting's provenance, and perhaps discovered one or two inconsistencies. Was the painting sold?'

'I believe not,' Winterton said.

'And you told the family that it was a bit doubtful.'

He nodded.

'There you are then. One quiet word, and Forster stops a sale which might have caused him considerable problems. Perhaps he was not as stupid as you think. Now, how about Forster's clients? Do you know any names?'

'Not many,' he said, replying now with great reluctance and scarcely concealed irritation. 'He did business at one stage helping families sell off their possessions, I know. When the market turned down he went into that line of business more or less full time. He virtually became an estate manager for the house near where he lived.'

'We know that.'

'That is the only name I know, I'm afraid, and I can't help you with any details, never having acted for the family myself. And I gather his work ended when a new owner took over. But as I say, I had little to do with him.

'Now, then,' he said, standing up in an end-of-interview way, 'please don't hesitate to contact me if you think I may be of further assistance to you . . .'

'Of course,' Flavia murmured. Indeed, she was surprised that they'd been there for so long, and that they'd got so much out of him.

'What did you think?' she asked Manstead as they emerged once more on to the street.

'Outrageous!' he replied.

'You are new at this game, aren't you?' she said with a faint smile.

'You mean that's common?'

'Refusing a decent commission merely because of a little matter like a painting being stolen? Very uncommon. He's more honest than I'd anticipated. Assuming he's telling the truth. He might have gone ahead and sold it anyway, using someone else as a cover. Could you check?'

'What is this picture? Another one on Bottando's list of Giotto's greatest hits?'

'Yes, it is. That's three connections. Uccello. Fra Angelico and Pollaiuolo. In fact, they're beginning to pop up so fast I'm amazed Forster stayed out of jail long enough to die at home. Can you look into this Belgian collection?'

'I don't know many people in Belgium.'

Flavia took out her notebook and scribbled a name and number on it. 'Try him. Tell him I sent you. He'll do his best.'

Manstead took the number and stuffed it in his pocket.

Flavia beamed at him. 'I bet you're getting sick of me.'
Manstead sighed. 'Not at all,' he said gallantly.

Argyll's own metropolitan labours – apart from picking up some clean clothes – took the form of a social call on an old friend of his called Lucy Garton. Old friend was, perhaps, pushing it a bit, considering that they had only vaguely known each other some years back, but it is amazing how fondly you begin to think of even virtual strangers when you need a favour of them.

Argyll's logic was simple. Although he had not talked to her for years now, idle gossip with mutual acquaintances had kept him approximately in touch with her movements since she had left university and hurled herself into the mêlée of the London art world, sliding elegantly up the greasy pole from being an assistant (read, secretary) to being an exhibition organizer, and on to the slightly more lofty heights as an expert valuer at one of the smaller auction houses which attempted to chip away at the duopoly of Christie's and Sotheby's.

More to the point, it was the same auction house at which Forster had bought and sold paintings, and Argyll, eager to find out more about the man's activities, thought that it would be a good idea to see exactly what he had been doing. His problem was Forster's position as effective curator of the Weller House paintings, a collection which had done quite nicely for the past century or so without being looked after at all. If Forster was spending his time running around Europe stealing paintings, why go to all the bother of seeking out Veronica Beaumont (as he had apparently done) and take on a job which provided an income that was little more than chickenfeed in comparison to what Fra Angelicos and the like must have brought in. Answer:

because it must have served a useful purpose. To Argyll's way of thinking that seemed obvious. Unfortunately, it wasn't at all obvious what that useful purpose was.

Besides which, he thought he might be able to render a small service to Mrs Verney, which he was keen on doing merely for its own sake, and not simply because it might make her think of using his services should she decide that selling off some paintings might be a way to restore herself to solvency.

Such was the aim, although as he was shown into Lucy's office (must be doing quite well if she had an office) he was not sufficiently naive as to think that achieving it was going to be so easy. What were your connections with this suspected criminal? Not many auction houses like such questions, and he remembered that Lucy was more than bright enough to work out what his questions meant, however carefully he might phrase them. No harm in trying, though.

Fortunately, she seemed perfectly pleased to see him, even though the surprise at his sudden materialization was evident. She had quite a sweet face, although Argyll remembered that behind the soft, almost chubby features lurked a mind that was surprisingly steely. The contrast between appearance and reality quite possibly accounted in some measure for her possession of an office. Argyll confessed that he had not come merely for the pleasure of seeing her.

'I sort of guessed that. You don't want a job, do you?'

'Oh, no,' he said, a little startled.

'That's good. We don't have any.'

'No. I've come to ask you a question or two about a client.'

Lucy raised an eyebrow in a that's confidential, you know that, we never disclose anything about clients, fashion.

'An ex-client, in fact. A man called Geoffrey Forster. Who is now safely dead.'

'Dead?'

'Fell down the stairs.'

She shrugged. 'That's all right, then. I vaguely remember the name.'

'He did buy and sell through you?'

'Think so. I can't remember any details. Why?'

'It's his pictures, you see,' Argyll said, nervously getting to the difficult bit. 'There's a certain amount of confusion about them which needs to be sorted out.'

She looked patiently at him.

'Where they came from. Where they went.'

'Who needs to sort it out?'

Argyll coughed. 'Well, the police, really. You see, they might not have been his.'

She was looking sufficiently alarmed by now for Argyll to realize he might as well jettison the subtle approach and tell her everything. Unless she had changed a good deal, she was a common-sensical sort of person who would probably be amenable to a dose of honesty. It seemed to work; or at least, the more detail he went into about Forster's possible career as a thief, the more she seemed to relax, and even to enjoy the account.

'But these were *Italian* pictures mainly, is that right? Is that what you're saying?'

'For the most part, yes. Fifteenth and sixteenth centuries.'

She shook her head. 'I do Dutch and English, you see. I'm not allowed to touch Italian. Alex does Italian.'

'Who's Alex?'

'My boss. He reckons he's the great expert. He doesn't like me. Tried to stop me getting a job here. Italian's the one thing I really know about, and he always makes a fuss if I so much as look at one of the pictures he sees as his. He is determined that no one but him will do them. His empire. He's worried about people finding out he's an idiot.'

'So if Forster slipped some stolen Italian paintings through here . . .'

'Alex would have assessed them. How very interesting,' she said and thought this over for a while. 'And if they turn out to be dodgy, and if there's any trouble about why we didn't notice . . . Hmm.'

There was another long pause, as Lucy thought some more and Argyll reflected about the adverse impact of office politics on character. 'Now. Tell me,' she went on, coming out of her reverie, 'what exactly do you want?'

'That depends on how much you're prepared to help.'

'We have a policy of the utmost cooperation with the police to assist them in trying to make the art market a more honest and reputable place.'

'Really?'

'No. But in this particular case I think we should make a start. What do you want?'

'Two things, then. Firstly a list of everything Forster sold through you. And bought, I suppose. Secondly, I'd like to know whether your firm did the inventory on Weller House.'

'Post-mortem?'

He nodded. 'Somebody did; it would have been official valuers and Forster was in charge then. It struck me he might well have chosen you. Your firm does that sort of thing, doesn't it?'

She grunted. 'Oh, yes. If the owners decide to sell it gives us a head start. That at least I can help you with. On the other hand, his trading might be a bit more difficult. All the details will be in Alex's office and I don't want to disturb him, if you see what I mean.'

'Of course.'

'Hold on.'

And she disappeared into the next office, carefully making sure that there was no one in it. Argyll heard the sound of file drawers being slid in and out, then a pause, then the whirring and clunking of a photocopying machine. Eventually, she returned, bearing a few sheets of paper.

'I've got the inventory at least. We did it at the end of January,' she said. 'I only copied the paintings for you; I'd have been there all day if I'd done the furniture as well.'

'That's fine.'

She handed the sheets over. 'Pretty motley collection,' she said. 'We're not the greatest auction house in the world, but even we get to deal with higher quality stuff. Ninety-nine in all.'

'Paintings?'

'Er, hold on.' She counted quickly. 'Seventy-two paintings. The rest are drawings. What's the matter? You look disappointed.'

'There's more than I was expecting.'

'Oh. Anyway, there's scarcely anything worth bothering about in the whole lot. Nearly all pretty ordinary family portraits. One supposed Kneller, but that apparently is a bit dubious. There's a note from the person who did it saying if that's a Kneller, he's a cucumber. The rest are even worse.'

He nodded. 'Now, I've taken more of your time than I should. I should leave you.'

'Not before you promise to keep me fully informed of everything that you find that concerns us.'

Argyll agreed.

'And put me up for a week when I come to Rome in September.'

Argyll agreed.

'And sell pictures through us if you ever use a London auction house.'

He agreed to that.

'And take me out for dinner before you leave.'

And that. As he left he wondered whether he could give the bill to Bottando.

11

He got back to Byrnes's gallery about half an hour after Flavia, and the two of them then slogged their way across central London to get to the station. Liverpool Street Station at five-thirty in the evening requires a strong stomach and nerves of steel even when you're used to it; for Flavia it resembled nothing so much as a scene from Dante's *Inferno*. A post-modern, recently-restored *Inferno*, no doubt, but even the fine restoration work on the station could not disguise the basic chaos of the transport.

'Dear God,' she said as she followed Argyll towards what was flagged as the 5.15 to Norwich, but which was still hanging around in the station, 'are you serious?'

She looked at the ancient carriages with the doors hanging open, the windows filthy with years of grime and the paint peeling off, then shook her head in disbelief. Then she peered through the caked mud and saw the hundreds of commuters crammed in with barely a square millimetre of space, each one gamely reading a newspaper and pretending this was a civilized way of spending their brief sojourn on earth. 'Is this the express service to Belsen, or something?' she asked.

Argyll coughed with embarrassment. It's always awkward, being in the position of feeling patriotically obliged to defend the indefensible. 'It'll get us there,' he said lamely. 'I hope.'

'But why don't these people just get off and put a match to the thing?' she asked with the incredulity that only someone who lives in a country with an effective train service can muster.

Argyll was halfway through explaining that British Rail would just transfer the charred wrecks to the Brighton line when a loud crackle was followed by an incomprehensible booming around the station.

'What?' asked Flavia, frowning and trying to make it out.

'I don't know.'

The grunting and mumbling seemed to be understood by the passengers on the train, however. With one huge collective sigh, they folded their newspapers, picked up their briefcases, got off and organized themselves on the platform. None seemed particularly perturbed by the fact that the train should have pulled out of the station twenty minutes ago.

'Excuse me,' Flavia asked a well-dressed, fifty-year-old man who had come to stand placidly nearby. 'What did that announcement say?'

He raised an eyebrow, surprised at the disturbance. 'The train has been cancelled again,' he explained. 'The next one's in an hour.'

'This is ridiculous,' she said firmly after she'd digested the information and decided that patience could be overdone. 'I'm not hanging around here for an hour to be squeezed into a cattle truck. If these people want to stand around like a bunch of sheep, that's their problem. I'm getting out of here.'

Suppressing a desire to point out that sheep don't travel in cattle trucks, Argyll trooped after her, out of the station and into a car rental place around the corner.

He reckoned they averaged about three miles an hour all the way to Norwich. He still thought they would have arrived faster if they'd waited for the train, but, in the circumstances, didn't want to say so. It did give them plenty of time to talk about the late Geoffrey Forster, and the varying possibilities that he was either a major criminal or, alternatively, the biggest waste of time for years. Argyll summarized his findings in the afternoon.

'So?' Flavia said as they slowed to a halt somewhere. 'What do you think?'

'Well. It's interesting, isn't it? All these little hints.'

'Which ones?'

'Forster busied himself for several years selling paintings from Weller House. Right?'

She nodded.

'Now, when Uncle Godfrey shuffled off the mortal coil fifteen years back, there were seventy-two paintings listed in the inventory taken when he died. When cousin Veronica followed suit another inventory was taken. And guess what?'

She shook her head. 'Amaze me.'

'Still seventy-two pictures in the collection.'

The queue of traffic got moving again, and Flavia paused while she tried to manoeuvre herself into a position to burst mightily through the twenty-miles-an-hour barrier.

'Which means,' she resumed as she gave up the effort a few moments later, 'that either he was buying new

143

ones, which I assume you can check from comparing the two lists, or he wasn't selling anything.'

Argyll nodded enthusiastically.

'Using Weller House as a sort of laundromat?' she suggested. 'Is that what you're getting at?'

'That's it. Forster steals a painting, which is bought by someone. Problem: how to disguise where it comes from, so it can satisfy the curious. For a picture not to have any provenance is a bit suspicious these days, and the last thing you want is to give the impression it might have come from Italy. So, you find an old country house collection that hasn't been examined by anyone for years. If there is any old documentation, you burn it so no one can double check. Then you begin to sell the pictures, perhaps going through an auction house to be doubly sure, claiming they came from there.'

'And,' Flavia continued, 'although some people might wonder, no one can ever prove it was stolen because Forster has made sure his targets were from badly catalogued, uninsured collections. And the new owners will be cautious enough to make sure no photographs of their new possession are taken either.'

'Exactly. There's some risk, but given the number of pictures in the world and the small number of people able to recognize them, it's not that big.'

Flavia nodded. 'This woman is going to send you a list of his sales and purchases, is she?'

'In a couple of days. She doesn't want anyone else to know.'

'I could do with the evidence now.'

Argyll thought this over. Some people are in such a hurry all the time. They'd only heard of Forster less than a week ago, after all.

'The statements about him aren't good enough?'

'One person, thirty years out of date and with a grudge. Sandano I'm not sure we can use: I promised him confidentiality. Della Quercia is too batty to be relied on. All Winterton says is that Forster recognized a possibly stolen painting. It's a pity Veronica Beaumont is dead. Evidence that Forster was selling pictures supposedly from Weller House, and proof that they didn't come from there, would be very useful. We might then be able to find out where they got to. Was there anything in his papers about his sales?'

'Not so far. But I haven't finished them yet.'

Then it was her turn to think and to change the subject. 'What do people in this village think of him? Nobody this afternoon seemed to have a high opinion. Winterton thought he had bad taste – which Bottando's Giotto most certainly did not have, if he existed. Byrnes sneers about Forster being charming. Why would anyone sneer at someone being charming?'

'Because this is England, my dear, and that's what we do here.'

'Why? I like people to be charming.'

'But you're Italian,' he explained patiently, as she slipped the car into gear and lurched forward a few hundred yards. 'In this country charm means you're superficial, have a tendency to flattery, are probably a bumptious social climber and, moreover, the term carries very distinct implications that you like women.'

'What's wrong with that?'

'A ladies' man,' Argyll said darkly. 'Few things can be worse. It suggests a propensity to slobber over people's hands and pay compliments like some continental. You can do that sort of thing with dogs, but not with the opposite sex.'

'You do come from a very strange country, you know.

Tell me about my new hostess. Am I going to enjoy her company?'

'Mrs Verney? Very much, I think. At least, I do. She's quite charming. And, before you ask, women can be charming. That's perfectly acceptable, even in England.'

'I see. And in what does her charm consist?'

'Comfort. She makes you feel relaxed and at home, even in that chilly great barn of a house. She's very intelligent, I think; a wry sense of humour, rather quick on her feet.'

'Why is she so obliging?' she asked suspiciously.

'Curiosity about you, probably. But as you're curious about her as well, that's all right. Besides, I suspect the real truth is that she's a bit lonely. She doesn't really have much of a life up there, you know.'

They arrived at the village at well past nine, and Flavia drove straight to Weller House. The rain was finally stopping as a way of welcoming them to Norfolk, and Mary greeted them like long-lost friends, led them into the kitchen – you must be hungry, so I kept a little food over for you – then settled them down so she and Flavia could cast an eye over each other and see what was mutually in store for them. Flavia was tired, Mary seemed unusually quiet and cautious.

But they got the measure of each other fairly quickly; Flavia was better with a drink beside her, and Mary relaxed. Argyll, in fact, felt rather left out, and a little affronted by the way they hit it off. Neither of them bothered to talk to him very much at all; rather, they chattered away, discussing the state of British transport, the weather, the horrors of living in London, Rome and Paris and the problem of getting good materials for salad to grow in an English climate.

'And have you reached a conclusion about Geoffrey?' she asked after a while.

'Not really,' Flavia said. 'Enquiries are continuing.'

'We may have linked him to another picture,' Argyll added, for no particular reason except for the fact that he hadn't been able to say anything for nearly quarter of an hour and needed to make his presence felt a little. 'A Pollaiuolo. But there is a bit of bad news for you as well, I'm afraid.'

'How's that?'

Flavia explained. Personally, she wasn't absolutely convinced that she wanted to talk about this case to someone she'd only met half an hour previously, but as Argyll seemed already to have told her everything, as she was her hostess and as she did indeed seem an eminently agreeable soul, there seemed to be little point in holding back.

'Forster might have been disguising the pictures he sold by saying they came from here,' she said.

Mary looked interested. 'Why? What would that accomplish?'

'You know crooks launder money so it can't be traced?'

'Of course.'

'Picture thieves often launder paintings. Give them a false pedigree to explain where they came from. An old collection like yours, full of pictures that no one has seen for a hundred years or more, would be absolutely perfect. Unless somebody checked with your family.'

'Which would have been a waste of breath. As I told Jonathan, Veronica wasn't exactly coherent all the time.'

'Even better.'

Mary looked thoughtful. 'That would explain why he

hid the documents on what actually was in the house, I suppose.'

'Probably.'

'Anything going on here while I've been away?' Argyll asked. 'More murders, arrests or anything?'

'No,' the older woman replied almost sadly. 'Quiet as the grave. Jessica's here, though.'

'Is that the wife?' Flavia asked.

'That's right. She came back this morning, poor thing. She's in a bit of a state; I suppose it must be a shock. So I asked whether she wanted to be put up as well; I couldn't imagine she wanted to stay in that house. But she said she was fine.'

'That was very kind of you.'

'Yes,' she agreed. 'It was. I must confess I was terrified that she might accept the offer. I'm all for helping the afflicted in their hour of need, of course, but frankly' – here she lowered her voice as though too many people might hear – 'the woman is so *wet* she makes me want to scream.'

'Have the police talked to her?'

She shrugged. 'How should I know? Even George Barton is in the dark about what's going on. And if he doesn't know, then a mere amateur like myself is unlikely to find anything out.'

After about another half hour of idle conversation – Argyll's lack of opportunity to talk meant he finished his food very much faster than did the other two – he decided to go to bed, leaving them comfortably ensconced in the sitting room wondering whether to have a brandy.

12

He was woken up by a loud bashing on the door and a head sticking itself inside.

'Oh, Jonathan. Sorry to wake you,' said Mary. 'The police have just arrived and could you get up as quickly as possible?'

Instead of a coherent response, he stuck his head out from underneath the blanket, into the dank, cold air and said 'Wha?' or something like that, as he tried to orientate himself.

'Coffee's in the kitchen,' she added brightly before disappearing.

Still fuddled, but doing as he was told, Argyll levered himself out of bed and reached for his clothes. He then wasted several precious minutes while he wondered where his left sock was, discovered it under the bed, along with generations of other debris, then dressed and went downstairs.

Inspector Wilson, with the sour look on his face of a man who has drunk too much coffee and not had enough breakfast, greeted him with a gruff sound that did little except communicate discontent.

Argyll peered at him cautiously. 'What's up?' he asked. 'You do not have the air of a man at peace with the world.'

'That's a way of putting it, Mr Argyll. I am not. I have a question to ask you.'

'Ask away.'

'Where were you yesterday afternoon?'

Argyll looked puzzled. 'I was in London,' he said cautiously. 'Why?'

'Can I take it, then, that you have no idea who went into Geoffrey Forster's house yesterday, broke through the seals, unlocked the door, and took all his papers?'

This time Argyll was surprised. 'Not a clue,' he said. 'But it wasn't me. Who'd want them, anyway?'

'Indeed.'

'When was this?'

'We're not sure. For once, the villagers were caught unawares. Nobody saw anyone go in or out. Except for police officers.'

'Must have been one of them, then,' he suggested. 'Are you sure no one took them away in a fit of diligence?'

Wilson didn't even answer. Instead, he turned his attention to the door, as a still-yawning Flavia came in. Mary Verney performed the introductions.

'Delighted,' Inspector Wilson said.

'Do I understand that a lot of papers have gone missing?' she asked mildly.

Wilson, slightly shamefaced now that he was confronted with a colleague, even though an unlikely-looking colleague, admitted that this was the case. And, to get it over and done with, also admitted that it did look bad, a load of evidence disappearing just like that from the house of someone who was possibly a victim of murder.

'I was hoping that Mr Argyll was going to tell me he'd taken all the papers so that he could study them at leisure here,' he said. 'Unfortunately, that's not the case.'

'Have you asked Forster's wife?' Mary chipped in. 'I suppose that she inherits whatever he may have had. So she would have an interest in them. Maybe she took them off to an accountant, or something.'

Wilson agreed that this was a possibility, but they had managed to think of this already and Jessica Forster had denied doing anything of the sort.

'Would you mind if I walked down and had a look around?' Flavia asked as he prepared to go. 'I'm sure I won't be able to contribute anything useful. But it would come in useful for my report.'

Wilson said that would be fine by him. But he'd be grateful if she didn't touch anything without his permission.

After a brief breakfast, therefore, the three of them wrapped themselves up in the warm clothing necessary for coping with an English summer morning, and set off on the short walk to Forster's house.

'This place used to belong to you, is that right?' Flavia asked as she and Mary walked in step and Argyll was distracted by the dog. 'Why did your cousin sell those cottages to him?'

'A good question. I thought of trying to get it overturned on grounds of undue influence, but the lawyers all told me I was wasting my time. Who knows, I might manage something now. I hope you don't decide I killed him just to get my property back.'

'I'll try not to. Was the Weller estate big once?'

'Oh, yes. It dwindled slowly. On the few occasions that I came here as a child, there were still half a dozen farms working like crazy to keep us in the style to which we were accustomed. But Uncle Godfrey was hopeless at business, and Veronica was too potty to care. Very big on family position, but not much use at providing the wherewithal to underpin it. Or so I found out when she died. She used to live very well and I never understood how. After she died I discovered it was basically by selling off the family silver. But, if it's good enough for the government, why not for Veronica, eh?'

'And more death duties when she died?'

She nodded. 'Not many. She transferred the place to my name some time ago. She had a turn, thought she was going to die and got frightened the taxman would get it. That was when I was asked to visit. We managed to avoid quite a lot of taxes, but there are still enough to keep me worried. The revenue men are beginning to nip at my heels a little. This is the house, by the way.'

She opened the door and then said that she'd leave Flavia to wander around at will. She'd walk around the grounds and see if anything needed doing.

'Perils of owning things,' she said. 'You're constantly eyeing up holes in fences and worrying about how much they'll cost to repair.'

'Shall I come with you?' Argyll asked.

'By all means.'

So she and Argyll set off down the small garden, leaving Flavia to examine Forster's house professionally. Argyll would have hung around, but she was quite capable of finding out everything she needed on her own and, at times like that when she was concentrating, he knew that she was better left in peace.

'I like Flavia,' Mary said eventually in a definite tone of voice. 'Hang on to her.'

'I'm going to. Where are we going, by the way?' he asked as they crossed through what seemed to be an old hedge.

'We're back in the grounds of Weller. That path over there leads back round to the front of the house. It gets a bit boggy at times. This path goes through that little copse. There's not much in it. Someone once had an idea about breeding pheasants, but got bored with it. You can still see some wandering around at times. They have a nice life. Nobody's bothered them for years. It's quite pretty.'

'Let's go down there, then. Tell me, why don't you just sell Weller and be shot of it? There must be something left over, mustn't there? Even after taxes?'

'After taxes, yes. But after taxes and paying off debts, no. Basically, we're chugging along courtesy of the bank manager. Uncle Godfrey refused to accept reality and kept on raising loans secured on what he persuaded bankers were his expectations.'

'What expectations?'

'That he would win his fight for compensation for the airbase, which was commandeered during the war. A complete waste of time, in my opinion. Or at least it was. Now they're going, there's a possibility I might get it back.'

'But not for several years, surely?'

'No. Frankly, I doubt if it will ever happen, although don't say I said so. The important thing is to persuade the banks, so I can borrow money on it.'

'Like Uncle Godfrey?'

'A bit. I suppose you think it's grossly irresponsible, borrowing money I know I will never pay back. But what the hell? What are banks for?'

They were crossing a small clearing, only a dozen or

so yards wide, and made a detour to avoid a volcano-shaped pile of garden rubbish that had been stacked up for burning. It still smelt slightly, the charred aroma of burnt material that has been wettened overnight when the rain started coming down again. On the other side, the source of the smell came into view, and Argyll stopped dead in his tracks. Then he went and peered closely at the large pile. An old manila file was only half-burnt, and it was labelled 'correspondence 1982'. Another bit of half-consumed paper had a letterhead from Bond Street. A third was the remains of some bill or other.

The pair of them looked at it for a while, then Jonathan said: 'Seems to solve the problem of the empty filing cabinet, doesn't it?'

'Yes,' she said eventually, sticking her hands in her pockets. 'It does, doesn't it?'

Now Argyll bent down, stuck his face close to the debris and sniffed. 'A whiff of petrol. Or paraffin,' he observed. 'What was the weather like here yesterday?'

'Rained in the morning, stopped in the afternoon, started again in the evening and kept going.'

He shrugged. 'Anyway, somebody must have worked very hard on this. Carrying all those files out of the house, bringing them all the way over here, setting light to them, watching them burn, then doing their best to scatter the debris. They must have been busy for quite a time. I wonder why?'

'Is that a rhetorical question, or do you think you know?'

'It destroys a lot of possible evidence about Forster, doesn't it? Come on. We'll have to walk back and find Inspector Wilson.'

*   *   *

154

Flavia, meanwhile, was having a cup of coffee and a little chat with Jessica Forster, whom she'd encountered just as she was beginning her cursory look around the site where the murdered man had been found. She was standing, hands in pocket, lost in thought, at the foot of the stairs, squinting up to get an idea of the man's descent, when there came a cough, half apologetic, half indignant, from behind her.

She turned round to greet the cougher, and apologize for coming in without knocking: in fact, she had entirely forgotten that Forster's widow was there. It was something, she decided later, that people did with Jessica Forster. The adjective mousy arose, quite unbidden, in her mind and despite all efforts to achieve a more balanced, subtle character analysis, it stayed there throughout, squeaking at her insistently.

Mrs Forster was over ten years younger than her husband, she guessed, and exuded none of the self-confidence and arrogance that the photographs of the dead man possessed. She had the pressed lips and tight jaw of suffering righteousness, of a martyr to the cause of doing things properly. She was also extremely nervous and manifestly in considerable distress, although this was, she decided charitably, more than reasonable in the circumstances. Either way, Flavia found her a difficult person to talk to, and discovered that the nervousness and twitchiness was mildly contagious.

Her opening remarks, along the lines of offering condolences on her husband's death, did not make much of an impact. 'It was a shock,' she said. 'I still can't believe it has happened.'

'I was wondering whether I could ask you . . .'

'You want to interview me as well? I've already told the police everything I know.'

Flavia hastened to reassure her and explained that she was interested in different things.

'So who are you then?'

She explained that as well, after a fashion. 'How much have the police told you?'

She shook her head. 'They haven't *told* me anything. Just asked me. It's been horrible. Almost as though it was none of my business.'

With some misgiving, Flavia told her what she knew, ending up with her quest for the Pollaiuolo. As long as she wasn't dissimulating, then she hadn't been told much. She appeared insignificant, so she was treated like that. It was hard to take her into consideration, but that was no reason for ignoring her. She seemed almost pathetically grateful for Flavia's efforts, and the Italian felt herself becoming more sympathetic.

When the explanation was finished, Mrs Forster shook her head. 'I didn't know anything about this at all,' she said.

'Would you expect to?'

'Maybe not. Of course, I didn't know anything about his business. Except that it hasn't been so easy recently. Because of Mrs Verney.'

With a bit of fire in her for the first time, Jessica Forster indicated that Mrs Verney and her husband had not got on at all well. 'I can't say who was at fault. She said she couldn't afford him any more. But Geoffrey was furious with her, far more so than I would have imagined. I'm afraid they just disliked each other. But I must say she has always been nice to me. She even offered to let me stay in Weller House if I couldn't face being here. That was kind, don't you think? You often find out the best of people in times of trouble.'

Flavia agreed it was frequently the case.

'I understood his reaction, of course,' she went on. 'Geoffrey had put in so much work for Miss Beaumont, and gave up his business in London to come here and work for her. Then Mrs Verney just ended it. He was deeply hurt. And I don't mind telling you, it hurt us financially as well.'

'And it was just because Mrs Verney couldn't afford it?'

Jessica Forster frowned. Flavia decided she was either very stupid or very simple. Or perhaps neither. 'What other reason could there be?'

'And you've been having a hard time? Financially, I mean?'

She nodded. 'But it was getting very much better. Geoffrey was re-establishing his business, and told me he expected to pull off a big deal very soon.'

'And what was that?'

'I've no idea. He never used to bother me with the details. I earn it, you spend it. That's what he used to say. He was a good man. I know what you've been told about him. But there was more to him than that. Much more.'

Flavia was left to guess what more she might have meant, and decided it was too complicated to pursue at the moment. 'This deal,' she said. 'What was it? A painting?'

'I suppose so. Unless he meant selling off the cottages. But I don't think it was that.'

'If he had valuable paintings, would he normally keep them here?'

'I've no idea. Maybe not. If they were really valuable. This isn't the most secure place, and so many people have keys, what with the cleaning ladies and such. And you do hear tales about burglars.'

'So if your husband wished to show a painting to a client, for example, it's possible that he would only bring it here at the last moment?'

She nodded. 'It's possible. He did have a safe deposit box at a bank in Norwich. I told all this to the police, you know.'

'He didn't mention the names of any clients?'

She shook her head.

'Did he have any contacts in Italy?'

Another shake.

'I see. Did your husband travel a great deal?'

'Of course. He was an art dealer. He was constantly on the move, seeing pictures and clients. Not that he enjoyed it much. He preferred to stay at home.'

'Did he go abroad?'

'Yes, sometimes. Not often, though. Why do you ask?'

'Just interest,' she said vaguely. 'Do you happen to know if he was in Scotland in July 1976?'

Another shake. 'I don't know.'

'In Padua in May 1991?'

Another.

'Milan in February 1992?'

'I don't think so. He went away often, but not for long and I wasn't always sure where he was.'

'Would anybody know?'

'Probably not. Geoffrey worked alone. You might ask that man Winterton. He might know something.'

'I see. Thank you. Can you tell me, how did he come to work for Veronica Beaumont?'

'She asked him, I think. Several years back, I believe they'd known each other. Socially. Geoffrey made a point of cultivating such people. Can't say I would have given most of them the time of day, myself. He said he'd given her informal advice for some time. But he really

158

started working here properly about three years ago. That was when we took the decision to move here.'

'They'd known each other for years, I understand. Since their twenties.'

She looked puzzled at this. 'Perhaps. I don't know. He never mentioned it. I must say I wasn't happy to come here. I know business was bad, but we would have managed. I was ready to go and get a job and help. And I wasn't sure that tying ourselves to the whim of one woman – who was a bit strange – was a good idea. But Geoff never listened to me. And it was no consolation when I was proven right. We should never have left London and buried ourselves here.'

An unfortunate choice of phrase, Flavia thought. And, come to think of it, it was a pity he hadn't listened to her. She might behave like a frightened rabbit, but if what she was saying was true, she had more sense – or better judgement – than her husband had. 'You don't know what happened to his papers?' she asked.

She looked nervous suddenly, and Flavia knew that she was not telling the truth when she shook her head and explained that she'd been out all day.

'I got back here last night, and spent all morning talking to the police. Then I went to Norwich to see the solicitors. After that, I spent the evening with friends. I didn't know anything about it until the police came round this morning, asked to see them and then started shouting when they discovered all the papers had gone.'

Flavia nodded thoughtfully. Such a rush of alibis, with all the tension vanishing as she spoke, almost as though she was reassuring herself as it came out. She was on the whole far too nervous, in Flavia's admittedly uncharitable view.

*   *   *

She sipped a glass of beer and pondered thoughtfully. No, she finally decided, she would go hungry. Safer that way. She had never seen food that looked quite like that before and didn't really care to experiment with what effect it might have on her stomach. Argyll did his best with a sausage roll and, to make up for their lack of appetite, Inspector Manstead, newly arrived from London to view proceedings, tucked enthusiastically into a second Scotch egg, then made the repast even more tasty by adding a large pickled onion to the mixture in his mouth. Flavia shuddered, and tried to concentrate.

'So what do they reckon? Your colleagues, I mean?' she asked.

Manstead chewed meditatively a while longer, then disposed of egg, sausage meat and pickled onion in one mighty swallow. 'I don't think they reckon anything yet. They want to think that our Gordon was responsible; nice and simple, no problems. But they don't, really. They're hanging on to him for want of anything better.'

'They've talked to Mrs Forster, I understand?'

'Yup.'

'She mentioned Forster's safe deposit box?'

Manstead smiled. 'Yes, she did. And it's been checked out.'

'And what's in it?'

'Nothing. It seems that Forster arrived that afternoon, just before closing time, and took everything out of it.'

'*What?* What did he take?'

'They don't know. Of course they don't. Wouldn't do to go snooping around in clients' boxes. It's not Switzerland, you know.'

Flavia frowned. 'So, if I understand this right, Jonathan telephones – when was it?'

'About two-thirty,' Argyll put in. 'A bit later, maybe.'

'And Forster immediately leaps into his car, rushes into Norwich and collects his package,' Manstead continued for her. 'It takes about forty-five minutes to get in. That evening he is dead, and when we look, there is nothing which appears out of place, as though it was collected from a safe deposit the previous day. But, of course, we don't know what we are looking for, do we?'

Flavia sniffed and scratched her nose. 'Jonathan?' Flavia asked, turning her attention on to him more completely. 'What *exactly* did you say when you rang him up?'

Argyll looked flustered, and tried to remember. 'That I was making enquiries about a picture I had heard about through an old friend of his.'

'And?'

'And that I'd heard he might know something about it.'

'And?'

'And that it might have been stolen. And that I wanted to talk to him about it. And that I didn't want to talk over the phone. He said I should come to see him here.'

'So it's possible that he thought you wanted to buy it?'

Argyll conceded this was possible.

'And also possible that he rushed off to get it so you could view the goods before making an offer?'

Another nod. 'I suppose. Except, of course, that I specifically mentioned the Palazzo Straga.'

'Ah.'

'And it still hardly explains why he's dead, does it?

161

Or why his papers got burned up. Can't blame me, this time.'

Manstead, who'd been listening to this with some pleasure, downed a good third of his pint then smacked his lips. 'Ah, country life,' he said with satisfaction. 'Good beer, good food, fresh air. What am I doing, living in London, eh? Perhaps,' he went on, 'pictures have got nothing to do with it.'

Flavia gave him a doubtful look. 'My friends in the force say there are lots of other more interesting lines of enquiry, and Gordon's refusal to say where he was is only one of them.'

'For example?'

'For example, the fact that Forster was carrying on with the cleaning girl, and Mrs Forster didn't like it one bit. She may look like a long-suffering simpleton, but even she must have got a bit annoyed by that. Can't say I blame her, either. And there is the problem of the London trip, of course.'

'Which problem is that?'

'Mrs Forster is in London, staying with her sister. But on the evening of Forster's death, she goes on her own to the cinema. She leaves the house at five, and comes back way after midnight. I know some films need some editing, but nine hours is a bit long, even for one of these avant-garde things. Acts a bit oddly, so the sister says, when asked why she was out so late.'

'And what does she say to you?'

'She says she was out, went for a walk, ate, saw a film, then, as it was a nice evening, walked home. Maybe she did.

'But now there's the affair of the burning papers,' he went on. 'And who could have burnt them but her? Safeguarding her position by destroying evidence of what he was up to? Not wanting her husband's estate confiscated by outraged victims?'

'Have you had any response from the Belgians about that picture Winterton mentioned?'

Manstead nodded. 'I have. A nice man, that, by the way. Kind of you to put me in contact. As for the picture, they sent this. It's still in the collection.'

He slipped out a slightly murky photograph from his file and, with a little smile of expectation, handed it to Flavia. It was very far from being a clear image. Flavia peered at it, and grunted.

'We've also shown it to the Earl of Dunkeld, who swears blind it's his. Pollaiuolo. St Mary the Egyptian.'

Flavia nodded, and sipped her beer. 'How was it stolen?'

'Simplicity itself. Big family wedding on' – here he paused and looked at his notes – 'the Saturday. 10th July 1976. Blushing bride marches down the aisle, organ plays, confetti thrown, party held in the ballroom – such useful things to have about the house, ballrooms, don't you think? Anyway, the whole thing is a huge success. Flawless. Everything right and proper and wonderful. Except that in the morning the library had this picture hanging up in it. Late at night a tired but proud father goes in for a quiet and relaxing sit down . . .'

'Blank spot on the wall?'

Manstead nodded. 'Exactly. By which time everybody had gone home. Could have been any one of seven hundred miscellaneous guests, relatives, caterers, musicians or vicars.'

'Has anyone cast an eye over the guest list?'

'I'm sure they did. But I assume nothing came of it.'

'Could they do it again?'

'I'll ask. Of course, if Forster was as good as your boss reckons, he would hardly have been there under his own name. Might not even have been on the guest list at all. Long time ago, as well. You can look at the file yourself, if you want.'

'Please. So. How did it get to Belgium?'

'That's the problem, of course,' Manstead said with a smile. 'The man who bought it is dead. And, naturally, his records don't say. Wouldn't, would they?'

'Any note about Forster selling them anything?'

'No.'

'Oh,' said a disappointed Flavia.

'Sorry about that.'

'But he did know about it. That's important. It means there are now hazy links between Forster and the disappearance of one Uccello, a Pollaiuolo, and a Fra Angelico. Three stolen paintings, dating between 1963 and 1991, and all on my boss's list of thefts by Giotto's hand. His own distinctive style, as you might say.'

'Impressive, and very hopeful. But there is nothing absolutely solid for any of them. Hazy, as you say. Now, where's that beer of mine?' he wondered.

In fact, Manstead's beer had been ambushed, or at least Argyll had. He had scarcely given the order to the barman when George, who might well have been lying in wait for hours, docked alongside him.

'Hello again, young man,' he said to open proceedings. 'What's been going on, then?'

'Not a lot,' Argyll said airily, as he watched the barman's wife, whose name, he gathered, was Sally, pull the pints. 'You probably know as much as I do.'

'In that case, they're not going to find anyone, are they? 'Cause I know nothing at all. Except that someone burnt all of Forster's papers, his wife's back, and that they're going to have to let Gordon Brown go sooner or later.'

'Oh? Why's that?'

'Because he didn't do it. He's got an alibi.'

'First I heard,' said Argyll, noticing that George was speaking in a remarkably loud voice.

'I know,' he said. 'But someone'll tell you soon enough. No doubt about that. Bound to. Even I know he didn't do it.' And, giving everybody in hearing distance what was unmistakably a significant look, George nodded sagely to himself, picked up the remains of his pint, and walked off to his corner seat. Argyll got the strong feeling that the man had delivered his message. He was just uncertain who the message had been delivered to. It certainly wasn't him.

He found out at about ten that evening, as the trio were clearing away the table in the morning room and beginning the task of carrying everything down to the kitchen. A good meal, except for a bumpy start: Flavia had been asked to cook some pasta and, despite her protestations that cooking really wasn't her area of expertise, she had given in eventually. Mary Verney had this certainty that all Italians are born cookers of pasta. Her opinion changed somewhat after the first course.

And then the doorbell went.

'Unexpected late-night calls seem to be popular all of a sudden,' Mary said as she got up and prepared to go on the long voyage across the saloon, through the entrance hallway to the door. It was a trip that took several minutes, and she returned only to poke her head through the door and summon them to the little sitting room which was the only properly comfortable part of the house.

'It's Sally,' she explained as she led them through the darkened hallway. 'The barman's wife. Don't know what she wants. But I'm feudally obliged to listen, and as it seems to be about Geoffrey, I thought you might want to hear as well.'

Sally, the barman's wife, was standing in her coat looking mightily uncomfortable, until Mary sat her down by the fire, beamed maternally and made appropriately reassuring noises.

'I said I had a headache and left Harry to close up,' she said. 'I'm so sorry to bother you but . . . oh!'

Her face fell as she turned round and saw Flavia and Argyll.

'What's the matter?'

'I think I've made a mistake. Perhaps I ought to go.'

'You'll do nothing of the sort,' Mary said firmly. 'If you need to talk to me on your own, then those two can go for a walk.'

'Oh, I don't know,' she replied, now panicking and wavering in her resolve. 'I'm sorry I came at all. But I thought you might tell me what to do . . .'

'Just so,' said a curiously unsurprised Mary. 'I think, if I can give you a little piece of advice, you would be well advised to tell Miss di Stefano your story as well. You can rely on her.'

'But what about him?' Sally said, pointing at Argyll. 'He gossips with George. All the time.'

Mary went into the hallway and let out a piercing whistle, putting both fingers into her mouth to produce the right effect. It echoed through the great rooms like an air-raid siren, and in response there was a muffled barking and a patter of eager canine feet. She picked Argyll's coat off the hook and tossed it at him.

'Please, Jonathan. A little favour. In the interests of

village serenity. Take Frederick for his evening constitutional. Walkies! Walkies!' she said, switching her attention to the beast that came running expectantly through the door.

'Women's business,' she went on, noting that Argyll seemed markedly less enthusiastic than Frederick at the prospect. 'Come back in half an hour.'

By the time he got halfway to the gate, Flavia was regarding the unhappy woman with what she hoped was an air of encouraging sympathy. Sally was in her late thirties, heavy in the face and pale from too much bad food and too many hours confined behind the bar of the pub. A pretty face though. With a little bit of care, she thought to herself . . . But, as Argyll constantly told her, that was not the way things were done here.

Whatever Sally had come for, she was not over eager to tell them about it. She sat in a sullen silence, staring down at the carpet, unable to begin.

'Perhaps if I helped,' Mary prompted. 'You've come about Gordon, is that right?'

'Oh, Mrs Verney, yes,' she said in a rush. It was as though the older woman had pulled the bung out of a barrel. The words suddenly started gushing out. 'He didn't do anything wrong. I suppose everybody knows he steals things and he can get rough. But not like that.'

'The police seem to like the idea,' Mary said.

'But they're wrong. I know they are.'

'And why is that?'

Sally lapsed into silence again.

'Because he was with you? Is that it?'

She nodded, and looked up with alarm.

'Tell us what happened,' Flavia suggested.

'Perhaps I should explain first of all,' Mary said. 'Gordon

is married to Louise. Formerly Louise Barton. George's daughter. That's why Sally didn't want Jonathan to overhear this.'

Then Sally began her tale. It was simple enough. Both she and her husband worked behind the bar only at busy periods. At weekends they got in help, but ordinarily they managed on their own. Most lunch-times and evenings either one or the other worked the bar. On the day Forster died, it was Harry, and his wife had the evening off. The bar of the pub was downstairs, and the living quarters upstairs at the back. At eight o'clock, just as it was getting busy and she knew her husband would be occupied until closing time, Gordon had left the bar, gone round the back and climbed up the drainpipe and into her room. He'd stayed there until he'd heard the bell for closing time, then disappeared the way he'd come.

'I see,' Flavia said, deciding to keep to facts, rather than go into motives. 'So he was with you from when, about eight to nearly eleven?'

'That's right.'

'Which covers him for all the period in which Forster might have been killed.'

'Yes,' she said. 'You see? That's what I mean.'

'By far the easiest thing would be for you to tell this to the police. Get it over and done with.'

'And you think they'll keep quiet about it? They arrested Gordon and they'll have to let him go. They'll say why and it'll be all over the village by the end of the week.'

'But Sally,' Mary said sadly, 'the only two people in Norfolk who don't know about you and Gordon are your husband and Gordon's wife. Surely you realize that?'

Sally's hand went up to her mouth in an expression of shock. 'No,' she said.

'Well, I know about it. And I'm not the nosiest person around here.'

'Excuse me,' Flavia said, breaking into this confessional. 'Can you tell me why Gordon didn't tell the police this? It's not as if he had a great deal to lose.'

'Because . . .' she began reluctantly.

'Because what?' Mary said sternly, picking up something that entirely passed Flavia by.

'Because Gordon saw George coming out of Forster's house.'

'Ah,' said Mary with concern. Flavia sat back in her seat. There was no point in her interfering or saying anything at all. Mary Verney was a much better interrogator than she was.

Gradually, Mary got Sally to say that Gordon had walked from his cottage past Forster's house and seen George coming out of the door. He'd hurried off with his head down, but seemed shaken and upset about something.

She shook her head. 'He didn't pay any attention at the time. But the next morning, when Gordon heard what had happened, he got worried that maybe George had done something drastic. You know about the cottage.'

'And rather than incriminate him, he kept quiet, even when he was arrested. Good for him,' Mary concluded unexpectedly.

Flavia sighed. She was having a hard time understanding the thick East Anglian accent, and was a little bemused by the way in which the façade of English village life was turning out to be just a little thin. On the other hand, she cast her mind back to some little towns she knew in Italy. Incest, wife-swapping and mass family murder seemed to be the local pastimes everywhere.

She leant forward in her chair. 'But this was before eight, wasn't it? It must have been.'

Sally nodded. 'Yes. On his way to the pub. About seven.'

'So what's he worried about? One thing the police seem sure of is that Forster didn't die until after nine. Maybe later. His evidence doesn't incriminate George at all, really. Especially as there is no motive.'

'There is a bit of a motive, though,' Mrs Verney explained. 'Or at least something that could be made into one. Did Jonathan not tell you about Forster threatening to evict him?'

'Ah.'

'George has lived there all his life, and wasn't at all happy. In fact, he hated Forster, and said some regrettable things about him on occasion.'

'Like "I'll kill the bastard"?'

'That's the general line.'

'I see. He said this to a lot of people?'

Mary Verney nodded.

Flavia considered this. 'In that case, it's only a matter of time before the police find out,' she said eventually. 'Gordon has to talk to them. If they find out on their own he'll be prosecuted for obstruction, or whatever they call it here. As for you, Sally, I suggest you tell Gordon that. There's no reason for you to get any more involved. The police have more pressing things to concern themselves with.'

Sally nodded reluctantly and stood up. 'I'd better get back,' she said. 'Otherwise Harry'll wonder where I got to.'

'Do you want me to have a word with George?' Mary asked. 'I'm sure there's nothing to it. But it might be better if he had his explanation ready. I could talk it over with him.'

'Oh, would you?' Sally said. 'That would make me feel better.'

'I'd be delighted. Then Gordon can say what he knows without having to bring you into it at all.'

Flavia smiled encouragingly, and Mary ushered a relieved woman out of the house again.

'Non-stop action in this place, isn't it?' she said once Mary had returned to the sitting room and placed herself in front of the fire to warm up.

Her hostess nodded. 'So it seems.'

'Were you surprised?' Flavia asked.

'That Gordon was innocent? Not at all.'

'About George.'

'Very much so. So surprised that frankly I don't believe it for a moment. I prefer to take a benevolent view of human nature, as Jonathan may have told you. Besides, what about the burning papers? I can't see George doing that.'

'Forster is dead.'

'Dead, yes. But perhaps not murdered. Besides, I thought you wanted it to have something to do with pictures. Or has poor Jessica become the front runner now?'

'We're doing our best, you know. Everybody is.'

'I know. I'm sorry. But I'm beginning to lose patience over this a little. You don't know Geoffrey was murdered and you don't know he was a thief. So why bash away at it? The village has been turned upside down by all this, you know. You can't have everybody under suspicion, one after the other.'

'Forster's death would have been investigated even without us. And if it's any consolation, the police seem to be losing heart. So am I, frankly.'

'Good.'

13

Seated behind the desk in his office that evening, as the sounds of the city dwindled and the rush hour came to its appointed end, General Bottando was feeling more than a little frustrated. It is very hard, the thought that investigations can get along perfectly well without you. It makes you feel old, and redundant. And, of course, he was vulnerable in that area, what with Argan trying to elevate this line of thought to the status of official policy.

That problem was temporarily quiescent at least, although Bottando thought that this was probably only a lull before the final storm. Apart from a little note again urging greater activity over the raid on the via Giulia, his secretary reported that Argan's word processor had fallen silent in the past day or so; no more memos were flying around documenting the iniquities of the Art Theft Department.

That said, it was probably because the air was already saturated. The quality of the man's information was also extraordinary. He had known that Flavia had seen della Quercia, had latched on to Sandano's withdrawing his confession, figured out the real reason why Flavia had gone to England.

Now, after subtle metamorphosis, Bottando was gullible about these silly theories, believed a convicted criminal because it fitted in with those theories and had now sent his obedient little girl to England at vast expense in a last ditch attempt to hang on to his job.

Well, true enough, if you wanted to look at it like that. But where was the information coming from? Who was feeding the information? Bottando, with the heightened senses of a man fighting for his life, reckoned he knew. Paolo. A good boy, he thought a little patronizingly, but wanted to get on faster than was seemly. In too much of a rush, he was, and attaching himself to a victorious Argan would undoubtedly speed things up a bit. Had Bottando neglected him? Maybe so.

But the rights and wrongs of it were irrelevant at the moment. Argan had his office mole. The question was, what to do about it?

Nothing, at the moment. That would have to wait.

The trouble was that the more he jotted down little notes, the more he was, very reluctantly, kicking and screaming and protesting all the way, coming to the appalling conclusion that, perhaps, the abominable Argan was right after all. Maybe he was losing his touch. He could just about encompass the latter, but the former proposition went so much against the fundamental laws of nature that it still made his head swim in bewilderment.

For the umpteenth time, he got out his notes, and read them once more, to see if he could spot any hole through which he, and the rest of the department could wriggle.

Forster implicated in theft of picture in 1963 from

Florence, Giotto number one. Connected loosely with disappearance of a Pollaiuolo from Scotland, 1976, Giotto number thirteen. Connected with theft of a Fra Angelico from Padua, 1991, Giotto number twenty-six.

Three connections, all popping up from nowhere, unbidden, in less than a week. Volunteered, you might say. And that was the thing that was giving Bottando a headache, making his bones creak and giving him the feeling that there was something wrong somewhere. Far too much of a coincidence that someone who, if he were Giotto, had successfully covered his tracks for a quarter of a century, should suddenly have his sticky fingerprints appearing everywhere.

And, of course, there was the other side of things. If you looked at it carefully, there was nothing whatsoever to show that Forster had stolen anything. He didn't have much money, and did not have an extravagant lifestyle. No one had proved he was anywhere in the vicinity when any of the pictures were stolen.

Bottando shook his head and ground his teeth. He was giving up the fight, he noticed. He was sitting here, waiting for fate to overtake him. And that wasn't good enough. It was time to put up a bit of a struggle. He could start with Fancelli and go on to Sandano.

He smiled to himself, and felt better. That was one problem solved already. He shovelled his papers into his bag, and marched with a very much more jaunty step out of his office.

His secretary had already gone home for the evening, and Bottando started to write her a little note.

Two things, he scribbled. *Firstly, could you ring Florence and get them to pull Sandano in for me. I'll be there by ten*

*in the morning. Secondly, could you ring Argan. Apologies,
but I've been called away. Urgent business. I'll let him know
when I'm back.*

And, having taken the first step towards taking control
of his universe, Bottando left.

Merely being on the road again made Bottando feel
better. Driving around, talking to people, gripping life
with both hands. That was the trouble really, he thought
to himself as he parked his car in a carefree manner in a
restricted zone in the centre of Florence and placed his
'police' card in a prominent place on the dashboard, he
had been deskbound for too long.

Even though the first visit, to Fancelli, had produced
nothing except to demonstrate that Flavia had done
a decent job, he was content. The ailing woman had
repeated her story more or less word for word, and the
indignation which the very idea of Forster produced in
her seemed genuine enough to him. Also, the birth
certificate of her son recovered from the municipal
authorities and naming Geoffrey Forster as the guilty
party, so to speak, was pretty convincing.

But no harm in checking. That was what real policing
was all about, and what he was trying to defend. It
wasn't Argan at all, really. In a way, he continued
philosophically as he walked to the Carabinieri station
where Sandano was being held, the dreadful man was
right. He *was* out of touch. But not for the reasons that
Argan thought. Rather, he'd spent too many hours
writing memoranda, sitting around while other people,
like Flavia, did the interesting work.

He was still in this reflective mood when he was
shown into the little cell in which a disgruntled Sandano
sat cross-legged on a pull-out bed. Bottando sat heavily

176

on the chair opposite and beamed affectionately at the man.

'Sandano.'

'General. I'm impressed. A visit from the big boss man himself. Just to torment me for no reason.'

'You know as well as I do that we don't torment people for no reason,' Bottando replied levelly. 'We always have a reason.'

'Oh,' said the crestfallen thief. 'You found out. I suppose my grandmother told you.'

The statement left Bottando a little bemused. Found out about what, he thought? Hadn't Flavia mentioned something about him looking unusually shifty?

'That's right,' he replied knowingly, hoping that Sandano's natural death wish would solve the problem. 'A responsible citizen. And I want to hear all about it. Even though I know everything already. It'll be easier for you in the long run, you know. Cooperation.'

Sandano scowled at him for a while, then puffed mightily, hesitated, and gave in.

'Oh, all right. But just you remember Flavia's promise.'

'I remember.'

'It was nothing to do with me, you know. I steal things, OK. But hitting nightwatchmen. That wasn't me. I just drove the truck.'

What the hell is he talking about? Bottando thought, trying to compose his features into a look of stern disapproval.

'He wouldn't pay up, you see. We broke into the shed on the dig site, took all the statues, and delivered them as required. And when my brother went round to get paid, this guy tells him to get lost. The deal had fallen through and he didn't have the money yet. It wasn't me who went back and drove a car through the window and took them back either, if that's what you're thinking. I just want you to know that. That's not my sort of thing. I was back in Florence by then.'

'Right,' said a faintly surprised Bottando.

'That man, he thinks he can do anything. Bastard. He's got all of you lot in his pocket. That's why he did it.'

'We'll see about that.' Really, poor old Sandano was dim. Whoever heard of criminals confessing before even being asked? 'And while you're in a confessional mode, you might want to tell me a little about the Fra Angelico.'

'Fra Angelico?'

'Florentine painter. Renaissance. Back of your car. Remember?'

'Oh. That. I've told you the truth. I told that girl of yours . . .'

Bottando held up his hand. 'A word of advice, dear boy. Not girl.'

'No?'

'No. Never.'

'OK. Anyway, I told Flavia the truth. I didn't steal it.'

'I know you didn't.'

'So what are you asking for?'

'I just want to hear your story again. For myself. Off you go.'

'Well, it's all true, what I told Flavia. I never stole that picture. I just got unlucky at the border.'

'Yes?'

'And I said I'd done it because the Carabinieri offered a deal.'

'And then this man Forster turned up to talk about it?'

'Like I said. About three, four months back. Just after I got out for those candlesticks in the church.'

'Did he say he'd stolen it?'

'Not exactly. But he knew all about it, like I say. And I know it was all hushed up. I mean, it was never in the papers, was it?'

'I see. So he turns up. Then?'

'He came and asked what had happened. About the theft, the handover and what had gone wrong. I told him, and he said he was sorry I'd gone to jail for something I hadn't done, and if I wanted to clear my name by retracting my confession that would be fine by him. And he gave me some money, like I said.'

'But he didn't actually say he'd done it?'

'Well, no. Not exactly.'

'So how did you know his name?'

'He told me. And gave me his card, in case I missed something and wanted to contact him.'

'Gave you his card. I see. Describe him, would you?'

'I'm not so good on that sort of thing. A bit short-sighted . . .'

'You should get glasses, then. Do your best. Remember your grandmother.'

'Well, now. He was English, like I say. Rotten Italian. Late fifties or older. Full head of hair, dark brown, almost black . . . well-cut. Almost well-dressed. Average height, well-built for his age.'

'Average this, average that,' Bottando commented. 'Very useful. No distinguishing features? Duelling scars or anything?'

'Not that I noticed. I'm doing my best.'

'Of course. So someone freely tells you his name, gives you his card, visits you in prison, asks you about lots of things that he should have known already had he stolen the painting. And you think that he was clearly responsible for the theft. You must think he was as stupid as you are, hmm?'

Sandano looked offended.

'I suppose you threw the card out?' Bottando asked, then nodded without surprise when Sandano said he had.

'Giacomo, please. As a friend, listen to me. Take my advice.'

'What?'

'Go straight. Give it up. Get a job.'

'Everybody tells me that. Even that judge.'

'You should listen. Now, one last thing. Those statues. What happened to them? Where are they?'

Sandano looked bashful.

'Come on. You might as well get it over and done with. I won't tell.'

'Promise?'

'Promise.'

'They're under my grandmother's bed. You must know that if she . . . Oh. I've done it again.'

Bottando nodded and beamed at him. 'That's what I say, give up.'

'Lovely man,' he said under his breath as he left.

He rang Flavia as soon as he'd finished having a thoughtful drink in the nearby bar to consider matters, and told her about Fra Angelico.

She was not happy to hear his interpretation, especially as it was obviously right: as Bottando said, it's what comes of underestimating the stupidity of the criminal classes.

'Little moron,' she said when he finished. 'When I get my hands on him next time . . .'

'You can torment him at your leisure. But you see what this means, don't you?'

'If Forster stole that painting, what the hell was he playing at by going back to talk to Sandano?'

'That's the problem. It would still be possible to make out a very good case for this all being a figment of my imagination. Especially if you now tell me that his death might not have had anything to do with his business at all. Is that what you're telling me?'

'It's a theory, and not a bad one.'

'That's the trouble. Everything's circumstantial. Can you get me something? One way or the other. Preferably proving that the time and money you've spent hasn't been a gross waste of department resources such as would be approved only by a senile old lunatic?'

'Ah. Argan. I was going to ask about him.'

'Yes,' said Bottando. 'Him. He seems to have laid off for the moment. Perhaps he's decided we were right to investigate. Certainly he seems to have stopped trying to use it as evidence against me. There's not been a memo for days now. But I'm convinced there will be; I can hardly wait. I'm sure it will come to nothing. Can you really see people supporting that little twerp rather than me?'

Flavia shook her head silently as she put the phone down. Poor old Bottando, she thought. He was really beginning to clutch at straws. Besides, a nasty thought had just occurred to her.

14

It was one of the great tragedies in the life of the senior partner in the local medical practice that his parents, Mr and Mrs Robert Johnson, of Ipswich, had christened him Samuel. It was similarly a tragedy of only slightly less proportions that the lad had, from an early age, desired to become a physician. All his life, it seemed, people had smirked when introduced to him. There could be no jest on the theme of Boswell that he had not heard many times over. The great lexicographer's comments on physicians he knew as well as if he'd written them himself, so often had they returned to haunt him.

Dr Samuel Johnson, MD, was, as a result, a man of resigned temperament. And, by some strange fluke of psychology, he had found himself growing, over the years, to look more and more like the eighteenth-century know-all who was the bane of his existence. He was short, round and dishevelled, his jacket splotched with old food, and his reading glasses always perched at an unnatural angle at the end of his nose.

He also had a tendency to be snappish with new-comers, on the grounds that if he presented a suitably ferocious appearance, he might head off some of the more timorous before they could make some supposedly whimsical comment. He wasn't very good at this, being naturally a lazy, amiable man, and so the result was more bizarre than frightening.

When Flavia marched into his room, stretched out her hand and pumped his up and down, then sat uninvited on his patient's chair, such pre-emptive strikes were unnecessary, and for a simple reason: Flavia had never heard of Samuel Johnson, and was absolutely unaware that there was anything even faintly amusing in the fact that a doctor should rejoice in both or either of two fairly common English names.

Dr Johnson found this quite a refreshing change and, as the woman was both perfectly pleasant and an agreeable physical presence, he found himself out-Johnsoning Johnson, overdoing the urbane and civilized Englishman routine in a fashion his family, friends and colleagues would have found embarrassing.

Flavia loved it, though, and thought the way he chuckled as he peered at her between thick shaggy eyebrows and the top of his reading glasses was perfectly delightful. She was a bit surprised at the only partly house-trained way he spilled his tea down his shirt and dabbed at it absent-mindedly with his tie while he talked, but this she put down to eccentricity.

In other words, they got on handsomely, and Dr Johnson found himself being far more forthcoming in his desire to charm than he would otherwise have been. Flavia's visit was one of desperation, searching after any smattering of detail which might give an insight into Forster and Veronica Beaumont. Argyll's thesis was all very well as far as it went, but it didn't go that far yet. And whatever their relationship was, it had been an odd one: they'd known each other in Italy, but had not got on. Then, over twenty years later, Forster appears, gets paid a salary which Miss Beaumont could scarcely afford to do a job which doesn't need doing. Or so it seemed. All right, perhaps he was merely using the position to launder paintings. But was Miss Beaumont really so batty she didn't notice?

The trouble was that sources of information were few and far between. Mrs Verncy had been only an irregular visitor before she'd inherited and was a bit vague on the details. There were few other relations and almost no friends. Apart from the vicar – an unobservant man who had been less than illuminating when the police had talked to him, and the cook who was similarly uncertain of details due to the fact that she was only in the house a few hours a day – no one had known the woman very well.

But Veronica Beaumont had been ill, and that meant doctors, and that led her to Dr Samuel Johnson, MD. Doctors frequently knew a great deal. The trouble was, they often had this finicky conscience about retelling it.

But at least the rubicund figure with the egg stains seemed as though he wanted to be helpful. Yes, indeed, he said, Miss Beaumont had been a patient of his after his predecessor retired about five years ago, although on the whole there was little wrong with her that he could treat. Her death had been a great tragedy, although for his part he was not entirely surprised. Although no psychiatrist, you understand . . .

'I gather she died of an overdose. Is that correct?'

He nodded. 'It's all in the coroner's report, and so there's nothing secret about it. She was on sleeping tablets. One day she took far too many of them and died.'

'Deliberately?'

Dr Johnson took off his glasses and rubbed them clean on the tail of his shirt, then put them back on, leaving the shirt tail hanging out. 'Officially, I think they concluded that there was no reason to think it was anything but an accident.'

'And unofficially?'

'Pills like that have an odd effect when taken with alcohol, so it's possible. Personally, though – and you must remember I'd known her for decades – I would very much doubt that she would take her own life deliberately. She was undoubtedly unbalanced. But not in that way. So I like to think it was an accident.'

'Unbalanced? Mrs Verney said she was crazy.'

'No, no,' the doctor replied. 'Only poor people are crazy. The Beaumont family has had a fair smattering of oddness, though. It was before my time, but Mrs Verney's mother was more than a little wayward, I understand. In the next generation it was poor Veronica.'

'What sort of unbalanced?'

'Delusions, insane fears, compulsions. That sort of thing. It sounds serious, but it was only very periodic. She could go for years perfectly normally, then have what the family called a little attack. Which was always discreetly covered up.'

'But what exactly did they cover up?'

Dr Johnson waggled his finger. 'There we risk trespassing on the medical secret. If you want to know that, you'll have to ask Mrs Verney. I couldn't possibly tell you.'

'Not even a hint?'

Dr Johnson wrestled with his medical conscience awhile. 'She came from a family which was not as rich as it had been. Still more than rich enough in my opinion, but perceptions in these matters are relative. Her experience was permanently one of not being able to afford things that were taken for granted in the family's past. Most of the time she coped quite well. When she didn't . . .'

He paused and wrestled some more.

'I gather she became jealous. Powerfully so.'

'Eh?'

'Covetous.'

'What?'

'I'm sorry, miss. I shouldn't even have said that. You will have to ask a member of the family for details. That is, after all, where I got them myself. Miss Beaumont hardly confided in me.'

'No. Hold on a second. Do you mean she stole things? Is that what you're discreetly hinting at?'

But this was pushing him too far. In a very medical fashion, he wrung his hands and became all technical. 'That is a broad and not very useful description,' he said. 'Indeed, I strongly doubt whether such forms of malady exist, in any real sense. Certainly there is no single illness, with identifiable or predictable symptoms.'

'Except for stealing things.'

Dr Johnson coughed with embarrassment at her way of phrasing it.

'She did steal things, is that right?'

'So I understand,' he said reluctantly, before recovering himself. 'A pair of gloves here, a tin of salmon there. Certain department stores in London were quite used to her. So Mrs Verney told me. Apparently it fell to her, in later years, to go round and sort things out with them, if you see what I mean. No. I cannot possibly comment further. I am no psychiatrist, and in any case, she was only my patient for the last few years of her life.

Such information as I have I got from members of the family, and you will have to apply to them. Naturally, they wanted to keep it as quiet as possible.'

'I see,' said an astonished Flavia. 'Now. What I really wanted to ask you about was her and Geoffrey Forster.'

Johnson looked stormy, and Flavia thought that maybe the medical secret was about to be invoked again.

'A most malign influence,' he said instead, however. 'Miss Beaumont was a weak and impressionable woman, and he manipulated her quite shamelessly. For his own ends, I believe.'

'To sell off the contents of Weller House?'

'I never knew the details. I do know that as he wormed his way into her affections, he was asked to do more and more, and that nothing ever came of any of it. If it wasn't for Mrs Verney, trying to keep him at bay, things would have been very much worse. Of course, there was little she could do. Near the end, I understand there was a serious fight between the two about Mr Forster's influence. After her death, she tried to undo some of the damage he had done. With only limited success.'

'You mean George Barton? Things like that?'

'Yes. Forster persuaded Miss Beaumont to transfer some of her remaining cottages into a development company he owned. The idea was that he would do them up and sell them, and they would share the profits. I gather the idea was to transfer even more; Forster told her it was a way of avoiding tax or some such nonsense. Fortunately, this did not happen. Personally, I doubt she would ever have seen a penny back. Mrs Verney spent some considerable amount of time trying to undo the damage but with little success, I gather. George Barton was being thrown out and there was little she could do about it.'

'I see. Now, to return to the suicide possibility. Is there any reason why she should have killed herself then?'

'None that I can think of, although in the case of depression you don't necessarily need anything. And, I must say, she had some reason to be depressed. She had many hypochondriacal tendencies, but in her last year – more than a year, in fact – she was genuinely ill.'

'How so?'

'She had a mild stroke in the summer of 1992. Not immediately life-threatening or disabling, but it frightened her – and she was easily frightened. She was not the sort to take adversity well. She spent a great deal of time in bed and rarely moved far from the house. Personally, I think she was fitter than she seemed, and should have taken exercise. But she never listened to me.'

'Was she depressed when she died? More so than usual, I mean?'

Dr Johnson thought this over. 'Perhaps. Although the last time I saw her, I think angry would have described her mood better. Again, that was not uncommon: she frequently fulminated against things – socialists, thieves, what she was pleased to call the lower classes, taxmen. What she was specifically angry about, I don't know. Possibly something to do with Forster. But, as I say, I doubt that was the cause of her death.'

Flavia stood up, shaking his hand once more. 'Thank you, Doctor. You've been most kind.'

In contrast to Flavia's preoccupation with the present, Argyll instead took much of the afternoon off. As there was little for him to do, and in any case the Italian

189

interest in Forster seemed to be winding down, he passed the time among the pictures. Loosely connected with the case, of course, but his main interest was merely to look at them, and check that they were all there. There was always the hope that, by mere mischance, something had been overlooked.

So, forgetful of thieves and murderers and with the two inventories of paintings in his hands, he padded quietly around the house, trying to identify the pictures mentioned in all these bits of paper with the ones which still hung on the walls of Weller House.

It was surprisingly easy; both inventories were virtually the same, and judging by the ease with which he found the paintings they referred to, he strongly suspected that they had not even been taken down for a good dusting in the past fifteen years. Possibly not since they'd been bought in the eighteenth or nineteenth century. So much for Forster's care and attention.

In many ways it was not a rewarding experience: there were seventy-two paintings in the inventories and he rapidly managed to count seventy-two hanging on the walls of the house. Fifty-three were nondescript family portraits. Portraits, anyway, as some were so filthy and dark that it was difficult to tell who they were; in many cases it would cost more to clean them up than one could hope to get by selling them. The dining room in particular was rather depressing, a glorious oak-panelled room which should have resounded to the tinkling of crystal, the scrape of mahogany on floorboards and the soft pad of a butler's footsteps. Instead, the windows were covered over, it was dark, unkempt and had a distinct smell of must. The huge mirror over the fireplace was cracked across its width and so decayed it reflected nothing at all. Not that there was much to reflect: the lights no longer worked and, although he tried to open the shutters, he found they'd been wedged shut.

The paintings of illustrious ancestors, which were meant to look down on the diners and impress them with the length of the lineage, were now little more than black patches surrounded by tarnished gilt frames. By peering carefully, and cheating by checking the few inscriptions on frames, Argyll could work out that these were the set of six seventeenth-century members of the Dunstan family, the aristocratic former owners who had been saved by reluctantly marrying their daughter Margaret to the lowly, but stinking rich, London merchant called Beaumont. The smallish half length of Margaret Dunstan-Beaumont was the one allegedly by Kneller, and was probably the only one which would fetch a halfway decent price. Although it was so unutterably filthy you could only just work out that it was a portrait. That it was a portrait of a young woman was as much guesswork as anything else. Even the attribution seemed doubtful, although Argyll did concede to himself that having to study it by the light of a match was not the best way of fully appreciating its subtleties. Still, it didn't look like Kneller to him. It seemed the valuer had been right on that one.

Giving up for fear of eye strain, Argyll thought that it was about time another rich merchant came along to refill the family coffers. Pity Mabel didn't do her duty. Otherwise, he concluded as he ticked the portraits off the list, her daughter is going to have to sell up pretty soon.

That completed, he returned to the attic to check out two old pictures which were said to be up there. They were. They were also said to be in bad condition and of no value and Argyll, again, could scarcely fault the acumen of the people who had drawn up the valuation. Once he'd done that, he settled down again with the pile of boxes he'd discovered, just on the off-chance that an old account book might contain some small details of when and where the pictures were bought. Even a date can do wonders for a painting's value.

But he drew a blank. He opened one box, discovered it contained pictures of Veronica's wedding and put it back with a shudder as he glimpsed the hairstyles. Then he tried another. Then another, and another, slowly, it seemed, reaching back into the past and the era when the family had enough money to buy paintings. The fifth box contained an old ledger, inscribed on the inside as concerning the marriage of Godfrey Beaumont to Margaret Dunstan. You never know, he thought, as he skimmed his eye down the accounts of the costs, and listings of presents and favours received; a social historian's dream as a way of picking out the networks of relations which bound English society together. The Dunstans were at least well-connected: earls and knights and baronets all clubbed in to wish the poor girl well. Even some courtiers of high rank and in favour with the King. Even the Earl of Arundel, who, with typical stinginess had skimped on the wedding present. While the others had presented furs and tapestries and even manor farms, he had sent along, so the ledger drily noted, 'an anatomy of Sgr Leoni'. Whoopee! Bet the bridegroom celebrated all night when he opened that.

Probably not. But then, Argyll thought with a sudden feeling of breathlessness in his lower abdomen, maybe he should have done.

He sat back in his chair, took a deep breath, and then

had a realization which was about as painful as being hit by a bolt of lightning. Two realizations, in fact, and, as it turned out, he had them in the wrong order. By the time it occurred to him that Arundel had died in 1646, and that Margaret Dunstan must have married before that, the significance of the fact was lost to him.

The thoughts that swamped this information derived from distant memories about the history of collecting. The Earl of Arundel was the biggest collector in England; he had bought the best paintings on offer with an unerring eye. Most importantly he had dealings with a man called Pompeo Leoni.

And Pompeo Leoni had sold him what is now almost every known drawing by Leonardo da Vinci. Seven hundred of them.

Argyll strained to remember. They vanished in the Civil War but six hundred were found, quite by accident, at the bottom of an old chest in Windsor Castle nearly a hundred and fifty years later. They are still there; but the other hundred vanished without trace.

He thought some more, mixing the written evidence with his knowledge and the evidence of his own eyes. And he became more and more convinced. He was as sure as he had ever been of anything that there were now only ninety-nine missing. The other one was in the bedroom with the damp patch. Anatomical indeed. And quite a wedding present. God only knew how much it would be worth. Perhaps not even him: it was decades since anything like that had been on the market. Time for a walk, he thought. This would take some digesting.

15

Bottando's return to his little office was not a pleasant one. Like most people, he had the tendency to assume that reality only existed within his eyesight and earshot; everybody else, he liked to think, froze into immobility whenever he was not around. If he left the office for the better part of the day, he fondly expected to find things pretty much the same when he got back again in the evening.

Such theories were severely undermined when he returned that particular evening to discover that, in fact, almost everybody had been in a frenzy of activity more or less since the moment that he'd left Rome that morning. Even worse, it appeared that Argan had used his absence to practise running the department.

'A nasty robbery in Naples,' the loathsome man said when Bottando came in and found him squatting at Bottando's own desk. 'While you were away.'

'Really?' Bottando said drily, unceremoniously easing him out of his chair and recapturing it for his own use.

'Yes. In your absence, I took control. I hope you don't mind.'

Bottando waved his hand in a be-my-guestish fashion.

'And a church ransacked outside Cremona.'

'Took control again, did you?'

Argan nodded. 'I thought it best. What with you being so preoccupied.'

'Ah-ha.'

'How are the researches?' Argan went on with the faint purr of a cat toying with an injured bird.

'What researches are those?'

'Into Giotto.'

'Good God! Has someone stolen Assisi in my absence as well? I hope you took control there too.'

Argan smirked. 'In a fashion. I talked this afternoon to one of the controllers of the budget.'

'Did you? I hope you found it passed the time.'

'A bit of a distressing conversation, in fact. He's very concerned – as are a lot of people in the Budget office, you know – about the cost/effectiveness ratio of this department.'

'You mean they think we should catch more people. Couldn't agree more.'

'Good. But I noticed a tone of hostility in his voice, you know.'

I wonder who put it there, Bottando thought.

'Anyway, you know me. Loyalty. So I came up with this brilliant idea for getting them off our backs.'

Our backs? Bottando thought. Here it comes.

'Of course, I should have consulted you. But as you weren't there . . .'

'You took control.'

'Exactly. Hope you don't mind.'

Bottando sighed.

'So I said that the perceptions of the department's ineffectiveness were quite misplaced. And I told them that the General was at this very moment working on a most important case that would produce an extraordinary result. I told them a bit about Forster, just how much time and effort you'd put into pursuing this man.'

'Did you?'

'And they asked for a full-scale meeting to discuss it with you. Tomorrow? At four o'clock?'

'Oh yes?'

'Yes. They're so keen to hear of how you tracked down this man, that the minister himself will be coming to hear about the triumph of your skill.'

'I shall look forward to it.'

'So will I,' said Argan. 'There are few things more rewarding than listening to an expert account of the virtues of experience. It will be very interesting.'

While Flavia was finishing with Dr Johnson and moving on to talk to the police once again, checking and cross-checking facts without, she hoped, giving much in return, Argyll went for a walk to take advantage of the brief spell of sun. He had a lot to think over and, as is usual in such circumstances, wandered about aimlessly, inspecting nothing in particular with great care before moving on again in a dream.

It was the Leonardo that occupied his mind. How to approach Mary Verney? He briefly toyed with not telling her, and concocting some story about wanting it because he liked it so much, giving her fifty pounds for it. Not worth it, of course, but . . .

Then he dismissed the idea. Not his sort of thing. He couldn't do it, and would only hate himself for all eternity if he even tried. So he'd tell her what it was, and hope she'd give him the commission to sell it. It would pay her debts and have more than enough left over to rebuild the house. He could tell Flavia at the same time. It would be something for them all to celebrate before they went back home, case resolutely unsolved.

He wandered in the direction of the church in the hope that a bit more exercise might clear his mind of the lingering regrets that he wasn't nastier and more unscrupulous. Nothing like a good church for cheering you up in such circumstances, he always considered, so he went through the churchyard gate and paused awhile to examine the noticeboard which had rotas for church wardens (George Barton the first Sunday, Henry Jones the second, Young Witherspoon the third and Old Witherspoon the fourth), a note, dated five months ago, of a parish council meeting, an announcement about the village fête on the second Saturday in July, as usual (with the proclamation that Mrs Mary Verney would graciously open it crossed out and the name of the vicar substituted instead) and a warning about not using hosepipes because of the drought.

He looked at it all, read it carefully, and forgot it just as quickly. That source of information exhausted, he went in and spent some time staring at the gravestones. One had fresh wild flowers; Joan Barton, beloved wife of George, and mother of Louise and Alice. Next to it was Harry Barton, beloved brother of George, and husband of Anne. Born 1935, died 1967. A bit young, poor soul. Didn't last long, these Bartons.

Thus rendered appropriately melancholic, he wandered around, past the black marble stones of the twentieth century, through the local stone slabs of the nineteenth and on to the more elaborately carved efforts of the sixteenth and seventeenth centuries. Some were as carefully tended as a suburban garden, others preferred the wild look. The same names cropped up again and again: dozens of Bartons, generations of Browns. He even found Veronica's husband: Henry Finsey-Groat, tragically drowned, beloved husband, fondly remembered, died 1966. Only the last seemed reliable: farcically drowned seemed more appropriate and, if the overgrown and entirely neglected grave was anything to go by, beloved husband, fondly remembered, seemed less than accurate.

Then he went into the church and examined its run of brasses and eighteenth-century monuments in memory of the various members of the Beaumont family. There had been rather a lot of them. He studied the simple plaque for Margaret Dunstan-Beaumont, she of the wedding present and Kneller portrait, and read how she'd died in 1680 at the age of sixty, greatly missed by her family and all who knew her as a pious wife, devoted mother of fifteen children, and generous giver of eight shillings a year to the poor of the parish. He wondered what Geoffrey Forster's memorial would say; even given the willingness of memorialists to stretch the truth, greatly missed might seem a little inappropriate. Nobody, so far, seemed to be greatly missing him. Except his wife, who was the only person who had a good word for him. Although how genuine that was seemed unsure.

Margaret Dunstan-Beaumont's tombstone was on the west wall of the north transept, spoiled only by having a huge pile of old parish magazines stacked beneath and around it. He looked through them at random standard contents: raffles and recipes, fêtes and fundraising and harvest festivals. Every year the same: the first cuckoo, the weather, and Miss Beaumont's gracious speech opening the fête. The very stuff of the rustic myth. Wonderful as long as you don't live near it.

Then back to the tombstones, especially the flashier eighteenth-century efforts, all Latin poetry and swooning maidens which got the prime space in the crossing and the choir. Much more ostentatious than the more modest tombstones in the graveyard outside. Joan Barton got a simple stone slab with carving, these people were inside in the dry church, with swags and ornaments and cherubs and paeans of praise for their goodness. Joan Barton, however, got fresh wild flowers; these were just objects of mild interest for the occasional passing tourist. Take your pick.

Jonathan Argyll, tourist, was tucked into the transept thinking about death and pictures, when he had a prickling feeling under his skin. Into his mind popped, quite unbidden and quite unconnected to anything else, the memory that Godfrey Kneller had come to England in the 1670s. And Margaret Dunstan-Beaumont had been married before 1646, must have been, so she could be given a natty little Leonardo sketch by Arundel. He was just about to pin down why this was important when his attention was distracted again. From the small door on the other side, the room where the vicar kept his vestments, and stacked spare prayer books and empty vases, came a murmur of voices. One he thought he recognized.

Argyll was not a nosy person, so he thought, although he would frequently admit to being inquisitive. And it was in the spirit of enquiry, rather than one of nosiness, that he found himself approaching the door softly, just to confirm who it was. He honestly believed that he had not the slightest intention of listening in, an activity he firmly thought was most impolite.

However, it is inevitable that, in order to ascertain the ownership of voices, you have to hear at least a little of what they are saying. Only a pedant would try to make a distinction between listening to the sound of voices, and listening to the words those sounds embody. Whether motivated by nosiness or curious enquiry, therefore, Argyll ended up listening to a conversation between Mary Verney and George Barton.

Overcoming his instincts for discretion, Argyll concentrated on the words they were saying.

'So what do you think you should do?' came the clear, melodious and kindly voice of Mary Verney.

'I dunno. Nothing, I guess.'

'It's very serious, as you know. If the police find out you'll go to jail. For a long time. Is there anything you want from me?'

'Oh, no. I don't know what you mean, Mrs Verney. As long as you say nothing, then everything will be fine, I reckon. So stupid, the whole thing. If I hadn't had the fight with him, I wouldn't have drunk too much, and if I hadn't drunk too much, I wouldn't have gone back there and . . .'

'Yes, I understand. But you did, and here you are, talking to me about it. But let me get this clear. You can live with it? You don't want just to go to the police and get it over with?'

'Nah. If that idiot Gordon were going to take the blame, then yes, I'd have to. Of course I would. I wouldn't let him go to jail, no matter what the cost. You know that. But Gordon's been let out.'

'Well. I don't know what to say.'

'He had it coming,' George said with a sudden intensity. 'He deserved it. You know something, Mrs Verney? The world's a better place without him. Do as you're done by, that's what I say. So he's no reason to complain. He was a nasty man and justice has been done, as far as I'm concerned. That's all there is to be said about it. I'm not going to lose one jot of sleep over him.'

Fascinating though it was, Argyll did not stay to hear any more. He felt a sneeze coming on and, rather than being caught red-handed, or rather red-eared, by the vestry door, he scuttled off behind a tomb and let rip there. It was the flower arrangements that did it, he decided later. Very pretty and showing proper community spirit, but the pollen really went up his nose. Any further conversation was, anyway, cut short fairly abruptly when his monumental sneeze erupted and echoed around the church. By the time Mary Verney emerged, he was to be found standing far away, oblivious to the world and staring enraptured at a mid-eighteenth-century tablet extolling the virtues of Sir Henry Beaumont, man of commerce and of charity, greatly missed by all who knew him.

'Oh, hello,' he said lightly and, to his mind with an utterly false tone of surprise in his voice. 'I thought I was alone in here. Where did you spring from?'

Mary Verney, for the first time since he had met her, seemed ill at ease. 'I was doing some tidying,' she said. 'In the vestry.'

As she talked, Argyll thought he heard a faint click of the door from the vestry into the churchyard closing. George Barton making his getaway.

'I didn't know you were a God-fearing member of the parish,' he rabbited on.

'I'm not. But one has to do one's bit. It's expected.'

'Oh, indeed. Although I must say I think that not having to do one's bit is one of the advantages of the big city. It is a lovely church, isn't it?'

'Beautiful. Wool money, you know. Did you see our misericords?'

Argyll confessed he hadn't. He'd only been in the church for a few seconds, he said, slipping the information in. It seemed to make her much more relaxed. Then he followed patiently while she gave him a guided tour of the misericords (one of the finest sets in the county, fourteenth-century, elbow rests with leaf work, underseats with monsters, birds and scenes of country life). Very pretty, but even Argyll, who normally liked nothing better than a nice misericord, found it hard to concentrate.

16

Flavia got back from talking to Manstead and the locals in a sombre and discontented mood. The essence of the discussion was that the Norfolk police were putting Forster on the backburner until such time as any actual evidence turned up. They had, so they said, quite enough thieves and murders on their hands already: there simply wasn't time to deal with something like this.

'You see,' Manstead said with a slight tone of apology in his voice, 'we can't even prove Forster was murdered. Not convincingly, anyway. And as for his being a thief . . .'

'No evidence, either? The Dunkeld wedding?'

'That was our one real chance, I think. And nothing. We even got them to look at his photograph to see if that rang any bells, but nothing. I mean, I hardly expected it to after all these years, but you can't say we haven't tried.'

'I know,' Flavia said. 'And I think I'd do the same, if I were you. I'm grateful for the effort.'

'As I say, if we had anything to go on at all . . .'

'Yes. Thank you. By the way, Veronica Beaumont *was* on the guest list, wasn't she?'

Manstead referred the question to Inspector Wilson, who nodded. 'That's right. As was most of *Burke's Peerage*, as far as I can see.'

'Ah. Did you, by any chance, reinterview George Barton?'

'Yes, we did, and thank you for that. But I'm afraid that his son-in-law was defending him quite unnecessarily. He did see Forster that evening, but it was long before Forster died. And then he went to see his daughter. Which, of course, Gordon would have known had he not been fooling around with Sally. Or if George had actually been on talking terms with him.'

'So that was a waste of time as well.'

'Yes. And Mrs Forster has been scratched too.'

'Why?'

'We demonstrated that she wasn't at the cinema that night.'

'Ah.'

'No. But her husband was having an affair, so she thought she'd do the same . . .'

'Jesus, not another one.'

'I know. Scratch the surface. But anyway, she's off the list.'

'I see. Tell me, when she was interviewed first time round, did she know that her husband was being investigated for theft?'

Manstead handed over a few sheets of paper. 'Look for yourself. It was a preliminary chat. Where were you, what were you doing? Nothing fancy like thefts at all. That came later. This morning, in fact. And she said the first she'd heard of it was from you. It may not be true, but can we prove differently? We cannot. And until we can . . .'

Then she came back and sat on a chair in the entrance hall to ring Bottando to report, which was where Argyll found her, listening with a pained expression on her face.

'The whole lot of them will be there,' Bottando told her after he'd monopolized the conversation by fulminating about Argan's plan for a final showdown. 'To listen to the fruits of my experience. Argan could hardly contain himself. I thought the little bastard was being unnaturally quiet. Now I know why. I've been going through his disks again. He's already written another detailed memorandum on the whole thing. You can guess what's in it.'

'Old fool, put him out to pasture?' Flavia said, a little tactlessly. There was a long silence from the Italian end.

'That's about it.'

'You seem very calm about it.'

'No point in being anything else. I'm sure everything will be fine once I give my explanation. I'm sure I can drag a rabbit or two out of a hat for the occasion. How are *you* doing?'

Flavia paused to consider. 'I hate to say this . . .'

'What?'

'Forster was a nasty bit of work. But I don't think I'll be able to prove he was Giotto. Certainly not by tomorrow afternoon. I'm doing my best, but the police here are shutting up shop.'

'Why's that?'

'Because basically there's nothing whatsoever to go on which is any more substantial than early morning mist.'

A long digestive pause from central Rome. 'Ah, well. No matter. It's not your fault. You can't create criminals

– or evidence – where none exist. If you can come back by tomorrow that would be helpful.'

She put the phone down, and sat quietly, lost in thought about the various options, all of them unsavoury, which presented themselves.

'Poor old Bottando,' Argyll commented.

'Hmm. I think he's deluding himself about the support he's going to get. Personally, I don't think anyone will help him. I think he's losing his grip on political realities, you know.'

'What are you going to do about it?'

She pursed her lips and thought. 'My best, I suppose,' she said without much conviction that this was going to be good enough. 'I'll have to go back. I can't say I relish watching the old fellow being gored to death, but at least I'll be able to give what support I can. Come on. I think I need a chat with Mrs Verney. And a stiff drink.'

It's awkward to go asking pointed questions of your hostess, not least because she might take offence and render you suddenly homeless. On top of that, Flavia rather liked the woman. She was generous, lively, and very good company.

But the fact remained that the clock was ticking. Flavia still had no proof of anything, but she was fairly certain, on such knowledge as she possessed, that she knew what had been going on. The only problem was that being right was as bad as not knowing anything at all.

'Ah, you're back,' Mary said cheerfully as they trooped into the kitchen. She gave the mixture in her pot a quick stir then replaced the lid. 'I hope you've had a profitable day.'

She looked up at them, and scrutinized their faces

carefully. 'Oh, dear,' she said. 'Graveyard looks. It's serious talk time, is it?'

'If you don't mind.'

She took off her apron, tossed it over the back of the chair, and got out a tray, some glasses and a bottle.

'These may be needed,' she observed. 'Come on, then. Back to the sitting room. Let's see what you want.'

Very much in control, she swept out of the kitchen, and up the stairs to the sitting room, with Flavia close behind and Argyll bringing up the rear with the tray. He was in full agreement that it was of central importance, and busied himself pouring and distributing while the other two settled themselves into position in the over-stuffed armchairs and prepared for combat.

'All right then,' Flavia began. 'I'll give you an account of the day Forster died. Round about lunch-time, Jonathan and Edward Byrnes are eating together. At two-thirty, or thereabouts, he rings Forster and says he wants to talk to him about a picture. A stolen one. Immediately afterwards, it seems, Forster leaves the house and heads for Norwich, where he visits and empties his safe deposit box. Later that evening, he is visited by George Barton, and has an acrimonious fight about George's forthcoming eviction. George leaves, and is seen by his son-in-law, Gordon. Around nine o'clock, Forster falls down the stairs, breaks his neck and dies.

'His body is discovered the next morning by Jonathan. Gordon, at the time of the death, is in bed with Sally, the barmaid; George was visiting his daughter and Mrs Forster was with her lover.'

'With her what?' Mary said with astonishment.

'True, apparently.'

'Good God! My opinion of her rises all the time.'

'Yes. Anyway, the point is that nobody saw, heard,

smelt, suspected, divined or guessed that anything was wrong. So much so that the police here, I gather, now agree. As far as they are concerned, the case of Forster's death is closed until such time as there is some evidence to justify reopening it.'

'That's a relief,' Mary said. 'Everybody will be very pleased.'

'So what do we conclude? That Forster's trip into Norwich had nothing to do with Jonathan. That his death was an accident. That his willingness to talk to him about a stolen Uccello was also unconnected to his death.'

Mary Verney looked placidly interested, but said nothing.

'Even so, there is evidence that Forster was connected in some way with the theft of pictures. Three statements from three people, none of whom know each other, all point to that. And, of course, there was the burning of Forster's papers, for which deed we must pencil in Mrs Forster. She returns to find her husband dead and also under investigation as a thief on a grand scale. Perhaps she knows it's true. So to protect what little money she has, she decides to bring the police investigation into this angle of her husband's life to an abrupt halt. End of story.'

Mary Verney continued to look calm, but companionably distressed at such an unsatisfactory conclusion.

'The trouble is, of course,' Flavia went on, 'that however agreeable this is as an explanation, it is not true.'

'Oh. Are you sure?'

'Fairly certain, yes.'

'Why?'

'Firstly, because the police say they went out of their way to make sure that Jessica Forster did not learn from them that her husband was suspected of any thefts. They say they asked her about matters surrounding his death. Nothing about anything else. She may have known he was a thief, but there was nothing to let her know that anyone else suspected and that she had to act. So, how did she know?'

There was a long silence as Mrs Verney drained her glass, then spoke: 'Simple. I told her.'

'Why?'

'Why do you think? I don't like her much, but living with Geoffrey was punishment enough for one lifetime. There was no need for her to suffer from him beyond the grave. I wanted to spare the poor thing the turmoil of having everything she owned – or he owned – taken away from her by vengeful victims. So when she came to visit that afternoon I told her that if she was going to do anything to defend herself, she'd have to move fast. Personally, I think it was good advice.'

'And she rushed out with the matches?'

'No. I rushed out with the matches. She was dithering too much to do anything herself. She asked my advice, and I gave it. She asked my help, and I gave that too.'

'That is a serious offence.'

Mrs Verney seemed blithely unconcerned. 'I can't see how it changes anything, myself.'

Flavia gave her a look of profound disapproval. 'Very humanitarian of you. It's a pity it's not true either.'

'I'm afraid it is. I nearly put my back out lifting all that paper.'

'I don't mean that. I mean your motives. You did not put the idea into her head to get rid of evidence indicating Forster was a thief. Nor did you do it when she came to visit.'

'No?'

211

'No. You did it to disguise the fact that there wasn't the slightest bit of evidence that he was a crook. And you went round to see to it after we got back from London and Jonathan said he'd be looking into his papers to see what he sold from here.'

'But it was raining.'

'It was stopping when we arrived.'

'And why would I do that? What was it to me?'

'Because the papers would have probably revealed that he was bleeding you and your family dry by threatening to reveal that for years your kleptomaniacal cousin had been touring the country houses of Europe lifting masterpieces.'

'Goodness! What a lovely idea. What leads you to that?'

'Enough, I think.'

'For example?'

'Forster, to start off with. What evidence is there that he stole paintings? Suggestions by three people, his comments to Jonathan, and his death. But he hardly lived like a vastly successful criminal; there were obvious signs of a shortage of money, and no indications at all that any is hidden away.

'He is meant to have spent ages touring round Europe stealing things, but his wife said he hated travelling and had hardly left Norfolk except for day trips to London since he moved here. He was, admittedly, in Florence when the Uccello disappeared. But so was your cousin Veronica, at della Quercia's. Virtually next door and with access to the Palazzo Straga. And your cousin was on the guest list for the Dunkeld wedding in 1976 and he was not. Your cousin had a reputation for taking things; whereas until last week, Forster did not.

'None of that is enough to acquit Forster or condemn

your cousin. But think of his relations with her. She didn't like him in Florence, it seems, but brings him in to help look after the collection. Why? It hardly needed looking after. She pays him a salary, virtually gives him a house, and begins to transfer other property in a way which made it entirely his when she died. A lot of money for not very much. If *he* was a thief it doesn't make sense. If he was blackmailing a thief, then it does.'

Mary Verney took a sip of her glass, and regarded Flavia with some affection. Flavia noted that she seemed neither indignant at listening to such a travesty, nor nervous about it either.

'I see. Interesting. But I wouldn't try going to court on it. Even Dr Johnson – indiscreet old buffer though he is – would have a hard time persuading a jury that someone as obviously scatty as my poor old cousin could manage the sort of planning your Giotto would have required for success. I mean, stealing things is only part of it, isn't it?'

'Oh, yes. And I'm sure that her success was largely because she stole things at random, knew only faded and impecunious aristocrats like herself whose collections are precisely the sort which aren't catalogued or insured too well. It took Bottando to turn lunacy into method, and see craziness as breathtaking skill. As for getting rid of them, she wouldn't have to. Winterton would do that.'

Mary looked surprised at the name. 'Winterton? Why him?'

'Come now,' Flavia said severely. 'You can do better than that. You know perfectly well why him. He's the man who went and talked to Sandano three months ago to find out what he knew about the Fra Angelico theft. Fifties or older with thick dark hair, so Sandano says.

That matches Winterton, but Forster was grey and a bit thin on top. Nice touch to give Sandano one of Forster's cards, though.'

'Old family friend helping out?'

Flavia frowned with disapproval at her lack of invention. 'Who gives a second-rater like Forster a place in his very exclusive gallery? And who risks his career by going to Italy to pay money to thieves and implicates Forster in the theft of the Pollaiuolo? He wouldn't touch something like that unless he had to. He's not the sort to do people favours like that. Not good enough. Perhaps you should tell me why? Save time and effort on the guessing games.'

'Maybe that's a good idea,' Mary replied, sipping the drink, then putting it down again and composing herself for the trial of being perfectly frank. At least, Flavia thought, they weren't going to have to batter their way through any more lies and evasions. One thing about Mary Verney, she was eminently sensible. She knew when she was beaten.

'He based his entire career on poor Veronica's little weaknesses,' she said with a sigh. 'He took a vast percentage, I gather. So much that the silly woman never really benefited much from her habit. Enough to keep things ticking over, not much more. Which was typical of her, really. I mean, if you're going to be a crook, you might as well make money out of it, don't you think?'

'Was it always part of the plan to kill Forster?'

'Certainly not,' she said robustly. 'If I'd wanted that, then I could have killed him and had done with it. No. I simply wanted him off my back. His dying made life appallingly complicated.'

'How did he get on your back in the first place?'

'Forster knew Veronica in Italy, and when she lifted

that Uccello, he offered to help her out by getting rid of it. It was just a way of worming himself into her affections, although I suspect he also made quite a lot of money out of it. Then communications ceased for years, until he was called in to organize the collection of someone in Belgium. He did it quite well, and noticed that a picture by Pollaiuolo wasn't all that it seemed. He worked quite hard, and found out what it really was, and absconded with all the sale documents concerning it.'

'Which were?'

'Which were, firstly a deed of sale countersigned by Veronica and by Winterton as the dealer who organized the deal, and secondly an export permission saying it came from the collection at Weller House.'

'Isn't that a risky way of selling hot pictures?'

'Evidently, as we are sitting here talking about it,' she said drily. 'But who am I to judge? If you think about it, I suppose you could say that the painting's original ownership was undocumented; it had been hidden away for some time, there was nothing to prove that it hadn't come from Weller House and the inventories here were vague. Forster got suspicious only because he knew Veronica and at some stage after Uncle Godfrey's death had gone through the Weller collection inventory so knew what was in it – and what certainly wasn't. Very bad luck on their part.

'Anyway, Forster figured out what might have happened, and decided to follow up. He wrote Veronica a letter, came to see her and put his cards on the table: "Hi. Remember me? I knew you in Florence. When you were stealing a Uccello. Nice to see you're still at it. Pollaiuolo now, eh? And I have documents to prove it. What's it worth?"

'At this stage, you see, he didn't even know the start of it, but once he was in the house, it didn't take him long to figure it out. He began dropping little hints; asking for favours, then money, then a house.'

'So what was the problem with your cousin? Couldn't she be stopped?'

'Again, you're asking the wrong person. *I* would have stopped her, but no one asked me. When she came back from Italy, she told my uncle everything and he panicked. He asked Winterton's advice. Personally, I think the obvious thing would have been to go to the police and help them recover the picture. "Sorry, Veronica had one of her little turns; you know how it is." Then followed it by locking her up or getting her good psychiatric treatment.

'But, of course, my family didn't think like that. The first thing that worried them was the shame of it all. All their instincts were to cover it up, and Winterton encouraged them to think that it would be easy to do this. I honestly don't think that it ever occurred to them that a *real* crime had been committed. That's what oiks like Gordon Brown do; Beaumonts are merely indiscreet. And, of course, they kept Veronica's cut from the sale.

'Besides, initially no one thought it would become a habit. And then it was too late: by the time Veronica had hung half a dozen little acquisitions on the wall and Winterton had got rid of them, they'd compromised themselves rather badly. Manufacturing fake provenances? Handling stolen goods? Benefiting from the sales? How could they explain that away? The only problem was Forster, but Winterton did a fine job of persuading him that he was just as guilty and more likely to go to jail if anyone said anything.

Fine for as long as Forster thought it was an isolated incident.

'As I say, Winterton built a lucrative clandestine career on it, and recycled the money into legitimate picture dealing. Did very nicely too, once he'd worked out who were the richest clients with the smallest scruples. He's a prig and a snob, but he's no fool either.

'Unlike Forster who, once he'd started, didn't know when to stop. He pushed too far, asking for this house and everything. He knew she was ill, and he had a vision of himself as Lord of Weller or something. Always a climber. Now, Veronica was crazy, but not that mad: and he attacked her in the one area where she would fight back – her family pride. She was determined to preserve Weller in the Beaumont family, even if that was me.

'So she dug in her heels, and told him to do his worst. Forster says he will do just that. Veronica realizes he means it and she reaches for the pills as the only way of stopping him. That's one interpretation.'

'What's another?'

'That Veronica decides to give herself up, confess all and denounce Forster as a blackmailer. And that Forster murders her.'

'Is that likely?'

She shrugged. 'I don't know. It's all a bit too much like a Victorian melodrama, really.'

'Why, then, did you revive it all? I assume it was you who prompted Fancelli to call in the Italian police?'

'Absolutely not. That wasn't the idea at all.'

'So what did happen?'

She sighed wearily, then nodded sadly. 'I was always on the outside of the family; I knew Veronica was a bit loopy, but never exactly how much. She died, I inherited this place, and realized the finances were catastrophic. So I decided to cut back, and the biggest – and pleasantest – saving was to get rid of Geoffrey Forster. And I got a little visit. It was the first I'd heard of any of it. At first I just laughed and said I didn't believe him. He suggested I go and ask Winterton. I did, and Winterton told me the whole story.

'It was a bit of a shock, as you can imagine. I inherit a stately home, and find that what I've really inherited is a rundown money sink kept afloat by thieving lunatics, up to its eyes in debt, pursued by the taxman and being blackmailed into the ground as well. I mean, Jesus. What a bloody mess.

'The trouble was knowing whether Forster really had enough proof. Winterton figured out who might have known something which would back him up, and the riskiest two characters – apart from himself – were Fancelli and Sandano. It wasn't certain if they knew anything, but it was important to find out. So, he visited them and made sure that, if asked, they would deny anything about Veronica and say that they thought Forster was the thief; and I went through all the papers here and destroyed any embarrassing ones. And there were quite a lot, believe me.'

'But Forster still had the vital evidence in the safe deposit box,' Flavia said, fascinated by the story now.

'Yes. And we still didn't know what it was. Which was why Winterton also got statements signed by Fancelli and Sandano saying more or less what they told you – that they knew Forster was a thief and had stolen these two pictures.

'He had statements *indicating* Veronica was a thief; we had statements *saying* he was. So I offered Forster

218

a draw: his documents for my documents and a lump sum to show there were no hard feelings.'

'This was the deal he told his wife about?'

'I assume so. I'd scraped away and raised the money, and got the documents ready and was just waiting for a final few thousand to be credited to my account. All we were waiting for was Forster's agreement.'

'So what happened?'

'Then all hell broke loose, because of that stupid woman Fancelli. She was rather taken with the idea of saying Forster had stolen the Uccello, you see, once the subject was raised. And after thirty years, she saw a means of getting her revenge.'

'Hold it. Forster was the father of her child?'

'Hmm? Oh, yes. That was all true. And behaved abominably, I gather. His child takes after him, as well.'

'He wasn't paying for the nursing home?'

She shook her head. 'I am. Or rather Winterton is. A fair exchange for her statement. Where was I?'

'Fancelli's revenge.'

'Oh, yes. Anyway, the trouble was that she wanted to do it before she died – Winterton said she was in a bad way, and I imagine that is what triggered it. So she gave the police a prod to start things off, and in due course Jonathan telephones Forster.

'Difficult. Especially as Forster thought that we were double-crossing him. I managed to persuade him that the best thing was to do the deal and destroy everything as fast as possible. Make sure there was nothing to investigate. So that wild allegations from a daft old woman and a confessed thief remained just that.

'And, as the situation had arisen, I confess I used it. He didn't have much time. He had to make up his mind. Did he accept or not? I put as much pressure on him as possible. I don't mind saying, I was getting a little panicky myself by then. I like a quiet, tranquil life, and this isn't.

'Anyway, eventually Forster saw my reasoning. I was due to go round to his house at ten with my evidence and a cheque. We'd do a swap.'

'And things went badly wrong?'

'Disastrously. I found Geoffrey on the foot of the stairs, stone dead. I was absolutely petrified. God only knows how long I stood there. But eventually I decided I might as well be hanged for a sheep as a lamb, and stepped over him. I went up the stairs, took the packet of papers, and left the way I'd come.'

'And destroyed them?'

'Of course, yes. Immediately.'

'And that's it?'

'Until Jonathan started going through his papers and found the inventory and started fussing through the pictures. There was always a chance something else might be in there as well. So I persuaded Jessica that it was in her interest to incinerate the rest of his papers, just to be on the safe side.'

'So who did kill Forster after all that?'

She shrugged. 'Did anybody?'

'Yes,' said a disappointed Argyll. 'You know that.'

There was a long silence here, as Argyll gave her the opportunity to speak. He wasn't entirely certain whether he should intervene or not, but knew that sooner or later it would come out. So he might as well get it over as fast as possible. As Mary still wasn't saying anything, he did.

'And so do I,' he went on. 'I heard you. In the church.'

'What do you mean, Jonathan?'

'George Barton killed him. I heard him say so. In the vestry. He said he was pleased about it, didn't feel bad about it at all and that Forster deserved it for the way he'd treated everybody.'

Mary Verney was giving him the sort of look you reserve for house guests who have been caught out slipping spoons into their pockets, feeding the dog too many chocolates and making it throw up on the Persian rug. Argyll gave her an apologetic smile.

'What could I say?' he asked plaintively.

She softened her gaze a little, then relaxed. 'I know. Duty, right?'

'Before we get into the finer nuances of etiquette here, can I ask whether it is true or not?'

She reluctantly nodded. 'I decided I'd have a little chat with him after what Sally told me. I thought it fitted, and feared the worst. Alas, I was right. He has a violent temper when he's got a drink in him. It was all a complete accident. Sweet as pie when sober. You heard about Forster wanting him out of his cottage?'

'Yes. So?'

She sighed a little, then explained. Simple enough. George had gone to Forster's asking him to be reasonable. Forster had virtually thrown him out. George went off and drank too much, worked himself into a fury and came back for a second go.

'I'm sure he didn't mean any harm, but apparently he just followed Forster up the stairs, pulled him by the arm, overdid it, and Forster went tumbling down and fell awkwardly.

'Of course, this is all speculation on my part. George has never actually said to me that he did it. His daughter will swear blind he was there all evening – as I gather she already has. And if asked, I would say

I would find it quite a ridiculous idea. Not a word from me.'

'What about justice? Law and order?'

She shrugged. 'Who am I to talk about that in current circumstances? To hell with all of it. I like George. What good would sticking him in prison do?'

'Isn't that for a court to decide?'

'I think that I will very arrogantly take the decision myself, and save everybody a lot of time and trouble.'

'But . . .'

'No,' she said firmly. 'No buts. My mind is made up. Do as you wish about me. But I will not give evidence against poor George. And I have a feeling that, without my help, there won't be nearly enough evidence to do anything.'

'Poor George snapped someone's neck. Then went off and left him,' Flavia said a little angrily. 'And you're not really concerned?'

'Not hugely.'

The room lapsed into silence after this pronouncement.

'So what happens to me now?'

'Obstruction of justice on innumerable occasions, at the very least, I imagine. Conspiracy as well.'

'Told you inheriting this place was a mistake,' Mary said sadly. 'Life was so easy and simple before. Bloody family. I am sorry for having caused you so much trouble. All I was trying to do was get out of a hole dug by other people.' Both her visitors looked at her sympathetically.

'I imagine Winterton will no more admit having had anything to do with selling the pictures than George will admit to having been in Forster's house,' Argyll said gloomily. 'You only know the whereabouts of one picture taken by Giotto, and Forster stole all the evidence of where it came from. And Mary here has just destroyed it. You might find something eventually, but it would be looking for a needle in a haystack. You certainly won't get anything useful in time for Bottando's meeting tomorrow.'

Another silence as Flavia contemplated how very correct he was.

'Doesn't look good, does it?' he went on remorselessly, vocalizing her own thoughts.

'What do you mean?'

'No pictures back out of thirty or more on the list. Nothing solid about Winterton except for the possibility that Sandano might agree to identify him, and who would believe Sandano, anyway? No murderer of Forster.

'And, worst of all, you have to announce that the sublime master thief Giotto was in reality nothing but a loony old lady. Once Argan puts it around that Bottando's been chasing a total nutter down every false trail set for him he'll be the laughing stock of policedom. He won't stand a chance, poor old soul.'

'I know. But what do you expect me to do about it?'

'Does Winterton know where all these pictures went?'

'Must do,' Mary said. 'That doesn't mean he'll tell you.'

'He must know that something will turn up sooner or later, if people keep looking hard enough. Whereas, if he was offered a cast-iron guarantee that the case would be closed forever . . . ?'

'Jonathan,' Flavia said impatiently, 'what is your point?'

'You're the one who keeps on telling me that it's often perfectly justifiable to cut corners a little bit.

And Bottando always goes on about how you're in business to recover pictures, first and foremost,' he said diffidently.

'He does say that, yes.'

'So maybe that's what you should do?'

She knew perfectly well what he was getting at. He was thinking exactly the things she was trying to avoid considering. That was the trouble of living with someone. She could, with an effort, subdue her own efforts towards self-preservation. She couldn't stop his as well.

So he explained himself, in a hesitant fashion to start off with, then more forcibly as he grew increasingly convinced that it was the only sensible way of proceeding. By the time he'd won his case, another hour or so had gone past. Then Mary Verney quickly drove Flavia to Norwich to get the last train to London. They left in such a rush that Flavia left behind most of her clothes. Argyll promised to bring them back with him.

At the station, she gave Argyll a quick kiss. 'See you in a few days,' she said. 'And thanks for the advice; I don't think I could have done this without you. I take it back about your not being sufficiently ruthless. Between us, I think we've just cut enough corners to last a lifetime.'

The meeting took place in the conference room of the ministry, and a sombre affair it was. About fifteen people in all were there to witness the public goring of Bottando and his sacrifice on the altar of streamlined efficiency. Many attended with reluctance; several liked Bottando and thought well of him. Several more were merely glad it was him and not them. Far more disliked Argan and what he represented.

But none of these could do much, and on the whole

were unwilling to try. Standing up for a colleague was one thing. But enough of Argan's complaints had been circulated to make them think that this time Bottando was in trouble. If you want to fight back, you have to choose the best possible battlefield. And the old guard had collectively decided to conserve its strength for a more auspicious occasion.

The moment Bottando walked into the room, with a very nervous Flavia with him, he knew she was the only person on his side. And she wasn't going to be much use. She was completely worn out, what with rushing down to London, and a long, hard bargaining session with Winterton which took three hours before he agreed to cooperate; then the flight back to Rome passing the time by anguishing about whether she was doing the right thing, and finally a rapid briefing of Bottando to give him some ammunition. She did all the talking; a remarkably calm Bottando did little but listen carefully, thank her, then bundle her into the car. The meeting, he explained, had been brought forward.

It was opened by the minister, a drab, if inoffensive man who was much too frail of spirit to go against the advice of his civil servants once they made up their minds. At least he kept things vague, a vocal washing of the hands which indicated that, whatever happened, he hoped no one was going to think he was in any way responsible for it. Next, routine business was gone through, and as a sort of warm-up session, an extraordinary argument broke out over a trivial matter of accounting procedure which did little except indicate how keyed up everybody was.

And then it was Argan's turn, mild, quiet and all the more dangerous for it.

He started off slowly, on structural matters, gradually

225

drawing the attention of the meeting to the way decisions were taken in the department and how Bottando was ultimately responsible for them. He then went through the statistics on the number of crimes and the number of recoveries and arrests. Even Bottando could hardly put his hand on his heart and say they were good.

'Numbing and meaningless figures,' Argan went on carelessly. 'And I hope that I can make the problem clearer by referring to some particular incidents. In the past couple of weeks there have been several crimes of varying seriousness and not a single one has been cleared up or even investigated competently. General Bottando will no doubt tell you that they could not be cleared up in such a short time. That art crimes need to ripen before they are ready for harvest. For generations, if necessary.

'I do not believe that. I believe that a properly organized and focused approach would have a much higher success rate. Strike while the iron is hot. That should be the watchword.

'It is clearly not the motto of the department as it is currently run. When an Etruscan site of major importance is looted, General Bottando sends off one of his girls to talk to some old woman with a grudge about a thirty-year-old crime. When a gallery in the via Giulia is raided, is it investigated? No; the same girl hares off instead to talk to a convicted criminal about some cock and bull story. The crimes and the thefts mount up and off we go to England, where any nonsense is chased after.

'And why? Because the General has a pet theory. For years now, despite all the evidence of how organized crime is responsible for much of art theft, and despite the fact that routine technology is demonstrably superior,

General Bottando has been obsessed with an outmoded, romantic notion. In brief, he believes in the master criminal, the shadowy figure who roams free and undetected. Nobody else even suspects the existence of this person, of course. Not a single policeman throughout Europe agrees with him. All common sense screams it is complete nonsense. But, by using entirely spurious reasoning, you can prove anything – and as a former art historian, believe me I know.'

A little jest, Bottando thought absently. He is confident. But then, of course, so he should be. He is using exactly the same techniques. He knows as well as I do that I never believed in Giotto. He knows that I hadn't even thought about it for years. He knows that Flavia saw Sandano for only a few minutes. And he knows, above all, that it would never have gone any further if he hadn't turned his attention on it and started manipulating. The slug.

And Argan was still talking, referring to the dangers of applying spurious theories to inadequate evidence, of wasting police effort as a result. Discipline, he was saying. Rigorous, coordinated control to keep attention focused where it was most needed. Times of economic stringency. No room in the modern world for the hunch, the flying-by-the-seat-of-the-pants approach. Need to conserve police – should he say the taxpayers'? – resources. Value for money. Cost-effectiveness. Productivity. Authority. Goal-oriented. Accountability.

Not a single buzzword left unused, not a single soft spot unprodded. Argan finished by saying all the right things; the civil servants positively glowed as he trotted out all the watchwords of their trade. They were lost to Bottando's cause anyway, probably. But even the policemen present looked uncomfortable. And they were the ones he was going to have to win back. Flavia, who deeply resented every word the man had said, especially the cracks about silly girls, glowered menacingly from her subordinate position at the end of the table, using up all her willpower to stop herself from going over and hitting him.

'General?' said the minister with an apologetic smile. 'I'm afraid you have had to listen to a fairly critical account of your department. I'm sure you would like to reply.'

'I suppose so,' Bottando said, leaning forward in his chair, taking out his reading glasses and perching them on the end of his nose so he could peer round the table in a more magisterial fashion. 'And I must say I am rather sad that Dottore Argan, after spending so much time in the department, appears to have formed such a low opinion of the way we go about things.

'I have tried to tell him that the department was set up to defend the national heritage and recover it where possible. On several occasions where there has been a conflict between catching a criminal and recovering an important work, we have always been instructed to do the latter. The attention we give is directly related to this; in the case of the Etruscan site robbery, an assault was committed and the case was taken up by the Carabinieri: we offered assistance and were told it wasn't necessary.'

'Petty bureaucratic demarcation dispute. Surely we are beyond that sort of thing by now?' Argan muttered darkly.

'Naturally,' Bottando went on, 'we kept our ears open nonetheless, using the networks of information that have been built up over the years. The *human* element of detection which, if I may be so bold, no computer will ever supplant.'

Argan snorted. 'And what did it produce?'

Bottando sighed as he thought about the comment. Then, not able to say anything which would answer the question adequately, he leant over and picked up a box stationed by his side. Slowly, piece by piece, he took out the contents and handed them around.

'Thirty-nine Etruscan figurines,' he said, watching carefully as they circulated around the table. 'Picked up this morning from underneath the bed of a little old lady in Viterbo.'

There was a pause at this small piece of theatre before Argan recovered himself.

'I hope they will be returned to their rightful owners quickly,' Argan said. 'We all know about your tendency to decorate your office with stolen goods.'

Bottando beamed at him. 'They will be, when all the paperwork is done. But I would like to put it on record now that I do *rather* resent the waste of time this little case involved. I mean, had Dottore Argan's brother-in-law paid the looters who stole the antiquities from the site for him in the first place, they would not have felt morally justified in raiding his gallery to get them back. Honour among thieves, you know.'

Bottando stole a quick glance around the room. A hit, he thought to himself, as he noticed the disapproving stares in Argan's direction. Argan was not smiling.

'Told you,' he said in a whisper to Flavia. 'Never attack an old lion till you're sure his teeth are gone.

'Now, the more important matter of the case called Giotto,' he went on more loudly, brushing aside Flavia as she tapped him on the arm and whispered urgently that she needed a little word with him outside. Not now, Flavia, he thought. I'm enjoying myself.

'As Dottore Argan has remarked, this was for a long

time only a string of vague suppositions on my part. I – my department – followed routine procedure. Unsolved crimes are reviewed at periodic intervals to see if they can be matched with new and apparently unrelated evidence. This process is where, if I may say so, *experience* comes in once more. To spot the possibility and to interrogate it. To see the *shape* of a crime. May I point out that, although Dottore Argan had full access to the original file and I understand studied it carefully, he failed to see any possibilities to be exploited.

'My experience,' he said loftily, 'and the practical skill of Signorina di Stefano here, did see those possibilities.'

For some reason Signorina di Stefano was looking more distraught than proud at this tribute. She did so much wish she could get him to shut up. He'd won. Did he really need to go for total victory?

He did.

'What Dottore Argan sneered at, we looked into. What he dismissed immediately as a tissue of nonsense, we followed up and pursued. And what Dottore Argan would have consigned to the wastepaper basket, we brought to a conclusion which, I do not mind saying, I am happy to count as the most considerable of my career. If my running of the department is to be judged, then I am more than content that it should be on this case.'

This bold statement produced a nice effect; it is, after all, quite rare in the world of bureaucracy that people go so far out on a limb with such unconditional claims. Flavia, still nervous, examined the top of the table, and fiddled with her pen.

'As for the man I labelled Giotto and of whose existence Dottore Argan is sceptical, I am now in a position to add substance to my original theory. His name was

Geoffrey Arnold Forster, and we can prove it. His identity was discovered because we listened to crooks and senile old women, and because we have the skill and experience to know when they are telling the truth and when they are lying.'

Proof? He went on as the questions erupted. Of course. Even if you disapproved of Sandano, there was the testimony of Signora Fancelli; Flavia had forgotten to tell him about the circumstances of its production. The statement of Arthur Winterton who, Bottando said, was renowned throughout the international art world as a dealer of the highest integrity. The testimony of Mary Verney that Forster had claimed to be selling pictures through Weller. Confirmation by Jonathan Argyll that he had not done so. His possible murder of Veronica Beaumont when she discovered how he was using the family name to trade in illegal paintings and had questioned him. The fact that his wife had burnt his papers in order to destroy evidence of his dealings. Finally, the possibility that he was himself murdered on the orders of a discontented client – although this was unlikely ever to be proven, due to the fact that it was in the hands of the English police who lacked a long-established Art Squad to investigate with skill.

Bottando paused for dramatic effect and to see how this was going down. They were all shifting uncertainly in their seats, unprepared for his vigorous self-defence. Argan, however, was looking a little relaxed once more, as he knew that so far Bottando had not produced the proof he had claimed. He was preparing to counter-attack. Bottando waited until the man was licking his lips with anticipation, then smiled sweetly at him, and took out a piece of paper.

'And, above all, there is this,' he went on, putting

the sheet on the table and glancing at it reverentially. He let it lie there for at least half a second, the room in silence, so that all present, even the dimmest, knew that the moment of climax was coming.

'Found in his files, again by one of my people. And what is it?' he asked rhetorically, peering around the room as though he expected hands to be raised. He shook his head as though 'twas a mere bagatelle. All in a day's routine.

'Just a list of his clients,' he said airily. 'The paintings they bought. And the places they were stolen from. That's all. Not complete, probably, but in my opinion one of the single greatest finds in the history of art theft. Nineteen works, twelve stolen from Italy alone, and painted by Uccello, Martini, Pollaiuolo, Masaccio, Bellini and many others. All on my list of deeds done by Giotto's hand, in whose existence Dottore Argan refused to believe. In themselves a major collection of which any museum would be very proud. We know where they are, and we can probably get many of them back. Their identification is,' he said firmly, glancing around and daring anyone to contradict him, 'a triumph for my entire department.'

Perhaps he went on a little remorselessly towards the end, but he was determined to leave nothing in doubt. He handed round the list which Flavia had bargained out of Winterton the evening before, so that all could look and admire. And as they examined, Bottando developed his variations on a theme of expertise and experience, on the dangers of thinking real life could be reduced to a flow chart of administrative responsibilities; on the need for long-term continuity, not constant change to keep up with the latest fad and fashion. On how policework is hard and time-consuming and could not be had on the cheap. On the need to be dispassionate, and not to end up defending crooks because you are related to them.

And above all, on the need for absolute and total dedication and integrity and honesty. This last with a glance in Argan's direction.

All delivered in a gentle, regretful, calm tone, and sheer music to the ears of the police members of the committee, who were regarding him almost with veneration by the time he'd finished. The mood of the meeting was entirely reversed. Now it was Argan's natural allies who found themselves unable to look steadily in his direction. They would be back, advocating reform, in due course. But they were not going to be shot to pieces defending a man who had so rashly led them into an ambush.

Bottando's vote of confidence was unanimous. Oddly, only Flavia still seemed unhappy. It must be the strain of it all, Bottando thought. It would take her a few days to recover, and for it to sink in what an extraordinary job she'd done.

Even Argan congratulated him on a fine piece of work. Bottando almost felt sorry for him.

Well, not really.

17

Bottando's triumph was Jonathan Argyll's nightmare. When Flavia left him at Norwich railway station, he'd been feeling quite content. He had, in his opinion, given good, if unorthodox, advice, the result of thinking through a process in a fashion that would end up to everyone's advantage. He had been quick, ruthless and decisive as recommended by all and sundry. He felt a little uncomfortable with this new and thrusting persona, but had no doubts that he would get used to it. Now all that remained was to transfer it to his job as a dealer and everything would be delightful. Soon he would have to talk to Mary Verney about the Leonardo. The mood lasted all the way back to Weller House, accompanied him to bed and sent him off to an exceptionally good sleep.

It did not, however, last very long in the morning; survived until he was halfway through his morning egg, in fact, at which point Mary Verney stuck her head through the door and summoned him to the telephone.

'Inspector Manstead,' she said. 'Wants to say hello.'

Manstead, being a courteous man, had rung solely for the purpose of thanking Argyll for his assistance, and to tell him how enormously impressed he was by Flavia's deductive skills.

'I never really believed Forster was a thief, you know,' he confessed. 'Just goes to show how wrong you can be. I doubt we'll ever figure out how he died,' he said. 'But that list of pictures you found is dynamite. A pity you didn't notice it the first time you looked through his desk. But at least you had the gumption to look again.'

'Ah, yes,' Argyll said. 'I left my pen behind. In the desk. I was just getting it back.'

'Amazing piece of luck it wasn't burnt with all the rest of the papers. That damned wife of his. If it wasn't for Flavia's plea for clemency I'd nail Jessica Forster to the wall, the time she wasted.'

'Mercy is a fine thing,' Argyll said. 'She suffered enough living with him, I think.'

'True. And she's all but penniless, I gather. God only knows where Forster's money went. He must have netted a packet from all the things he nicked.'

'Someone said something about gambling,' Argyll offered.

'Did they?' Manstead said in surprise. 'I'd not heard that. I suppose that's art dealers' gossip, is it?'

'That sort of thing.'

'It's not really important. If we recover the Pollaiuolo, that will be more than sufficient reward. I mean, we knew where it was, but now we have more indication that it was knowingly bought as a stolen painting it'll be easier to get it back.'

'Was that on the list?' Argyll said with a sudden lurching feeling in his stomach as a penny dropped and clattered around somewhere at the bottom of his stomach.

'Of course. Why?'

'Nothing. Just that I didn't notice. Too excited, I suppose. Tell me, was the Uccello on it as well?'

'Of course. The first one. Didn't you read it at all? You must have been in a real daze.'

'Yes. A daze. That's about it.'

His good mood dissipating fast as little details swept through his mind, laughing at him, he went back more sombrely to his half-cold egg. What had gone wrong? It was quite possible that he could make a mistake, but he didn't believe that Flavia would have done. After all, she was good at this sort of thing. But of course, she was relying unusually heavily on information he had gathered. Left to her own devices, she would have made the connections. But as Argyll hadn't detailed his burrowing in the Weller House archives, or his trips around graveyards, how could she possibly put the pieces together?

Still, maybe it was just a figment of his imagination, he told himself as he stared moodily at the toast. And maybe not, he added a few moments later when he opened and read a letter that the postman had delivered while he was on the phone. It delivered the *coup de grâce*.

It was from Lucy Garton, reporting that Italy Alex had finally taken a long lunch after an unprecedented period of devotion to duty, and she had grasped the opportunity to rummage through his files. It was not a happy letter. Peeved, in fact, as she reported that, despite Argyll's firm belief, Geoffrey Forster had not sold any Italian paintings through her auction house.

Argyll more or less knew this by now, of course,

so it came as no great shock. What did surprise him a little was the indignant announcement that in fact Forster had sold four pictures in the last couple of years and they had all been English. More to the point, one was attributed as being from the Weller House collection and it had been assessed by Lucy herself. She would stake her reputation on the assertion that it was, indeed, what he had said it was, and enclosed the auction catalogue to prove it. What, exactly was all this about, she went on? How was she supposed to win much-deserved promotion if Argyll didn't deliver the goods? Did he realize how much that meal was going to cost him now?

Argyll looked at the indicated spot of the catalogue, and cursed the day he'd ever thought of going to see the damned woman. She had ringed lot forty-seven. A portrait, school of Kneller, of Margaret Dunstan-Beaumont, sold for £1,250, provenance Weller House. A photocopied receipt for the sale was signed by Veronica Beaumont.

He shook his head in virtual disbelief. How could he have missed it? That bloody drawing had confused him, that was the reason, he thought. And it was just a question of simple arithmetic, really. Margaret Dunstan-Beaumont had died in 1680 at the age of sixty. Kneller had begun work in England in the mid-1670s. Therefore a Kneller portrait of Margaret Dunstan-Beaumont would have to show a woman of at least fifty-five.

His mind reeling with alarm as the implications came sweeping in on him, he walked down to the dining room and looked at the painting said to be of her with far more attention. It was filthy and still dark. Nonetheless, try as he might, there was no way he could persuade himself that it was the portrait of a fifty-year-old woman. The sitter was no more than twenty-five at best. So he looked closer, and even wetted his finger and rubbed it on the canvas.

Oh, you idiot, he thought miserably as the dirt thinned a little. It *is* a young woman. You don't even need to clean it to see that. You even know what it is. You saw it on the wall of Bottando's office a couple of years ago. Never again, he thought bitterly, will I think that good visual recall is a blessing.

He knew he should ring Flavia immediately, but also knew that, if he did turn out to be wrong, then his constant changing his mind would make Bottando seem like a complete fool. And his confidence about his ability to be right on anything was dwindling fast. On the other hand, if he *was* finally right, then this whole risky subterfuge that he'd recommended was unnecessary, if not worse. What should he do? Suddenly he felt his old self again, and the thrusting and dynamic alter ego withered and vanished. Damn good thing, considering how much trouble its brief appearance had caused.

To postpone the decision as long as possible, he walked to the bedroom and examined his beloved drawing once more, no longer the neglected orphan but now revealed as a prince in disguise. Now he knew the author, he was disappointed in himself for not having recognized the style the moment he first clapped eyes on it. The broad, confident and assured strokes of the pencil, the subtle way in which light and shade were merely suggested by a stroke here and there, the completeness of the whole thing. But it wasn't the same: he had loved it; now he also knew that it was Leonardo, and had a watertight provenance traceable back to the artist's pencil, he was merely awed by it.

He decided to give himself another half hour. Then he would make up his mind.

Forty-five minutes later, he concluded, reluctantly, that he had no choice. Flavia would have to know the full and complete truth. He could not, in good conscience, do anything other. It would be very difficult, but not disastrous as long as she got to Bottando before he started talking to the committee.

'Jonathan, it was awful,' she burbled down the phone before he could even finish saying hello.

'He's already done it? I thought it was at four?'

'Brought forward.'

'Oh, my God! He told them the whole thing? About Forster being Giotto? He didn't have any qualms about it?'

'Why should *he* have any qualms?'

There was a long pause as Argyll digested this.

'You mean you didn't tell him?' he asked, rocking in anguished astonishment. 'He went in to deliver this story about Forster not knowing it was entirely fictitious?'

'I didn't have time,' she said a little defensively. 'As I say, it was brought forward. And I knew he would have balked at the idea anyway. The damnable thing is that it wasn't necessary. Bottando had already nobbled Argan. He proved that his brother-in-law was handling stolen goods and raiding archaeological sites. He didn't need all that stuff on Forster we concocted. So I should never have listened to you in the first place.'

'Well,' said Argyll defensively. 'You didn't have to.'

'I know. I'm sorry. And there's no harm done, I suppose.'

'You do get some pictures back. I thought that was the most important thing.'

'In theory. And I suppose it was worth it. Veronica is dead, and we couldn't get Winterton anyway, so it's not as if we were letting anyone off the hook.'

There was a long pause as Argyll tried to stop his head spinning. 'Oh. Well. Just as well then. But what if the, um, truth ever seeps out?'

'I don't see why it should. I'm going to be in charge of writing the reports and the current owners aren't going to go out of their way to advertise what happened. Nor will Mary or Winterton, if they have any sense.'

'What about the other pictures?'

'Which other pictures?'

'The ones Bottando had on his list that Winterton didn't own up to? What about them? The Velásquez, for example?'

'Pouf! I suppose he was wrong. I can't see that she did that one. I mean, Bottando isn't infallible. He was only guessing, a lot of the time.'

'Ah. That's all right, then.'

'When are you coming back?'

'I'm leaving for London in a few hours. I just have one or two details to clear up.'

'Well, hurry home. Bottando wants to take us both out for a celebration.'

By the time he'd cleaned up his room and packed his bag and made ready to go, he decided that the only person who could offer any form of useful advice was Mary Verney. If anyone was going to know what he should do, she was the one.

He found her in the sitting room, the only comfortable room in the bloody place, as she called it, curled up on a vast Victorian armchair, reading a book.

'Jonathan, dear,' she said, looking up with a smile

and taking her reading glasses off. 'Are you about to leave me?'

'I think so, yes.'

'What's the matter, darling? You look dreadfully anxious.'

'A problem. I was wondering . . .'

'You want to ask me? How flattering. Of course. Go ahead. What is it? I can't guarantee to be much use, though. I'm still quite flustered from yesterday. Too much excitement.'

Sweet as ever, but this time Argyll didn't react so warmly. He was too preoccupied. 'There are little anomalies, you see,' he said. 'Holes in the evidence.'

'Dear me. Can you let me in on the secret? Tell me what they are?'

Despite himself, Argyll smiled at last. She was a very easy woman to like. That was part of the trouble. 'Oh, yes. I think maybe you're just the person to tell. Maybe even the only one.'

'I am fascinated,' she said. 'But I'm also thirsty. Whatever it is, I'm sure it will sound better with a gin in hand. I do hope your problems are not so serious that they've turned you into a teetotaller.'

Argyll nodded his assent, and she poured a brace of her habitually vast drinks, then he waited while she went down to the kitchen and got some ice and lemon.

'So,' she said as she finally sat down again and turned her full attention on to him. 'Your anomalies. Why do they make you so furrowed of brow?'

He took a gulp at his gin. 'Because they mean you have not been entirely truthful,' he said more apologetically than was strictly warranted.

There was a long pause and she studied him with

242

perplexed concern. 'But you know that,' she said after a while.

'I mean, we end up feeling sorry for you and work out a way of retrieving the situation so you don't have to suffer because of your relations,' he went on, following his own thoughts.

'Which was appreciated,' she replied. 'And it was to Flavia's own advantage as much as mine.'

'So I thought. But then I find out you're lying again.'

'I'm afraid you've lost me.'

He shook his head almost angrily. 'No, I haven't. You've never been lost. And the fact that it's all my fault just makes it worse.'

'Meaning?'

'I liked you. So I wasn't paying attention. And Flavia was in a hurry and allowed me to push her against her instincts and better judgement. So it's all my fault, you see.'

She looked at him oddly, and suggested he got to the point.

'If your story is true, then cousin Veronica must have stolen all the pictures in the list Winterton handed over. Otherwise, how would he have known where they were now?'

'True. Have an olive?'

'No, thank you. Now. If there were pictures on the list which she didn't steal, couldn't possibly have stolen, then your explanation yesterday becomes inadequate.'

'I'm still not with you, my love, but go on anyway. I'm sure you'll make sense soon.'

'Two pictures she couldn't possibly have stolen were very much on the list.'

'Extraordinary.'

'The Uccello, to start with. Supposedly stolen by her

while she was at that finishing school. Except she wasn't. She never went anywhere near della Quercia's. Of course she didn't.'

'What makes you think that?'

'Because she was married by then. Her husband died at their fifth wedding anniversary party. His gravestone says that was 1966. Therefore they were married in 1961. You don't go to a finishing school to find a husband if you've already got one. I mean, that's silly. You don't have fastidious snobs like della Quercia calling you Miss Beaumont if you are Mrs Finsey-Groat, nor saying how you married someone awfully suitable later. And judging by how people talk about cousin Veronica, you don't have the old bat reminiscing about how nice you are either. She wasn't sent there to find a husband. You were.'

'Hmm.'

'Then there's the Pollaiuolo.'

'I thought that nice Inspector Manstead had established she was on the guest list.'

'He did, and she was. But she didn't go. She couldn't have because she was, in fact, opening the fête here. 10th July 1976. A Saturday, and obviously the second Saturday in the month. The traditional day of the fête. Which she never missed. So I looked it up. She got a good write-up in the parish magazine. A charming and gracious speech over the tombola stands. As George said, she never missed a single one.'

'Amazing.'

'And finally there is the little matter of the theft of the Velásquez portrait of Francesca Arunta. Taken two months after Veronica had a stroke. Frankly, the vision of her hobbling through the streets with a Velásquez tied to her Zimmer frame is too much to countenance.'

'Is that on the list?'

'Not on the list Winterton provided. Flavia discounted it because there was no real evidence who took it, even though it was on Bottando's list of Giotto's greatest hits.'

'So Bottando was wrong and Flavia is right, then,' Mary suggested kindly. 'She obviously can't have stolen that, can she?'

'My point exactly.'

'So?'

'So what is it doing in your dining room?'

'Ah,' she said. 'A good point. I must say, that one is a bit difficult to answer. What conclusions do you draw from all this?'

'Simple enough. Forster wasn't Giotto. And cousin Veronica wasn't Giotto. But you are.'

'And what do you expect me to say to that?' she said with a bright laugh.

'I expect you to look faintly amused, and ask how it was that I could come to such an entertaining but, alas, erroneous conclusion.'

'No, I won't do that. But I will point out a problem with your basic premise. Why would I risk an investigation on my own doorstep, when doing nothing would mean that police attention would never head in my direction? What sort of sense does that make?'

'It makes perfect sense, although the implications are upsetting.'

'What do you mean?'

'Your cousin gets wind of something fishy. She doesn't know what to do, so she asks Forster, who has assisted the family in the past. He looks hard, and eventually produces proof that your money is more than a little dodgy. Nails it down just after you'd stolen the Velásquez.

'She confronts you with it. And dies. I don't think she killed herself, nor do I think Forster killed her. You murder her because she has found out about you. You slip her the extra pills and leave her.

'Forster's mistake is to try to blackmail you, rather than going straight to the police. You decide to murder him as well at the appropriate moment.

'But before you do that, you have to make sure that you can get your hands on whatever evidence he might have accumulated. So, instead of that nonsense about Fancelli telling the police against your wishes, you actually tell her to go to the police, to stir Forster up.

'It works very nicely. The moment I talk to him, he makes an appointment to see me and goes out to get his evidence. Winterton tells you the bait has been taken, you go down, kill him and take it all away.'

'And George Barton's confession? You heard it, after all.'

'George Barton didn't say anything about killing him. The whole conversation could just as easily have been about how he'd seen you coming out of Forster's house that evening. Because he likes you, and didn't like Forster, he was telling you he wouldn't say anything.'

'And hasn't.'

'No. And probably won't. This is an extraordinary tight-lipped place. Anyway, Forster's dead, you've destroyed the evidence, and you think you're in the clear. Until you realize that we are looking for more evidence. So you do the next best thing: you burn his papers, in the hope we'll stick with Forster, and as a fall-back you keep on dropping hints here and there about your crazy cousin. Not knowing how she kept the place going with so little money. Going on fugues. Interested in art.

Dr Johnson said she stole things, but he also said that you told him that.

'And all along, right in front of our noses, there is the reason: the Velásquez stolen from Milan a couple of years back; waiting, I assume, to be collected.'

Mary Verney gave a heavy sigh, and looked at him sadly. 'I am sorry, Jonathan,' she said eventually after debating how to approach the issue and then deciding that there was little point in being anything but straightforward. 'You must be feeling quite dreadfully abused.'

This was the trouble. Not only was she a thief and a murderer, he had just proven it. Morally, at least. But she was still charming and he still liked her. Damn the woman.

'That is putting it mildly.'

'I suppose you don't think too highly of me.'

'Two murders, God knows how many thefts, framing Forster and your cousin, manipulating Jessica Forster, lying through your teeth to me and Flavia and the police. I've come across people who are better socially adapted. I mean, why? You're really nice. You have intelligence, and presence . . .'

'And I could have been an honest woman. Married to someone I didn't care for, doing a job that bored me, growing old and frightened about not having enough money to retire on, living in a poky little flat somewhere, which was all I had to look forward to after this family of mine had done their worst. Yes. I could have done that. But why the hell should I have done?'

'And instead you chose to steal other people's property.'

She sniffed. 'If you like. So I'm a thief. But I never destroyed anything or took from people who couldn't

247

afford it. Most of them didn't even know the value of the paintings I took. They only made a fuss later. I have stolen thirty-one paintings. The nineteen we told you about will soon be back in the hands of their original owners. Of the remainder, one by one they will drift back into the public gaze. In essence, they are borrowed, as all paintings are, really. You cannot own a painting; you are merely its custodian for greater or shorter periods. They all still exist, after all, and many are better looked after than they were before.'

'But property, and legitimate ownership . . .'

'Oh, Jonathan, really. Stop puffing up like that. Even though I only met you a few days ago, I know you better.'

'Do you indeed?'

'Well enough to know that such statements don't mean much to you. The Calleone Velásquez. Do you know where the money came to buy that? Centuries of screwing the peasants, and massacring the natives in South America. The Dunkeld Pollaiuolo, owned by an English aristocrat who'd squeezed Ireland dry for two hundred years. What I do is wrong, I suppose. But at least I don't pretend I'm a public benefactor.'

'If that's all there was to it, I would be half-inclined to agree with you. But there's more than that, isn't there? You killed two people. Don't you feel guilty about that? Just a little.'

'I'm not happy about it,' she said slightly indignantly. 'I'm not a psychopath, you know. But I've already told you there's no point in feeling guilty. Do it, or don't do it. Simple as that. In their case, I was merely defending myself. They were blackmailers and leeches, who didn't even have the courage of their own greed. Both of them were content to profit from what I did, but had the gall to sneer, and criticize me for actually doing it. Veronica, the model of noblesse oblige. She ignored me and was vilely rude to me for years. She persuaded Uncle Godfrey not to help my mother when she was dying. She would have nothing to do with me until she heard I had money. Then she was all over me, wanting me to put it into restoring Weller to its former glory.

'She never earned a penny in her life, and didn't care one jot where I got mine as long as she got her hands on it. I agreed, and kept her afloat. In fact, it was a wonderful way of storing away illicit money. But I did it only on condition that I got this place in return, so that eventually I'd get the money back. My mother liked the place, and so did I. She should have inherited it; I was damned sure I would. I'd already paid for it a couple of times over by the time Veronica died.

'Veronica had no choice, and agreed. But, once she'd got a large infusion of cash, she began to try and get out of it and wanted to give Weller – which would have been sold long since without me – to some cousin. Anything to make sure I didn't get it.'

'This is when Forster came in?'

'That's right. The old cow started trying to find some pretext to weasel out of the deal and still keep my money. So she brought in Forster. I suppose she must have realized there was something odd, as I had so much money which seemed to come from nowhere, but she couldn't pin it down. She explored my past life, people I'd known, and came across Forster, who told her that I'd been up to something in Florence. So she told him to find out more. He did, with the Pollaiuolo. And Veronica summoned me, at the end of the last year, produced his evidence and told me that I'd seen the last of my money. And could forget about

Weller, which would go into a trust where I couldn't touch it.

'She was dying anyway, that's why she was in a hurry. I thought about it for a bit, then hurried the natural process along a little. That was all. What else could I have done? I was damned if she was going to steal my money before she went.'

'And Forster?'

'He was a piece of scum,' she said thoughtfully, the words contrasting strangely with the soft and melodious voice. 'He got Fancelli pregnant and left her. Not him, says he. The girl was a slut. Could have been anyone. The Stragas said that if della Quercia was going to continue associating with them, Fancelli would have to go. Primitive, intolerant times. I felt for her. My own origins weren't so much more respectable.

'So she was out on her ear. I was appalled. If no one else was going to help her, I would. I'd been sent to Italy to find a husband to get me off their hands. I didn't want to go to a finishing school to find a husband, for God's sake. I wanted to look after myself.

'I didn't have any money to give Fancelli, so I thought it only fair that the Stragas should provide it. They all trooped off to Mass on Sunday at ten on the dot. There was always a side door left open so lunch could be delivered. I slipped in, took the picture and left.

'It was *so* easy,' she said with a tone of fond nostalgia. 'I don't think they even noticed it had gone for a couple of days. The next stage was to slip it off to an old friend of my mother who sold it. Again, very easy.'

'So Forster didn't take it? That stuff Fancelli said was just lies?'

'He took her to Switzerland, and delivered the parcel for me. I had very carefully sealed it up. He, of course, simply opened it. I gave him some money to shut him up, and the rest to Fancelli. I paid for her to have her kid, just as I'm paying now for her to die. I liked her. So she was prepared to help me.'

'And Forster didn't try to blackmail you then?'

'He couldn't. It would have been my word against his. Getting rid of him then was very simple. The whole thing was simple, in fact. As far as I was concerned, what I got out of the Straga episode was the knowledge that stealing paintings is a cinch, if you know what you're doing. One other lesson: I had a natural alibi. When my thefts were discovered, the police always looked for a man. "He must have got in through . . ."; "He took the picture off the wall . . ." I knew it would never occur to them that a woman was responsible unless I made a bad mistake. I very much regret the feminist movement, you know. It made life more difficult.

'So I went on. The first few solved my financial woes for a while. I came back to England, married Verney and retired. Then the bastard left me with the kids to support. So I decided that full-time art theft was as good an option as any. I learned about art history until the money ran out, worked at an auction house and an insurance company or two as a secretary, slowly built up contacts and got to know Winterton, who I spotted as someone who was unscrupulous, ambitious and – this may sound odd – entirely trustworthy.

'After four years' patient research, I was ready. I had detailed breakdowns of the whereabouts of paintings in a dozen houses, as well as plans of such security systems as existed, and knew which ones had been photographed. It was then merely a question of picking them off, one by one.'

'How much did you get?'

'I was doing quite nicely by then. The art market was going up, of course. Between 1971 and 1975, I netted nearly $600,000; '75 to '80, over a million. From then on, I worked to commission, when a specific client had been lined up – and had paid – in advance. One intermediary, who never came into personal contact with the clients either, no assistants. Always smallish paintings, nothing I couldn't carry easily myself. And I was always very, very careful. If I didn't like the prospects, I'd hand the money back. And I always insisted on the painting going into hiding for a couple of years so it wouldn't pop up until the police had stopped looking.'

'Fra Angelico?'

'My only failure and the reason we are sitting here now. I'd got into the house by working as a cleaning lady – a useful way of doing it, by the way. So, of course, I had to stay on afterwards for several months: it would have been too obvious to have disappeared. That was why I had to use that idiot Sandano to get the thing out of the country. Bad mistake. I'd not approached him directly, of course, so there was no danger, but I lost the picture.'

'The Milan Velásquez?'

'I had to do that, because I'd already been paid for the Fra Angelico. It went wrong, so I offered them an alternative. They insisted on the Velásquez. I wasn't happy, because I knew a print had been made which could identify it; it was too well-known for my normal way of doing things. But I wanted the contract off my hands and I wanted to retire. I'm getting much too old for this sort of work. But I insisted it went out of circulation for a couple of years before delivery. When I got Weller, I decided it was a perfect place to put it.'

'Why? Wasn't that asking for trouble?'

'I had to put it somewhere, and there's no bigger giveaway than stashing these things in safe deposit boxes. I know bankers aren't meant to peek. But I did not intend to trust my continued liberty to the promise of a banker. Besides, once I'd hidden the documentation, stuck it in an appropriate frame and dirtied it up, it looked quite convincing. Then I called in the morons from the auction house. They swept through in about half an hour – for which they charged an outrageous sum – and scarcely gave it a second glance.

'So for export purposes I now have certificates from English Heritage, the auctioneers and the Inland Revenue itself saying it is a mock-Kneller scarcely worth £500 due to its poor condition. Perfect. That's the great virtue of experts: people believe them. But my worries were right. There was a print, and you recognized the picture from it. Even though you did take some time over it.'

'So what happened with Forster?' Argyll asked, brushing aside the criticism of his abilities. 'What did he have on you?'

'His account of Florence, documents on the Pollaiuolo and a fair smattering of stuff he'd picked up from comparing auction house records and inventories here. I mean, he couldn't prove anything about Veronica's death, but there was enough to link me positively with two thefts. And once an investigation starts . . . So he wanted me to buy them back.'

'And you killed him instead?'

Mary looked sad that he should have such a low opinion of her. 'No, I agreed,' she said reproachfully. 'I don't make a habit of killing people, you know. I agreed. And every time I agreed, he upped the price. I got a million for the picture, with another million on delivery in a month or so. Bargain basement, but what the hell. Forster wanted three million for his grubby bits of paper. He pushed me further than I could go. That was when I lost patience. I went to Fancelli and sent Winterton to Sandano. The police took the bait, you turned up, Forster got his evidence.'

'And you got Forster. Dear God.' Argyll rubbed his face in his hands, and closed his eyes as he digested all this information and realized the enormity of his mistake.

'I'm so sorry, Jonathan,' she said gently. 'You must be feeling very badly used. And I can't blame you. I've grown quite fond of you in the past few days; I would much rather it had ended in a different way. But what could I do? You can't expect me to go to jail just because I like you?'

Argyll nodded silently. He didn't really know what he thought at the moment.

Mary Verney continued to regard him with what seemed very like genuine sympathy and affection. 'The thing is, what are *you* going to do?'

'Hmm?'

'Be the straight arrow, as our American friends say? Go to Flavia, and tell her what you know? I'm not going to leap at you with an axe or anything, if that's what you're worried about. There is a difference, you know. Between you and them.'

Argyll sighed. 'I'm glad to hear it.'

'So?'

'In different circumstances, I would have happily sought your advice. I had a high opinion of your good sense.'

'Thank you. I can lay out the options, if you like. I'll be biased, of course, but you can tell how accurate I am.'

'Go on.'

'The upright good citizen approach,' she said briskly. 'You go straight off to Manstead. Please sir. Mrs Verney is a thief. With the Velásquez and the leads you provide he would certainly get enough to convict me and Winterton. I doubt I would be even charged with the murder of either Forster or Veronica, though. Absolutely no evidence. Zilch; George would never say anything.

'Still, justice gets done: I atone for a misspent life. Splendid. But, for the satisfaction of locking me up for a few years and getting one extra picture, there will be costs. Mainly borne by Flavia who will have to give a very good account for having deceived her own boss, told lies to the English police and, in effect, conspired to pervert the course of justice in a major way. All of which she did on your recommendation, if I remember. She is, I gather, already unhappy about it. You wait till she hears this one.'

Argyll rubbed his eyes and groaned quietly.

'From what you tell me, her boss won't come out of it too well either, as he's just told a pack of lies to his superiors,' she went on. 'Saying he didn't know what was going on won't exactly impress them, and I imagine the man he has just humiliated will be more than ready to take his revenge.'

Argyll looked at her stonily. 'Go on.'

'The other option is to take the advice you are so willing to give others. Forget all about me and Forster and Veronica and Winterton and Velásquez. You have made a mess. You now have the choice of making it worse, or . . .'

'Or?'

'Or not. Don't do anything. Forget it.'

He slumped back in the armchair and stared at the ceiling as he thought about this.

'Here,' she said. 'Maybe it's not appropriate any more. But I was going to give you this as a parting present.'

She handed him a box. He unwrapped it, and pulled off the cardboard lid. Inside, wrapped in tissue paper, lay a drawing of a hand.

A Leonardo da Vinci. Just what he'd always wanted.

'I suppose we can take the profuse thanks as read on this occasion,' Mary said drily. 'But you seemed to like it and it means nothing to me. A token of affection. Not a precious one, I'm afraid, but I hoped it would indicate my pleasure in your company over the last few days. Which was real enough, although I can't expect you to believe that any more. I'm very sorry it's gone sour, but I hope you'll take it anyway. As an apology.'

Argyll looked at her and it sadly. Oh, sod. Of all the times for someone to give him a bloody Leonardo, this was about the worst. This is a nightmare, he thought.

In the old days, this morning, he would instantly have told Mary Verney exactly what it was. They would have celebrated his cleverness and her good fortune, and sealed a friendship on it. He would never have taken it and kept quiet, even if it was what a real art dealer, a Winterton, would do. But now? Honesty on his part seemed hardly appropriate, given the circumstances.

He looked at it again, in its dusty frame with the cracked glass. Selling it would set him up as a dealer with enough finance to succeed. Good God, he wouldn't have to succeed any more. He could retire. That's how you get ahead in this business, he thought. Spotting the opportunity and grabbing it with both hands. Look at Winterton. That's how he began.

'And if I prefer to go to the police?'

'Then you preserve your purity and self-esteem but would have to live with the knowledge that the costs of your particular brand of principled indecision are being borne by everyone else. Particularly your fiancée.

'Do that if you want: no one can stop you. Not even me any more. But if you do, I'd advise you to start looking for another girlfriend; she'll find it difficult to forgive you. I know I would. You told her it was her duty to recast the truth for Bottando, and she listened and did just that. Are you not prepared to do the same for her?

'But,' she said firmly, giving him a long, hard look, 'whatever you do, make up your mind more quickly this time: indecisiveness and irrelevant feelings of guilt really are your biggest faults. But whatever you do, take that drawing.'

'I don't want it.'

She picked it up and took out a cigarette lighter, which she held underneath it. 'Nor do I. Either you have it or nobody does.'

'I'll take it. I'll take it,' he said hurriedly.

'Good. I don't know why it's important to me. But it is.'

She shrugged, slightly bemused by herself, then picked up the glasses and bottle and loaded them on the tray, leaving Argyll moodily staring at the fireplace. For the last ten days, it seemed, everybody he'd met had been telling him to make up his mind. He'd never really thought of himself as being so feeble, but majority opinion seemed against him. A bit much for a murderer to give him lectures, but certainly no one could say she was overburdened by doubt and uncertainty.

And she was quite right in one thing. This time he had to make a choice quickly. He looked at the drawing.

So very beautiful, and certainly more than he'd ever dreamt of. The Moresby Museum would be happy to give him a fortune for it. But, however lovely it was, it now represented all the silly mistakes he'd made in the past day or so. He stared glumly at the drawing; odd how he was thinking about that, not about Forster. Think, he told himself. Was she right? He envisioned the scene. Flavia would believe him. The police would come back. There would be no Velásquez. Nobody in the village would say a peep. There wasn't much chance of making much progress.

And the disadvantages? They'd have to call in the English police, who would be bound to make a formal protest. Flavia would certainly not come out of it well. And as for Bottando . . . No. She was right there, too.

And the Leonardo. Was he really prepared to see something so pretty destroyed simply because he was upset at being beaten? Wouldn't that make things worse? Yes. But, if he took it, he'd be compromised. That was the point of the gift, of course.

'Well?' she said. 'What's it to be?'

'Tell me one thing. You say you stole thirty-one pictures?'

'Thirty-two including the Fra Angelico. I don't count that.'

'And the nineteen that Winterton told Flavia about?'

'Were the ones whose new owners could not identify us. The others will have to stay in hiding in case someone speaks out of turn. I'm sure Flavia realized that when she was talking to him.'

Put like that, there wasn't a great deal to be said about it. She was right. There was nothing he could do anyway. So, feigning a certainty he was far from feeling, Argyll stood and picked up the drawing. The move was his answer to all the questions, and Mary saw that instantly.

'Good,' she said seriously. 'I hope you don't take it amiss if I say you are taking the right decision. And having leapt that hurdle, why don't you follow up by marrying her as well?'

Argyll smiled sadly and walked silently to the door.

'Jonathan.'

He turned round and looked at her.

'I really am sorry, you know.'

He nodded, and left.

A few minutes later, Weller House was disappearing in his rear view mirror and he was driving along the road which led to the motorway, London and the airport. He pulled out into the middle of the road to avoid George Barton walking home to his cottage. He at least came out of this well. He waved, then came up to the patch of road he had pranced up and down on a few days previously to attract the attention of PC Hanson. He was deeply miserable, and could not get out of his head what had happened. Every time he tried, all that happened was that he thought of the beautiful, hateful drawing on the passenger seat. His greatest triumph, and look what had to happen before he could achieve it.

Without even suspecting himself of what he was going to do, he slowed down and turned the car down the narrow driveway, stopped and got out. OK, he thought. Flavia can lie for Bottando, then I can do the same for her. Serves me right. But I am damned if I'm going to turn into Arthur Winterton. Sod that.

There was a light on in the house, and Jessica Forster opened up when he knocked at the door. He thought he'd say hello. He sort of identified with her. Used,

259

manipulated, exploited. The only difference was that she didn't appear to feel sorry for herself on quite the grand scale that Argyll did.

'I'm just going,' Argyll explained. 'I thought I'd see how you were doing. My name's Argyll, by the way.'

Mrs Forster smiled with sad pleasure and insisted he get out of the rain. 'Come in, please, Mr Argyll. It was kind of you to call. You're the friend of that Italian woman, aren't you?'

Argyll said he was. She had gone back to Italy in a bit of a rush, he explained, which was why she hadn't said goodbye personally. So she'd asked him to do it instead.

Jessica Forster nodded. 'Thank her for the thought. She's a kind woman. Do you know, the only people who have shown any kindness to me since all this happened are Miss di Stefano – who I don't know – and Mrs Verney, whom I'd never really liked. Everyone else has been avoiding me as though I had a contagious disease. I suppose they thought that I was about to be arrested for Geoff's murder.'

'How are you feeling now?'

She shrugged. 'I'm recovering, I suppose. Trying to get my life together again. That's what I have to concentrate on, now. At least I don't have to worry about anything. The police tell me it was definitely just an accident. Do you know, I'm glad? Geoff had his faults, I knew that better than anyone; but it would have been a horrid way to die.'

'Yes. Well, I imagine it will take some time. Do you know what you'll do?'

'I've scarcely thought. I shall probably go and live in London. See if I can find someone to give me a job, although God only knows what I'll do. It's not as if I'm qualified or anything. But I always hated country life, and now I have no one to look after but myself, I can get away from it. I hate cows and local gossip and village fêtes. I suppose I'll have to stay for a while, to sort out Geoff's things. Although there isn't a great deal to sort out. There doesn't seem to be anything but debts. I can still hardly believe what's happened.'

Argyll sympathized, and said he could hardly believe it either. He thought Mrs Verney had been a bit hard on Jessica Forster. No dynamo, certainly, but resilient, and, in her way, courageous. She deserved better treatment than she had received. 'He really left a mess, did he?'

'I'm afraid so,' she said, smiling bravely. 'I'm on my own, now. There's no savings, no insurance, and a lot of debts and mortgages. Even his pictures aren't worth much, I'm told.'

'Oh dear. In fact,' he went on, 'I didn't just come to ask how you were. I've got something for you.'

He produced the little packet. 'It belonged to your husband. It's something he left you.'

She grimaced. 'I suppose I shall have to find its rightful owner, then.'

'No. It really did belong to him. No hanky-panky at all. He bought it; quite above board. I thought you'd like it.'

She opened it up and looked inside sceptically. 'I don't know that I do. Small, isn't it?'

'It is small, yes. But if I were you I'd sell it. It might help your finances quite a lot. There's a place called the Moresby Museum in Los Angeles which is always on the look-out. I'll contact the director and send the details of what it is, if you want. I have all the information he'll require.'

'Is it worth a little money? Can't be, surely. It's not even finished.'

'Let me take care of the money angle,' Argyll reassured her. 'I'll tell him what price you'll accept and make sure you get it.'

Mrs Forster shrugged again, perplexed at the strangeness of the world, then tucked the drawing away and put it on a shelf above the television.

'That's very kind of you,' she said. 'I appreciate the thought. I will of course pay you for your trouble . . .'

'No,' he said sharply, and saw her recoil a little from his vehemence. 'No,' he repeated more gently. 'That's quite all right. My pleasure.'

'Well, thank you,' she said simply.

'Think nothing of it. Just don't tell anyone about this until you contact the Moresby, OK?'

'Why?'

'Funny business, the art world. You wouldn't want Gordon to pay you an unexpected call before you leave. Besides, if the taxmen decide it's part of your husband's estate, you might not be allowed to sell it for months.'

Mrs Forster nodded.

'Listen,' Argyll went on, shaking her hand, 'I've got to go and catch a plane. Good luck. And *please* don't lose that drawing.'

And Jonathan Argyll, former art dealer, left Weller and all it contained.

As he drove, he found himself breathing more easily, and he began to compose a letter in his mind to the international university accepting their kind offer of a position. He even began to wonder how on earth he was going to teach a load of ignorant, spotty-faced adolescents to appreciate the subtlety, grace and profundity of baroque art.

But he hadn't a clue; so he forgot all about it, and hummed to himself instead.

The Portrait
Iain Pears

The windswept isle of Houat, off the coast of Brittany, is no picturesque artists' colony. So why did Henry MacAlpine forsake London – where he had been fêted by critics and gallery owners, his works exhibited alongside the likes of Cezanne and Van Gogh – to make his home in this remote outpost?

The truth begins to emerge when, four years into his exile, MacAlpine receives his first visitor: the influential art critic William Nasmyth, who has come to the island to sit for a portrait. Over the course of the sitting, the power balance between the two men shifts dramatically as the critic whose pen could anoint or destroy careers becomes a passive subject. And as the painter struggles to capture Nasmyth's true character on canvas, a story unfolds – one of betrayal, hypocrisy, forbidden love, suicide and ultimately murder.

'A tense tale of revenge, where the creative bites the critical back' *Observer*

'A wonderful, grimly entertaining novel' *Sunday Telegraph*

'This is an atmospheric tour de force of historical writing, and of narrative skill' *Independent*

'A revenge fantasy to relish' *Independent on Sunday*

ISBN: 0-00-720277-6

Death and Restoration

Iain Pears

The monastery of San Giovanni has few treasures – only a painting doubtfully attributed to Caravaggio. So Flavia di Stefano of Rome's Art Squad is surprised to receive a tip-off that a raid is being planned on the building.

When the raid takes place, the thieves are disturbed and snatch the wrong painting, a curious icon of the Madonna, remarkable only for the affection in which it is held by the local population. Or is this what they wanted all along? Does the legend of the icon's miraculous powers hold any clue? And who murdered the French dealer found in the Tiber soon afterwards?

With the help of Jonathan Argyll, Flavia immerses herself in the intrigues of monastic and police politics in an attempt to solve the double mystery. But the solution is murkier and more complex than anyone could have known.

'Pears is a delightful writer, with a light, ironic touch'
FRANCES HEGARTY, *Mail on Sunday*

ISBN: 0 00 649875 2

The Immaculate Deception

Iain Pears

When a major painting is kidnapped days before an important international exhibition opens in Rome, Flavia di Stefano, newly appointed head of the Italian Art Squad, has a feeling her life is suddenly going to get very complicated.

Things start badly when Flavia is told to get the painting back at all costs without causing any embarrassment to the country and without paying the ransom to the thieves. She knows she will be blamed if something goes wrong, and finds herself pushed ever further into unorthodox tactics to save both the painting and her job.

Encouraged by her art-dealing husband Jonathan Argyll and her old boss, Taddeo Bottando, she delves deeply into past cases to try and identify those responsible for the kidnapping before it is too late, and in the process discovers a secret, lying hidden for decades, which gives her the biggest shock of her career.

'An intricately plotted, entertaining murder mystery'
PETER GUTTERIDGE, *Observer Review*

ISBN: 0 00 232660 4

The Bernini Bust

Iain Pears

British art historian Jonathan Argyll has just sold a minor Titian to an American museum for a highly inflated price. But as he complacently awaits his cheque in the Californian sunshine, trouble erupts: the museum's billionaire owner is murdered, a dubious art dealer disappears, and a Bernini bust, apparently smuggled out of Italy, is missing.

Things could hardly be worse, and the situation calls for assistance from his friends General Bottando and Flavia di Stefano of the Italian National Art Theft Squad . . . especially as things very definitely *do* get worse when the killer's attention turns to Jonathan himself.

Cleverly mixing murder with art, *The Bernini Bust* is a witty and intriguing mystery from the bestselling author of *An Instance of the Fingerpost*.

'Excellent'   GERALD KAUFMAN, *Scotsman*

ISBN 0 00 651114 7

The Titian Committee

Iain Pears

When Louis Masterson, a member of the famous Titian Committee, is found stabbed to death in a Venetian public garden, General Bottando of Rome's Art Theft Squad sends Flavia di Stefano to Venice to assist the local carabinieri. But it seems they don't want her help or expertise, and are convinced a Sicilian mugger is responsible for the killing.

Flavia has her own ideas, and persuades English art dealer Jonathan Argyll to come to Venice and buy a picture from the Marchesa di Mulino's collection. But then another member of the committee is found dead, and the Marchesa's collection is stolen. Following a tortuous trail in their attempts to discover the truth behind both murders and theft, Flavia and Argyll not only stumble across another murder, but come close to unravelling a mystery from Titian's own life.

'Admirable.'   MARCEL BERLINS, *The Times*

ISBN 0 00 651113 9

The Raphael Affair

Iain Pears

When English art historian Jonathan Argyll is caught breaking into a church in Rome, he has an astonishing story to tell. He claims that the church contains a genuine Raphael, hidden under a painting by Mantini. Further investigation reveals that the painting has disappeared . . . to reappear later in the hands of top English art dealer, Edward Byrnes.

Soon Byrnes is able to unveil the Raphael before an amazed world. But how had he found out about the hidden masterpiece? And there is also the curious matter of the forger whose safety deposit box contains some highly suspicious sketches.

Then a hideous act of vandalism is perpetrated. Murder is to follow . . . and General Bottando of Italy's Art Theft Squad faces the most critical challenge of his whole career.

'Pears is a delightful writer, with a light, ironic touch.'
FRANCES HEGARTY, *Mail on Sunday*

ISBN 0 00 651112 0